A Killer Donation

Blue Dragon
Publishing

A Killer Donation
Published by Blue Dragon Publishing, LLC
Williamsburg, VA
www.BlueDragonPublishing.com
Copyright © 2025 by Dawn Brotherton
https://DawnBrothertonAuthor.com

ISBN 978-1-939696-96-0 (paperback)
ISBN 978-1-969416-00-2(large print)

ISBN 978-1-939696-97-7 (ePub)

Library of Congress Control Number: 2025936840

Printed in the U.S.A

29 28 27 26 25   1 2 3 4 5 6 7

Bookclub discussion questions available on author's website: www.DawnBrothertonAuthor.com

A Killer Donation

Eastover Treasure Mystery Book 3

Dawn Brotherton

Chapter 1

Sweat dripped down her neck as Aury St. Clair wrestled with the bulky bundle. The sour stench turned her stomach. She let it fall to the floor, kicking up a billow of dust. Coughing, she turned away, waving her hand to clear the air. Her eyes burned, but she resisted the urge to touch them with her filthy hands.

"Are you okay in there?" a voice called from outside the building.

"I'm fine." Aury grunted as she hefted the well-worn mattress by the edge and slid it across the floor through the open doorway. Red and yellow leaves clung to the grubby fabric as she tugged it into place against the others stacked outside. Dust covered Aury's faded jeans and flannel shirt. She paused to roll her sleeves to the elbow.

Her grandmother Liza wrinkled her nose and shifted in her lawn chair to avoid the dust plume drifting her way. "Those are going straight to the dump, right?"

"Absolutely. They've been in this old building with no climate control for too many years. Just look at these holes." As if to emphasize her point, something with wings fluttered past her face. Aury swatted at it in disgust.

A horn beeped. Aury turned toward the rusty red pickup truck bumping its way over the dirt path to the cottage.

"Figures you'd show up after the hard work was done," she said as Scott Bell and Alan Rolfe climbed out of the truck.

Scott kissed Aury quickly and nodded at Gran. "You had supervision. We would have just gotten in your way."

"Good morning, Alan," Gran said to the handyman and caretaker for the Eastover Retreat Center. "How's that daughter of yours?"

Alan touched the brim of his dirty baseball cap with two fingers. "Mornin', Liza. She's doing mighty fine. She's off the crutches and has a walkin' cast, so she's getting about on her own. Good thing, because her little ones weren't slowing down for nothing."

Liza smiled. "I'm sure Scott and Aury are glad to have you back. They need you here, especially with Aury's latest project."

Alan squinted as he stuck his head inside the dimly lit cottage. "You've got your work cut out for you, cleaning this place up. Scott tells me you're gonna teach classes or somethin' in here."

Sweeping her right arm as if in presentation mode, Aury announced, "The Crafters' Cottage."

Alan's dubious look made Aury laugh.

"Really, it'll be great. Just wait and see." She was glad to have Alan on their team as she and Scott built the Eastover Retreat Center. The 283-acre property in Surry, Virginia, had been in Scott's family for years. His parents had always talked about using this property as an escape for city folks, but his mother passed away from cancer when Scott was a teenager, and his father died soon after.

When Scott left for college, he piled the responsibility of running the retreat center on Alan. The handyman had worked for Scott's parents for over thirty years and did his best to stretch the very thin budget he was given after all the medical bills were paid. It was only after working at a DC engineering firm for ten years that Scott could invest money to fix up the property.

Aury admired the muscles in Scott's tan forearm, accentuated when he hoisted a metal toolbox from the truck bed.

"This should have what you need to take those frames apart." He carried it into the musty cottage. "I wonder if we can add bigger windows to let in more light. We'll have to look at the structure."

Returning to the truck, he pulled an industrial-size broom from the truck and handed it to Gran. "And I have something for you too."

She playfully swatted him with it. "Aury, you better get your fiancé in line. Didn't he just say I was the supervisor?"

Alan and Scott proceeded to toss the mattresses into the truck bed as if they weighed nothing. When they finished and climbed back into the cab, Scott leaned out the window. "We're going to drop these at the dump, then go into town to rent a stump grinder. We shouldn't be long. How about I bring back lunch?"

"Sounds good." Aury waved as the truck trundled away.

"You got yourself a good one there." Gran pushed herself out of the chair, her colorful jacket hanging loosely below her knees and crocheted scarf wrapped around her neck. "Let's get these old bones moving."

Gran may have lived many years, but no one would dare call her old. She was still active, doing yoga three times a week and walking a few miles every day. Aury prayed that she inherited her grandmother's genes and would be as trim when she was in her seventies.

When she passed through the door, the older woman's face pinched, and her nostrils flared. "I think something died in here."

Aury handed Gran a wrench from the toolbox without comment.

Gran pulled her scarf up over her nose. "When do you plan to have this place finished?"

Aury ignored the stench, focusing on one of the eight sets of bunk beds. "With the lodge and motel done, I'll have more time to devote to this project. We'll see how long Scott thinks it'll take to add windows and maybe another door."

When a hurricane planted a tree through the motel roof two years ago, Scott's methodical plans for renovating the property were scrambled. He had to reprioritize his projects. Aury smiled inwardly as she thought of how that storm brought them together. It also reawakened Scott's interest in working outdoors with his hands, and he moved here from DC permanently. Aury followed the rise in his happiness level as he got excited by new projects.

It had taken over a year of hard work to get to the stage where the property wasn't a money pit. Even with Aury's accounting background, balancing the budget was a feat. The discovery of the treasure Scott's ancestor had hidden on the property provided a nice backstop, but they were trying to make the funds last as long as possible.

When Scott and Aury got engaged, she gladly resigned from her accounting job to work alongside him. With his knowledge of architecture and engineering, and her number crunching and analytical thinking, they were good business partners. The bookings for the cabins and the lodge were almost always full.

She glanced around at the cobwebs in the high corners, then back to where her grandmother loosened nuts on the frame opposite her. "Maybe skylights would be better. That will leave more room to hang artwork."

Previously used only as a bunkhouse, the building had no modern conveniences. Four sets of bunk beds lined each long wall with two small windows hugging the ceiling opposite each other. No other furniture took up space, as the occupants were expected to spend most of their time outside.

Gran grunted her approval, straining with a corroded bolt. "So another couple of months?"

Aury pushed hair off her face. "I don't think it'll take that long. I already posted fliers around town announcing that classes will start soon. We can keep making improvements around the class schedule."

"I love how you found a way to share enthusiasm of all things crafty with the campers."

"And the locals, I hope. I got the idea because so many of the groups we host are quilters, scrapbookers, knitters, and weavers. Most of the church groups that stay have some artsy aspect to their events. This will give them a place to try new things."

"And you too, I suspect." Gran chuckled. "What classes are you starting with?"

"I'm thinking the basics, like clay bead making and jewelry. I've asked my friend Karmine to teach painting. I'll try to get others involved once I see what most people are interested in. Swedish weaving might be fun." Aury paused to tighten her ponytail.

Gran gawked at her. "You don't sit still for a moment, do you?"

Aury's eyes widened in mock surprise. "I wonder where I got that." The bolt she was working on clattered to the floor. "Grab that end of the frame, will you?"

Jiggling the structure slightly to loosen the connection, they lifted the upper bed frame and placed it on the well-worn planks that made up the floor. As they started the deconstruction project, Aury said, "I was hoping you'd teach a class or two. I'm sure the folks at Halo Inspirations would appreciate having more quilters around here."

"Of course. Thank goodness we finally have a quilt store in Williamsburg. I hated that traffic into Newport News when I needed to pick up something quick." Gran tossed hardware into the pile and pulled off the headboard.

"Since when was a trip to a fabric store ever quick for you? You spend hours wandering the aisles."

"It makes me happy. What can I say?" Gran's cheerful voice matched the mischievous twinkle in her eye.

Aury had inherited her creative expression from her grandmother, as well as her love of colors. She removed the footboard, and the side rails clanked to the floor. "I'll carry this out."

Gran turned to the next frame. "Are you sure this project isn't just an excuse to put off planning for something more important?"

Aury's jaw tightened as she bit back her first thought before it could escape. Outside, she tossed the bed pieces with a little more oomph than necessary, and they scattered across the brown grass. Returning to the cottage, she pasted on a smile. "We have plenty of time."

Aury mouthed the words as they left Gran's mouth. "Not if you want to have kids."

The older woman placed a gentle hand on Aury's shoulder. "I understand you get tired of hearing me say it, but you have nothing to be afraid of. Scott loves you. It's obvious to everyone who sees you together. He is not Todd."

Aury shuddered. It was reflex really. Most days she tried not to think of him at all.

"I realize Scott isn't anything like Todd. Would I have said yes if I thought he was?" The words came out harsher than she meant them to.

Gran's face fell.

"Sorry," Aury added quietly.

Gran returned to the bedframes.

"Honestly, Gran. I don't know what my problem is, but for sure it isn't you." Aury hugged her tightly. She was always safest in her grandmother's arms.

Gran patted her back. "I trust you more than you do."

Aury kept silent as she started the next bunk bed but couldn't return Gran's confident smile. As much as she wanted to share her grandmother's faith in her, Aury couldn't help but believe she had good reason to doubt.

Chapter 2

Aury held the shaky ladder as Scott climbed down from the cottage roof. Bits of dirt from the rungs floated onto her face. She snapped her head down to avoid getting crud in her eyes.

Once on the ground, Scott wiped his hands on the back of his cargo shorts, already dark with stains and soot. "The seal looks good on the skylights. You shouldn't have any problems with them."

She used the bottom of her oversized t-shirt to clean a spot on his sweat-soaked face and planted a kiss there. "Thank you for getting them done so quickly."

"We got lucky that the building store had some in stock." Scott glanced at the sky. "And I wanted to finish while we had a dry spell. Probably would have been helpful while you and Liza finished cleaning inside."

"It's all good. It didn't take us that long. There wasn't much to move out." Aury's mind raced with ideas on how to arrange the easels and tables to best utilize the natural light. As she turned to look at the cottage, a warmth in her chest brought a smile to her lips. Having a project of her own gave her a sense of satisfaction she didn't realize she was missing.

Scott pushed in the quick-release levers, allowing the ladder to slide down the rails into a more compact size. He loaded it into the back of his truck.

Aury stood with her hands on her hips, staring at the cottage. Despite being close to eighty years old, the bones of the building were solid. The rough-hewn outer boards had been painted a dark green as if to camouflage the building into the evergreen and deciduous trees behind it.

Scott slipped his arms around her waist. "Don't go dreaming up more work for me. In addition to running water lines out here, filling potholes, and keeping up with routine maintenance, Alan and I want to take down trees along the path to the beach to make it safe again for hikers. That project will take at least a month."

Aury grimaced and wormed free of him. "You're all sweaty."

"I thought you liked me sweaty." He wiggled his eyebrows.

She laughed. "Not from being on the roof."

He stole a kiss. "Alan's making chicken parmesan for the guests on the scrapbooking retreat. I thought we could eat the leftovers when they're finished."

"Sounds good to me." Aury slid her hand over his shoulder, appreciating the feel of hard muscles beneath his shirt.

He climbed into the truck.

A dust cloud in the distance signaled an arriving vehicle. Aury shielded her eyes with her hand, trying to make out the driver. When she recognized the director of the local Fresh Start organization, her face brightened. Michelle Paris had dedicated her life to finding homes for single women who had come on tough times, so they didn't end up on the streets.

The dark gray panel van stopped in front of Aury. Scott waved to them as he pulled away.

"I hoped he wasn't leaving on my account." Michelle adjusted the strap of her overalls that had slipped from her shoulder. In her sixties, she didn't fit into any traditional convention for clothing style.

"No, he's going to play Paul Bunyan." Aury took in the large flowers imprinted on Michelle's denim. "Did you make those yourself? I've never seen anything like it."

Michelle spun in a circle to show Aury the full effect. "I got the material online and had one of the women in the shelter make them for me. Aren't they to die for?"

"They're perfect. Maybe I can get her to teach a sewing class here."

"That's one of the reasons I'm here. I saw your sign at the diner. I have some things for you." Michelle swung open the back doors to the van. Stacks of canvases rested against the sides, held in place by bungee cords.

Aury's eyes grew wide. She had to stop herself from immediately diving into the treasure trove of castoffs. "Wow! Where did these come from?"

"You know the large yellow house with gray shutters on Goodson Path?" When Aury nodded, Michelle went on. "Penny Warren donated it to Fresh Start. Now I can house women right away until we can find them a suitable home in the community."

Michelle mimed pulling out her hair. The shoulder-length strands fell neatly back into place. "Now all I have to do is get rid of all the stuff inside, clean it up, bring it up to the city's building code, and redecorate."

Aury chuckled. "That'll keep you busy for a while."

Yet again, the denim strap slipped off as Michelle made a sweeping gesture to the canvases. "I've already started. I found these in one of the upstairs rooms. The owner of the art gallery appraised them. They don't have any monetary value as works of art. The painter was a novice, and these look like practice canvases. I thought you might be able to use them for your classes."

After unhooking the bungee cords, Aury pulled a painting from the stack and held it at arm's length. "This is pretty good for just practice."

"I took snapshots of some of the best ones and sent them to the previous owner, but Penny doesn't want them. She was thrilled with the idea of donating them to you."

"I'll make sure to send her a thank you letter if you'll pass on her address." Aury picked up as many canvases as she could carry. "We can store these against the back wall until we build a storage closet."

The ladies made several trips to empty the van.

Michelle closed the door. "I also found old canning jars. Maybe you can use them for paintbrushes. Why don't you stop over when you get a chance and see what else might be helpful? I'm at the house most of the time."

"Is anyone helping you?"

She rolled her eyes. "My nephew Brandon is supposed to be, but he expends more energy thinking of ways to get out of working. It was a miracle he was around to help me load the van this time."

"If you want, Gran and I can chip in."

Michelle brushed aside the suggestion. "You have enough to do. The ladies who will be living there can help out. I think that will make them appreciate it all the more."

As Michelle drove away, Aury returned to the canvases, taking more time to look through them. Some were still blank, but others had scenes of farming life from the late 1800s. She set a few aside, thinking Michelle might change her mind and want to hang them once the house was redecorated.

A particular painting caught her eye. At first glance, Aury thought it was just a run-of-the-mill picture of a little plant, but closer inspection revealed its roots nestled in someone's cupped palms, the soil spilling off the side. Though the perspective didn't include the person's face, the brown hands were small compared to the torso, so they didn't belong to a man. In the background, Aury could make out hints of green, rolling fields. Something about the limited frame intrigued her. Somehow the artist had managed to produce only one piece of a scene but left the viewer with no doubt that there was something more to this painting.

The next morning, Aury propped the painting against the wall in Gran's cozy Williamsburg kitchen. She kept her eyes on it as she took her usual seat at the table.

Gran refilled Aury's coffee mug and gave the canvas the once-over. "That painting is lovely. What are you going to do with it?"

"I haven't decided yet. I may take it to Karmine for a good cleaning." Aury added sugar to her coffee. "At the very least, I want time to study the shading. The artist had a good eye for perspective."

As she regarded the palette of the canvas, Aury's mind wandered to her latest quilt project. She had set it aside when she began fixing up the crafters' cottage and hadn't gotten back to it in weeks. Now her fingers itched to touch the fabric. "Let's go by the quilt store before lunch. I need some yellows to go with the purples I picked up in Ithaca."

While visiting Scott's cousins in the Finger Lakes region of New York, Aury and Gran had purchased many fabrics featuring the purples and greens of the wine country. Aury planned to make bedspreads for the newly rebuilt lodge that housed many of their large groups. Besides having an excuse to try out different patterns, the quilts acted as a motivator for the creatives who frequented the Eastover Retreat Center.

"Speaking of shading, I'm starting your wedding ring quilt soon. Do you have a preference for colors?"

Aury cringed. Her grandmother had been eager to make her a wedding ring quilt for years. She hadn't done it for Aury's first marriage. There was always tension between Gran and Todd. She had certainly seen something that Aury hadn't. Eventually, they stopped visiting because Aury's nerves couldn't take the tug-of-war between her ex-husband and her grandmother.

But since Scott and Aury had started dating, Gran had been nothing but smiles and compliments. It hadn't gone without notice when Gran pulled out old books with variations on the wedding ring quilt, and that was even before they got engaged.

"You have plenty of time," Aury hedged.

"I'm not that young, and I want to make sure you have one before I meet my maker."

Aury sighed. She couldn't hold up against guilt trips, especially when they included comments about Gran's age. Aury was well aware Gran wouldn't be around forever.

She gave in. "You know how much I love purple, but Scott is more of a blue person."

"I can work with that." Gran picked a pattern book from the bookshelf in the attached sitting area. "Finish up your coffee. I have a coupon for Halo Inspirations Quilt Shop."

A short drive later and they were entering through the door, greeted by the chime of a bell.

"Aury, Liza! Always a pleasure to see you." Ralene, owner of the quilt shop and member of the Williamsburg Guild, was resplendent in her jacket of sparkly black and flowery purples. "What are you working on this week?"

Gran filled Ralene in on their latest projects while Aury drifted among the frenzy of flamboyant textiles. She ran her hand over the bolts of fabrics, lined up by tones on the color wheel. The abundance of shade variation always lightened her soul.

A particular powder blue caught her eye. When she looked more closely, the miniature ducks and sailing ships spoke to her. She reached for it but caught herself in time. Her grandmother was already overly excited about the wedding. Aury didn't want her hinting for a great-grandchild as well.

It wasn't that Aury didn't want a baby. She had wanted one for as long as she could remember, but then her first marriage failed. How could she be sure things would be better this time?

Her vision blurred through tears threatening to escape. Aury moved away from baby fabrics and searched for cheery yellows and sun-kissed oranges.

As she started toward the cutting table carrying four bolts, Aury gave a slow, disbelieving shake of her head and didn't try to hide her smile. Gran was still chatting at the register. A few ladies from the guild had entered the store, and they were exchanging gossip.

Debbie hugged Aury when she got close. "I'm really looking forward to the next quilt retreat. Hopefully less excitement than last time."

Aury smiled. Their last retreat at Eastover had ended in disaster when hurricane-force winds uprooted trees and destroyed the rooms they were staying in. "The new lodge is a respectable distance from the tree line."

"I hear you added a second floor," Pat chimed in. "Hope there's an elevator. I don't think these knees can handle the climb."

"We know how you hurt your knees." Debbie elbowed her friend, who only rolled her eyes.

Aury laughed inwardly at the sexual innuendo, shaking her head. The first time she heard Debbie tease Pat like this, Aury was surprised. Now she didn't expect anything less.

"It's not that I don't trust you, but I'm packing my emergency phone, just in case," Pat said.

Debbie touched Aury's arm. "Did you hear about the fight on the ferry?"

When Aury shook her head, Debbie went on. "Linda told me she was sitting in her car, minding her own business, when two men got out of vehicles on either side of her. They started arguing right in front of her."

Pat jumped in. "One threw a punch, and they just went at it."

"What were they fighting about?" Gran asked.

Debbie lowered her voice as if ready to impart a great secret. "Linda couldn't hear them, but no one came to break up the fight. They kept it up until the boat docked and people were returning to their cars."

"Then they just got in their cars and pulled away?" Aury waited for the great reveal, but Debbie only waited with a satisfied smile.

"That sounds anticlimactic," Aury said.

"I can only report what Linda told me." Debbie huffed. "You'll have to complain to her if you want more details." She stalked off in a pout.

Pat eyed her as she left. "Linda mentioned a gaudy bumper sticker on one of the cars. *Moore Is Better.*"

"That's the obnoxious man from those commercials." Gran closed her eyes and tapped her forehead in concentration. Her eyes snapped open, and she stabbed her right index finger in the air. "Hamilton Moore!"

"He's grabbing up land all over the area and erecting more shopping centers," Aury said.

"As if we need more! There are empty buildings all over the peninsula." Gran sniffed her disapproval.

"As long as it isn't another quilt store." Ralene took Aury's arm. "Show me what you picked out. How many yards do you need?"

Aury let herself be led to the cutting table. "Five yards of each should get me started."

"That's a big project. Are you working on a quilt for your *trousseau*?"

"*Trousseau* is a little outdated, don't you think? Did Gran put you up to this?"

Ralene shrugged and squeezed Aury's arm a little tighter. "She's excited for you. I hear Scott is a wonderful man."

Aury's mouth went dry. She licked her lips, trying to unstick her tongue. "He's great."

"And handsome, I'll bet. You'll make great parents."

Aury pried her arm free. "Now I'm sure Gran has gotten to you. We're taking our time."

The fabric snapped as Ralene shook it out over the table. Methodically, she brushed out the wrinkles and aligned the selvage to the ruler on the cutting mat. "Hey, I'm just excited for you. It could be the beginning of so much. That's the thing with family—anything can happen."

"That's true," Aury said wearily. "Anything can happen."

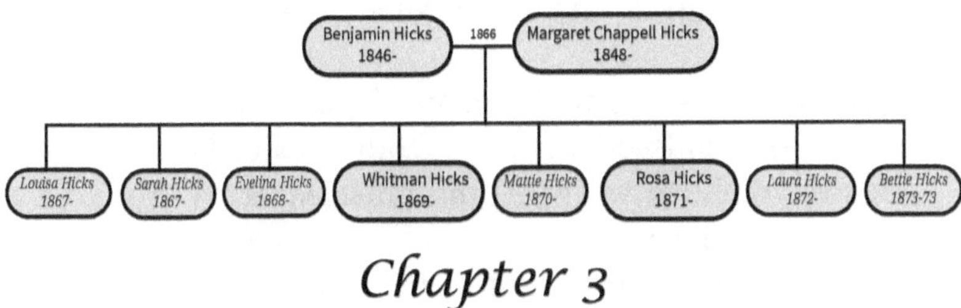

Chapter 3

1875

Something hit the back of Margaret's knees. If it weren't for Benjamin's arms, she would have fallen.

"Mama! Mama!"

Margaret Hicks pried the four-year-old's arms from her long skirt as a feisty six-year-old tore into the dusty yard.

Locking eyes with his father, the young boy slid to an abrupt halt.

"Whitman, what's that you're holdin'?" Benjamin Hicks asked.

"Just taking Freddy for a walk."

The boy's pretense of innocence wasn't about to fool Margaret. "Since when does a frog need a walk? Looks more like you were running when you should have been hopping."

The little girl peeked out from behind her mother's skirt. "He says if I kiss Freddy, he'll turn into a prince. But, Mama, I don't want to kiss nobody."

Benjamin swept her up. "That's right, Rosa. You save all your kisses for your pa. Prince or not."

She giggled when he tickled her neck.

Benjamin stood and held his floppy straw hat over his heart. Bowing his head over his wife's hand, he became the picture of charm. "Miss Margaret, I sure would be delighted to have your company at the church picnic."

Love swelled in her heart as she took in the sweat from the Virginian summer heat already glistening on his dark black neck. She kissed the close-cropped, curly hair on the top of his head. "As if I'd be seen with anyone but you, you silly thing. What's got you acting so courtly?"

"I'm just thinkin' my lovely wife deserves some courtly manners."

"You're wantin' something, aren't you?" The smile in her caramel eyes dismissed any sting from her words.

"Only you." He wrapped his muscled arms around her and pulled her close.

She breathed in his scent of fresh dirt, hay, and horses. This was safety, security, and love.

But they had someplace to be. She released him and turned to the house.

"You are supposed to be getting ready for church. Are the others coming?" Margaret yelled, "Let's go, y'all."

"Whitman, put Freddy away and wash your hands. Tell the others to get out here." Benjamin set Rosa down and straightened her dress. "You look a might pretty today."

Rosa held her skirt on the sides and bowed. "Why, thank you."

Margaret took her hand as the other four children poured out of the house, some still adjusting suspenders or fiddling with their hats. Their eldest daughter placed the three-year-old carefully in a wagon Benjamin had devised just for this purpose. Margaret and the girls had added the extra padding and cushions to make the ride smoother. Two picnic baskets for the Sunday picnic after church sandwiched the toddler, making it easier for her to sit up but not climb out.

After one last inspection of their offspring, Margaret took Benjamin's offered elbow as they started their journey to church.

Whitman ran to catch up. He fell in line with his siblings, sweat glossy on his dark face.

It was a beautiful spring morning for the half-mile walk to church. The older children dutifully took turns pulling the wagon.

"Brother Benjamin, so nice to see you!" The pastor's large hand enveloped Benjamin's. "And where did you come across these angels? You are mighty lucky to have God favor you with so many blessings."

Whitman kicked at the dirt. "Ah, you say that every Sunday."

Margaret swatted the top of his head, while the pastor guffawed.

"Don't you worry, Sister Margaret. It's good for them to be reminded often that they are God's blessings."

Benjamin ushered his wife and seven blessings into the church. The air was already stuffy with so many people. The front and back doors were both open to create a breeze, but the current was barely moving.

Throughout the service, Margaret caught Benjamin staring at the ceiling more than once, and she didn't think he was praying.

"We need to rig up a fan in here to get the air circulating." Benjamin pointed to the rafters. "Wouldn't take much to put some blades on a crank right up there."

Margaret bounced the toddler on her lap as she followed his gaze. "I can probably get the ladies to help me weave the panels to make the fan. We'll chat about it at the picnic. Hush now and pay attention."

She put her hand over his and squeezed.

After the service, the Hicks family filed into the churchyard with the other congregants. Finding a smooth spot under a red maple tree, Benjamin and the older children spread two quilts on the grass. The fresh white paint on the church façade was almost blinding in the sun, so they sat facing the trees at the back of the property. Other families were also staking their spots wherever they could find shade.

The kids dropped the picnic baskets to hold the corners, then they kicked off their shoes to go play with their friends. Even Rosa plucked up her rag doll and deserted her parents to sit with her companion, whose yarn-haired toy was already sipping tea. The dolls struck up an immediate conversation.

Margaret settled the sleeping toddler on the blanket and covered her with a light blanket. Even the ruckus of the children burning off their restless energy wouldn't wake this one.

Benjamin sighed, keeping a watchful eye on his brood. "We have been blessed."

Margaret thought about the ups and downs they had been through in their short eight years of marriage. The life of a farmer was hard. Successful crops were never guaranteed, and the last few poor seasons had taken a toll on the money and seed they had been setting aside. But the biggest loss was that of her sweet baby Bettie. She only lived a few days on this earth, but Margaret had loved her much longer than that.

She batted her eyes, willing tears away. She knew she had to do better and be stronger for her husband and her family. Nothing would bring her baby back, but life would go on. It had to.

Studying his profile, she found strength. "We surely have. Know what would make it even better?"

He gave her one of his dazzling smiles, showing his dimples. "You know I do."

She elbowed him playfully, then became serious. "What about if we had one more mouth to feed?"

His eyes popped open. Then he let out a whoop of joy. He picked her up and swung her about.

Curious eyes watched them, but Margaret was allowing herself to be happy; she didn't care. They had always wanted a large family. Perhaps the Lord would see fit to give them a healthy babe this time.

From the time they took up residence as sharecroppers on old White-man Dugal's property, life had graced them with bounty. First with their crops, then with their children, and even with Benjamin's blacksmith work he did on the side. Their abundant harvests early in their marriage had allowed them to survive the rough weather of the last few seasons.

After the War Between the States, Dugal couldn't afford to continue running the plantation. He had lost too many workers and all his sons in battle. He moved north and leased his property to Benjamin and a collection of farmers to work the fields.

A year later, Benjamin had earned enough money and respect to be named the manager of the property. Along with the promotion came the right to live in the big house. Dugal had no desire to return to Virginia, and they needed the space for their growing family, so the timing was perfect.

With the landowner offsite, the farmers flourished. Margaret and the other wives banded together during canning season, quickly preparing for the winter with food to spare. The families took turns hauling their goods to the Williamsburg market every Saturday, which provided them a little extra money as a cushion in case of a bad harvest.

Good thing, with their growing family.

"What are we celebrating over here?" The pastor stood with his hands on his hips.

"Another angel to add to the Hicks family line! And this one will be just as precious as the other seven." Benjamin kept his arm around Margaret's shoulders.

"God bless you! Again!" The pastor laughed at his own joke. "We'll have to extend the church at this rate."

The couple chuckled as the pastor moved off, leaving another lanky Black man in his place, hat in hand. "Congratulations and blessings to you both." He glanced at Margaret before speaking to Benjamin. "Perhaps this isn't the best time to talk business."

"It is the Lord's Day." Benjamin regarded him closely. "But we can talk some generalities. What seems to be bothering you?"

"I don't think I'm cut out to be a farmer. I'm fallin' further and further behind each year." The man stared at his boots as he talked. "I don't suppose you know anyone who would be interested in taking over my lease. My father-in-law has asked me to come work with him at the factory in Smithfield."

Benjamin stroked his chin as he stared off into the distance. Margaret recognized the concentration on his face as he deliberated the pros and cons.

After a few minutes, he stuck out his hand. "I do believe I can help you out with this. Leave it to me."

The man's relieved expression spoke volumes. He pumped Benjamin's hand enthusiastically.

"You got anything planted yet?" Benjamin asked.

A worried look fell over the failed farmer's face. "I was fixin' to next week, but then this other opportunity came up."

"That's fine. That's fine. Don't you worry none about it. We'll meet up tomorrow and draw up some papers."

The man rushed off, probably hoping to get away before Benjamin had a chance to change his mind.

Margaret hugged her husband's arm. "That's a wonderful thing you did for him. His wife was not cut out to be a farmer."

"It wasn't entirely a selfless move, I will admit. I've been thinking about trying my hand at growing soybeans, but the peanuts have been doing so well, I hate the idea of displacing them just to try something new. I reckon if I can get the seeds quick enough, I can get at least a small crop this year."

"You're always coming up with something new, aren't you?"

He placed a hand on her belly. "Well, I need to try to stay ahead of this brood. Gotta have enough to give them each a little piece of this land that fed them."

Chapter 4

Present day

Aury dropped Gran at her house and headed home. The twenty-minute ferry ride across the James River was typically a highlight of her trips to Williamsburg, where she could relax and daydream. Today, as she stood at the ferry railing watching seagulls soar and dive alongside the boat, thoughts wrestled for her attention.

Niggling doubts about remarrying haunted her. She was afraid to be wrong about Scott like she was her first husband. He was nice at the beginning too. Was Scott's kindness simply an act that would disappear once they said their vows?

Since their first treasure hunt, Aury and Scott had been almost inseparable, and just a look from him set her heart racing. That was a good sign, right?

When they were apart, she collected stories to share with him, knowing he was interested in her life and what she had to say. What would he think about the fight on the ferry? Maybe he had also heard about it and could fill in details. Williamsburg wasn't a large town, and Surry was smaller still.

As the ferry approached the shore, Aury wound her way back to her car, the cries of the seagulls following her. A shiver ran up her spine. She didn't believe in omens, but if this was a horror movie, that sinister call would make the soundtrack.

Two rows over, the neon blues and pinks of a bumper sticker caught her eye. It didn't take much to make out the words *Moore Is Better*. She stood outside her car until a tall,

White man with dark hair approached the silver Volvo with the bumper sticker. He was clean-shaven and didn't appear to sport any cuts or bruises that Aury could see.

When the ferry bumped against the dock, Aury climbed into her car and fastened her seatbelt. The Volvo's row filed off the ferry well ahead of Aury, so she didn't see which way it turned at the crossroads.

When she arrived home, she found the note Scott left her, saying he was on the beach trail. Aury made them sandwiches and packed a few other goodies into a basket for an impromptu picnic. She swung it back and forth while she strolled to where he was working.

As she drew nearer, she watched him with an appreciative eye. He had removed his shirt, and his muscles rippled as he swung the pickaxe. His facial features were chiseled with concentration but not frustration. He was the type of man who approached a situation looking for opportunities, not problems to be overcome. Aury loved that about him.

He stopped to mop the sweat from his brow, then stuffed the kerchief into his back pocket.

A sudden crash through the brush drew his notice as Treasure bounded onto the path. A squirrel darted away, scampering up the nearest tree. The puppy placed her forepaws on the trunk and yapped a few times, but the squirrel stayed just outside her reach.

"C'mon, girl." Scott tapped his leg, and Treasure broke off her pursuit in exchange for a scratch behind the ears.

"She listens to you much better than to me," Aury said.

Looking up, Scott broke into a grin. "Did you come to get your hands dirty?"

"Better. I brought lunch." She produced a bottle of water from the basket and handed it to him. The warm fall day had Aury working up a sweat with the short walk from the house. She wouldn't want to be the one swinging an ax in this heat.

He guzzled it before pouring the last little bit over his head and face. When he ran his hand through his hair, it stuck up in patches.

"You need a haircut." Aury handed him a sandwich.

He sat on a nearby log, gesturing for her to sit on the golf cart nearby. "I'm sure you have enough scissors in your collection that you can find a pair that would work."

She raised her arms, palms out. "No way. I don't see that working out well. Remember, I cut things into little pieces to sew them back together again."

He unwrapped his sandwich. "Thanks for lunch. How's Liza?"

"Persistent."

He chuckled.

"But I did learn something interesting at the quilt shop. Did you hear about a fight on the ferry?" She opened the bag of chips.

"The Jamestown ferry? No."

Aury filled him in on the few details she had picked up from the quilt ladies.

"I'll keep my ears open. Alan's more in tune with Surry. He's been here a lot longer. You might want to ask him."

"Good idea." Aury collected the remains of the picnic, tossing it in the basket. "I'm going to pick up the paint for the cottage, then I'll visit Michelle. She said she might have more items I can use for classes."

Aury drove with the windows down in the late-fall afternoon. The crisp air was refreshing without being chilly. The band AJR blasted on the radio as she sang along. She pulled in the driveway behind Michelle's car but waited until the end of the song to shut off the engine.

Still singing along in her head, Aury approached the front door. When she raised her fist to knock, she noticed the door was ajar. She pushed it open and called out, "Michelle? Are you in there?"

Getting no reply, she stepped in and called again, aiming her voice up the staircase.

Still hearing nothing, Aury wandered toward the back of the house where she assumed the kitchen would be. The house was eerily quiet, and the hairs on the back of her neck tingled. The hall's wallpaper, with miniature three-dimensional printed carriages and horses, assaulted her already-heightened senses. The overall effect was that the carriages were chasing her down the passageway.

She pushed through the swinging door, expecting to find Michelle finally taking a break. The large room was empty.

Walking around the large butcher-block island, Aury peered through the window over the sink into the backyard. No sign of Michelle, and she apparently hadn't been working outside. Tall weeds swayed in the breeze, and thorny rose bushes overran the path.

The kitchen sink was piled high with dishes soaking in suds. Michelle had to be around somewhere. Aury headed for the back staircase that led out of the kitchen.

The banister was free from dust, and the stair treads felt secure under Aury's feet as she climbed. With a house this old, Aury was surprised not to hear creaks and groans from the old boards. At the second floor, she stepped into the hall, although the staircase continued upward.

"Michelle?" The early afternoon sunlight streamed through a series of tall bay windows. Aury stuck her head into open doorways, admiring the large rooms, some already empty, others with boxes waiting to be moved.

One closed door proved to be locked when Aury jiggled the handle. Curiosity piqued, she made a mental note to circle back to that room once she located Michelle. When she poked her head into the next room, her heart skipped a beat.

A figure lay prone on the polished hardwood floor, blood glistening in the sunlight.

Chapter 5

"**M**ichelle!" Aury rushed in, dropping to her knees beside her friend.

She felt for a pulse. Nothing.

This couldn't be happening. Not Michelle.

Aury's hands shook, and her mouth went dry.

What was she supposed to do?

Focus! Aury took a deep breath, willing herself to be calm. This wasn't the first dead body she had seen, but that time, there were other people who could help.

"What are you doing here?"

The booming voice shocked Aury out of her spiral. Her heart pounded in her ears, but at least her brain was reengaged.

She shot a look at the young man in the doorway. "Call nine-one-one!"

Aury bent back over the body, hoping against hope that she had missed the pulse. The back of the woman's head was matted with dark red blood.

"What have you done?" The question from the man came out in a harsh rasp as he grabbed Aury's shoulder.

A slice of fear cut through her as she realized this might be the man who attacked Michelle. She spun quickly in a half crouch, ready to defend herself.

The man stared at the bloody mess, not at Aury. "Aunty Michelle?"

Aunty? A closer look at him revealed no blood on his hands or clothes. With his scrawny frame and the blond scruff on his chin, Aury put him in his early twenties. His furrowed brow and look of confusion reminded her of a leery mutt ready to bolt.

Dismissing him as a threat, she focused on helping Michelle.

Aury rolled her friend onto her back. An earbud fell into the pool of blood. With the initial shock over, she realized this woman was much younger than Michelle, although their hair length and color were the same.

The man froze in place. "That's not Aunty Michelle."

Aury quickly scanned the woman from head to foot, checking for other injuries besides the back of her head. She didn't want to make things worse. Nothing obvious. She ensured the woman's body was flat against the floor so she could perform CPR.

The man went from petrified to aggressive before Aury had time to process her next move. He fixated on the body and yelled, "What did you do to her?"

"I'm trying to help. I said call nine-one-one!" Aury started chest compressions, although she had little faith it would make a difference.

The man stepped back as he continued to yell at Aury. "You better believe I'm calling the cops. How dare you break in here!"

The man punched buttons and only stopped his muttering when someone on the other end answered.

Aury half-registered his words as she concentrated on keeping her compressions steady, running the tune of "Stayin' Alive" through her head as she had been taught. The AJR song from the car earlier played atop it in her mind, a discordant harmony reminding her how fast everything had changed. The bouncing melody of the college band singing about Legos was so different than the steady rhythm meant to imitate an absent heartbeat.

She picked up on *break-in* and *dead* before the twenty-something man was standing over her again.

All signs of shock gone, he stood with his arms folded across his chest, watching Aury perform CPR. "What are you doing? She's gone. Isn't it obvious?"

His callousness only revived Aury's determination, and she got her second wind.

Her arms ached by the time paramedics arrived and gently moved her aside. The taller medic in a blue uniform checked for a pulse while the other pulled out an automated external defibrillator. The medic checking for a pulse shook his head and ripped opened the bloody woman's shirt.

The other unsealed the defibrillator pads and handed them to her partner, while she flipped on the machine to charge. The man placed the pads on the chest of the downed woman.

As the whine of the machine revved up, the female paramedic placed the paddles on the pads. "Clear!"

The other paramedic sat back and raised his hands.

The body jumped as the beep indicated the released shock. Immediately, the male paramedic continued CPR.

Aury watched as the scene played out in slow motion. She rubbed her upper arms, trying to stop her shaking. Silently, she prayed over and over for the woman to live.

The medic shocked the woman two more times before setting the paddles aside. "No pulse and no response."

"Agree," the second one answered. Addressing Aury, he asked, "How long did you perform compressions?"

Aury shook her head. "I'm not really sure, to be honest." She tipped her chin toward the surly man in saggy pants who stood near the window, a cell phone still in his hand. "I told that man to call nine-one-one, then I started compressions. I didn't know what else to do."

A shudder ran through her as she took in the body and the crimson smears on the floor. Bloody footprints led from the puddle to where the belligerent man stood, slapping his phone against his palm.

The first paramedic jotted down something on a pad.

Someone cleared his throat, catching everyone's attention. He wore a suit, but the tie was loose and the jacket open. "Are you done here?"

"Yes, Lieutenant," the male paramedic said. "We'll wait outside."

Aury was too stunned to move. She continued to stare at the body, now discarded among the equipment and debris from the AED pads. *What had just happened?*

The man with the phone turned to the officer. His yellow boxer shorts showed above his belt. He pointed an angry finger at Aury. "I found her assaulting that poor woman."

Aury could only blink at them. Her mind couldn't form words, and she struggled to understand what the angry man was saying.

"Sir, wait with the police officers outside." The lieutenant guided Saggy Pants around the body and to the bedroom door to where two uniformed officers were standing. "They'll take your statement."

"But where is Aunty Michelle? What if she did something to my aunty?"

"I'm right here. What is going on?" Michelle tried to push into the room, but a patrolman stopped her.

"Oh, Aunty! I'm so relieved you're okay. I thought she hurt you." Michelle's nephew threw himself into her arms.

The fluctuation in his attitude had Aury wondering if this was the same man who had been yelling at her. Had he yelled at her, or was that her imagination? Confusion swirled in her foggy brain.

Michelle patted his back awkwardly three times, then pushed him away. "Of course I'm all right. Will someone tell me what's going on?"

"That woman killed one of your guests!" The young man disengaged from his aunt and brandished his accusatory finger at Aury again. This time his voice came across more whiny than threatening.

The patrolman took the man's arm. "You can give me your statement outside. Ma'am, why don't you come with me as well?"

Michelle spotted Aury over the patrolman's head. "Aury? Are you okay?"

When Aury didn't answer, Michelle tried to brush the patrolman aside again.

"She wasn't harmed," the cop said. "Lieutenant Elliott is taking her statement now. Let's go downstairs and let Lieutenant Elliott do his job." The man in uniform politely but firmly herded Michelle and her nephew down the stairs.

The lieutenant returned to Aury. "Can you tell me your name?"

She couldn't stop staring at the body.

He cleared his throat.

Her breath hitched as she answered, "Aury. Aury St. Clair."

"Aury, I'm Lieutenant Jack Elliott. I'm a detective with the Surry Police Department. Let's sit down. I think you're suffering from shock." He guided her into the hallway where an armchair rested on the second-floor landing. "You aren't hurt, are you? That's not your blood, right?"

She regarded her hands and work-weathered calluses splotched with red. Numbly, she shook her head. "I found her."

"You did good. There was nothing you could have done, but you tried. Many others wouldn't have in your shoes." He produced a handkerchief from his pocket and handed it to her.

Lot of good it did. Half of her almost wished she hadn't. Then maybe the sensation of the woman's still chest wouldn't be lingering on her palm. Then maybe the fingernails caked with blood wouldn't seem so alien. She used the cloth to scrub the blood from her hands.

Elliott took out a small notebook. "What about the woman? Do you know who she is?"

She shook her head. "Why was she in Michelle's house?"

Elliott jotted something down. "Michelle who? Is that the woman who lives here?"

Aury licked her lips. Her tongue felt swollen in her mouth. "No, not exactly."

Elliott waited.

"Paris. Her last name's Paris. She's fixing up the house. It's part of Fresh Start." Aury rubbed her palms against the fabric of her jeans. Her mouth was dry, but her hands were wet. Was that normal?

"Ah, I've heard of Fresh Start. Good program. What brought you here today?"

Aury met his gaze. "Michelle. She told me to come by to pick up things for the crafters' cottage."

"Good. That explains that." The lieutenant's voice was calming, but his eyes were sharp. "Where was Michelle when you got here?"

Aury cleared her throat. "I'm not sure. I looked for her. Her car was here. Then I found . . ."

"I understand. Did you come with the gentleman?"

"Who?" Realization dawned on her. He meant the man shouting at her while she tried to revive the woman. Aury's nose wrinkled. "I don't know him. He came in after."

"Did you know Michelle had a nephew?"

She started to shake her head and changed her mind when a flash of an old conversation resurfaced in her memory. "Michelle told me her nephew was supposed to be helping her clean out the house. I hadn't met him before."

Elliott closed his notebook and rose. "Are you able to go to the station and make a statement?"

Reflexively, Aury also stood. "I want to call Scott."

"Scott?"

"My fiancé."

"You can call him from the station. Let's go." He reached out to help her up, but she pulled away.

Clarity settled in Aury's chest, replacing the haze that had been clouding her mind. "I want to call him now."

She stared the officer down. Her set jaw left no room for argument.

He tilted his head back to stare at the ceiling. After a deep sigh, Elliott gestured for her to lead the way out.

Aury pulled out her phone as they made their way down the stairs and out of the house. Things seemed to move in slow motion until Scott answered. His jovial manner grated her raw nerves that were strung tight from the last thirty minutes. She spoke over him to get the needed words out. Elliott lurked nearby, so she kept the call short.

As she disconnected, an elderly man charged up to Elliott. His tweed coat was frayed at the cuffs and didn't match his gray-striped pants at all. Something about his short, curly, black hair with tuffs of white felt familiar to Aury, but she couldn't place him. Maybe she had seen him around town.

She sidled closer to the pair while staying out of the officer's line of sight. The odor of whiskey reached her across the distance, and though Aury was no connoisseur, she doubted such a reek came from anything on the top shelf.

"What's going on here, officer?" the man demanded.

Elliott took his time turning, his expression slightly annoyed. "And who might you be?"

The man planted his feet and gestured toward the house next door, puffing out his narrow chest. "I'm Thomas Freeman. I'm in charge of the neighborhood watch in this community and have a duty to keep my neighbors safe."

"What a coincidence, Mr. Freeman. I'm Lieutenant Elliott, the police officer tasked with keeping Surry safe. I hope you can see our goals here are aligned and that you will be an asset instead of an obstacle during our investigation." Elliott gave Freeman a stern look from under his bushy eyebrows.

Aury got the sense that Elliott had met people like Freeman before and was unlikely to be bullied. That earned him a notch up on her respect scale.

Perhaps the man also realized Elliott wouldn't be bullied, and that was why his face turned a deep, angry purple. "It's my neighborhood! I have the right to know what's happening next door to me."

"Well, Mr. Freeman, I'll send a patrolman to talk to you shortly, and he will be happy to have a nice long conversation on your rights or anything else you may have ferreted out while on your neighborhood watch." Elliott turned as if that was the end of it, but Freeman clearly wasn't finished.

Freeman cast his gaze around frantically, landing on the man in the saggy pants. He nodded to where Brandon slumped sullenly against a police car. "You've got young Brandon there. He's a feisty one, that."

Seeming reluctant to entertain Freeman's interference any longer, Elliott's eyebrows squeezed together, and he rolled his eyes. He cast a tired glance at Brandon. "Doesn't look that way to me. What makes you say so?"

Freeman crossed his arms and slowed his response to a casual pace. "Everyone in the neighborhood heard him and his aunt carrying on ever since they started working over there. He wasn't one to do anything without a fight."

Aury didn't miss the bluster in his words.

This time the lieutenant observed Brandon more closely. "Have they had one of these arguments lately?"

"Just this morning." The neighbor had changed from angry to eager now that he had the officer's attention. "That's what I figured all this fuss was about, but I can't believe Michelle would call the cops on him. She has the patience of a saint, that one. Why is the ambulance here?"

Though curiosity furrowed Elliott's brow briefly, he put on a neutral mask in light of Freeman's excitement. "Go home for now. I'll have a patrolman stop by to get your statement." Elliott locked his eyes on Aury. "Miss St. Clair? Are you ready to go now?"

She nodded; however, she was more absorbed with watching Freeman's nostrils flare in renewed frustration at the lieutenant's repeated dismissal than their impending departure.

"There's nothing to worry about," the lieutenant said, misinterpreting Aury's frown. "The statement we'll need from you is just a confirmation of what we already talked about."

"That's fine." Aury's eyes followed Freeman as the elderly neighbor stomped away, stumbling a bit when he reached the curb. She tipped her head in his direction. "Only I can't promise my statement will be anywhere near as exciting as his promises to be."

Elliott shot Aury a wry smile. "Thank goodness for the neighborhood watch."

Aury attempted a smile, but she couldn't erase the image of the figure sprawled across the floor upstairs.

"I feel safer already."

Chapter 6

When Aury finished giving her statement, she was released into the police station waiting room. A desk sergeant sat in a tall chair behind a counter, plucking away at a computer keyboard. The stark, white walls were blinding after the windowless office where the policewoman made her relive the experience of finding the body.

Scott was the only one waiting in the row of gray metal folding chairs against the wall. He jumped to his feet when she emerged. "Are you okay?"

She fell into his arms and nodded against his shoulder, letting his earthy scent soothe her. Relief flooded her as she finally let herself be comforted after the unexpected ordeal of the afternoon.

The outer door to the station waiting room banged open. "Who's in charge here?"

A forty-something-year-old man dressed in creased blue jeans and a brown leather bomber jacket charged toward the counter.

The patrolman stepped around the desk, intercepting the man before he could storm into the deeper reaches of the station. "What can I help you with, sir?"

"I need to talk to the person in charge of the investigation at the Warren house. It belongs to my family. I want to know what's going on." The man tugged at the bottom of his jacket, pulling it tighter across his bulging belly.

"Why don't you have a seat, and I'll get Lieutenant Elliott for you?" The patrolman squinted and inclined his head. "That's quite the shiner you got there. Is there something you need to report?"

The man waved a hand in a frustrated dismissal. "It's got nothing to do with this. Let me talk to Elliott."

The cop pointed to a metal chair. He didn't make a move until the blustery man sat.

He was breathing hard as he dropped onto the chair. Sweat glistened along the man's receding, blond hairline. He ran a hand over his forehead, wiping the wetness away on his jeans.

"Michelle said the house was donated to her nonprofit. I wonder why this guy says he owns it," Aury whispered to Scott.

"We're sticking around to find out, aren't we?" Scott winked at her.

She gave him a squeeze in response. She tried to hold very still and go unnoticed, but she felt stifled laughter shaking Scott's shoulders.

Elliott entered the lobby. His red silk tie was tightened now, and Aury noted the cut of his suit was not off the rack. She didn't know a lot about men's fashions, but it fit him too well not to be tailormade.

The balding man sprang from his seat and tugged at his jacket again.

"I'm Lieutenant Elliott." The officer held out his hand for the visitor to shake. "I understand you have some information for me. Let's start with your name."

Grudgingly, the man shook his hand. "David Willard. My family owns the Warren house. I heard there was a murder. I demand to be informed."

Two overly interested men in one hour, both equally forceful with their questions and confident in their entitlement to the answers, Aury mused. Clearly the similarity wasn't lost on the lieutenant either.

Lieutenant Elliott inhaled deeply through his nose as he retracted his hand. "'Demand' is such a harsh word," he said calmly. "Besides, I was led to believe Michelle Paris owns the house, or at least Fresh Start does. Are you two related?"

Willard scoffed. "She doesn't own the house. Not yet. My aunt Penny Warren does, and it sounds like she needs to hang on to it. This is what she gets for trying to do something nice."

"I don't see how a young woman's death affects Ms. Warren, unless there's something you aren't telling me."

Aury admired how smoothly Elliott spoke. He didn't let this blowhard ruffle him either.

"It's her reputation, of course! Why should she be involved with people who go around getting themselves killed?"

Elliott lifted a single eyebrow. "I'm sure that wasn't the victim's intention when she got out of bed this morning."

The door to the back offices opened, and Michelle slipped out. Dressed in an old flannel shirt and baggy khakis, she appeared to have aged twenty years since she had visited Aury at Eastover.

When Michelle spotted Aury, tears filled her already puffy eyes, and Michelle hurried to her, arms outstretched. "I'm so glad you're okay. I feel terrible that you got involved with this tragedy."

Aury returned the tight squeeze and then took hold of Michelle's hands. "Are you okay? Who was that woman?"

Before Michelle had a chance to answer, Willard turned on her. "I demand you give up on this crazy scheme of yours before someone else gets hurt!"

"There you go, *demanding* again," Elliott said in a bored tone. "Mr. Willard, let's go in the back, and I'll take your statement."

"Statement? About what? I'm waiting for *you* to tell *me* what happened."

"Perhaps, but that's not how it works here. Let's go." Elliott took Willard's elbow and steered him to the door.

Michelle focused on Aury. "Izzie was one of the single women who was slated to move in once we got the house fixed up. She's been painting the bedrooms." She held a hand to her mouth. "Is this my fault?"

"No, of course not. Why would it be your fault?"

"She was only there because I asked her to help me. If I didn't, would she still be alive?" Silent tears streamed down Michelle's face.

"There was no way you could know something would happen." Aury embraced her again, understanding the need to take the blame. She had asked herself the same question about her parents' deaths hundreds of times. "Don't think like that."

Scott placed a gentle hand on Michelle's shoulder. "Come on. We'll give you a ride home."

As they made their way outside, a flash went off. Questions bombarded them from the waiting reporters.

"Were you the one who found the body?"

"What'll happen to Fresh Start now?"

"How was she killed?"

"Did you see the murder weapon?"

Aury ducked her head and turned protectively toward Michelle. She didn't understand how people could be so insensitive, but she also knew responding was out of the question.

Scott stepped in front of the ladies to shield them. The trio ignored the shouts as patrolmen cleared their way to Scott's pickup truck.

Safely behind locked doors, Scott glanced first at Aury and then Michelle. "Are you okay? The media can be brutal."

Michelle stared out the window, eyes glazed over. "Izzie is dead."

Scott and Aury exchanged a concerned look. Aury didn't know Izzie, but she knew her friend. Michelle would beat herself up about this forever. Aury's mind went into overdrive trying to figure out a way to help.

Scott put the truck in gear. "Let's get her home and settled."

They rode through the quiet neighborhoods of Surry. The lots were large, leaving open space between the modest-sized houses. Aury couldn't help but compare them to the tightly packed developments in Newport News. She had felt suffocated by the ability to touch her house and the one next door at the same time. Here, there was room for kids to play safely in a yard rather than the street.

Their next turn took them into a newer area. The lots had been subdivided. The buildings were closer together but still sat a respectable distance apart. The houses were mostly two-story with vinyl siding and dormer windows. The variety of neutral colors were only distinguished by flower gardens and bushes, which were now closing up for the coming winter. The current warm temperatures had fooled a few bushes into sprouting one last bloom.

Michelle's house was pale green with forest-green shutters. Flower boxes hung off the rails of the front porch that ran the width of the house. Only a few stubborn pansies lent any color to the beds. When they pulled into the empty driveway, Aury offered, "Scott and I can go get your car."

"Don't bother. Brandon can take me over when he finishes up. Why don't you come in for coffee or tea?" Michelle climbed the front steps to her house slowly, as if in pain.

She opened the heavy wooden door with its lovely etched glass. Taking a deep breath, Michelle appeared to collect herself, then headed toward the back of the house.

As Aury and Scott stepped into the brightly lit entry hall, she paused to gather her thoughts and feelings. Yes, she had been through an ordeal, but Michelle needed her support right now. Izzie was her friend, and her murder occurred on Michelle's property, or at least property she was responsible for. What would this mean for Fresh Start?

Aury would find time later to process her part in this horrible day. And to wash her hands again. They still felt sticky from the blood, even though she had washed her hands thoroughly at the station.

Scott took Aury's elbow, stopping her from following right away. "How are you handling all this? Are you up to visiting?"

"I'm fine." She moved to follow Michelle, and he squeezed her elbow gently, halting her in her tracks. Pent-up energy from the day and a surge of adrenaline activated her fight-or-flight response. It took all her concentration to not run away from him. She recognized that her heightened senses were putting her on edge; she wasn't really in danger. She needed to take control of her emotions.

"I can make an excuse to get us out of here," he went on.

Something about those words triggered a memory—not a good one. "I don't need you to make excuses for me." Her heart raced, but she forced herself to stay calm. "Let go of my arm please."

He dropped his hand immediately but stepped closer to her. "It's been a horrific day. It would be totally understandable if you wanted to take some time alone to process this."

"Time alone or time with you?" Her voice sounded cold to her ears, but she couldn't help herself. *He's not my ex,* she chided herself.

"Of course I'll be there for you. Always." He reached for her hand.

Todd had offered her the same type of comfort after her parents died. It lasted only long enough to get her alone to reshape the events leading up to the night of their car accident.

Gran had to come to the house and supervise as Aury packed her things. Gran spent months pulling her out of her funk. After that, Aury had sworn to be stronger.

Aury straightened her shoulders and stepped back. She couldn't meet his eyes. "I'll be fine."

She had to be fine.

"I'm here for you whenever you need me." Scott stepped closer but didn't attempt to touch her this time.

Her resolve started to slip. She would love him to wrap his arms around her and keep her safe, but that put her fate in someone else's hands. She didn't want to depend on anyone that much.

She cleared her throat and willed herself to speak rationally. "If you'll remember, this isn't the first dead body I've seen."

His shoulders slumped as if he were carrying a great weight. "Well, yeah, I know that, but this is different—"

Aury couldn't help herself. Her walls of protection slammed into place. She had to act strong to be strong. "I would guess this *is* the first murder victim Michelle has run across on property she's responsible for. Let's focus on her."

As she put her hand up to stop any further argument he might offer, she had to confess inwardly that she was still shaken from finding Izzie. The blood on her hands . . . she shuddered. But she didn't want to be treated like she was helpless. She would work through the madness filling her head—sadness for Izzie, fear that a killer was out there, relief she wasn't dead. They all vied for her attention. She had to hold it together.

Relaxing her shoulders, Aury washed the traces of irritation from her face before she emerged into the kitchen, where Michelle was filling a kettle and placing it on the stove.

Like the rest of the house suggested, the room was modest but comfortable. There was a coziness that all lived-in kitchens had, from the cartoon snail theme among the fridge magnets to the quilted potholders hanging from the cabinet handles. A large air fryer and a shiny food processor showed the house wasn't frozen in time. Michelle may have been on the older side of middle-age, but she was clearly not one to turn her nose up at new gadgetry.

"Have you had any trouble at the Warren house since you started working there?" Aury asked as Michelle fetched three mugs from the shelf above the stove.

Michelle sighed. "Just the usual. It's been empty for some time now, and I suspect kids used it as a hangout. I upgraded all the locks. Occasionally kids will see if they can pry open a window, but they haven't been able to get in." She dropped into her seat. "Surely none of the kids in the neighborhood would be capable of this!"

Aury thought of the brutality of the room at Fresh Start, the cold way the woman had been left face down in her own blood. This was the same image she told Scott was nothing to worry about, but here it was, burnt into her eyelids.

Pushing that thought aside, she patted her friend's hand. "I don't think this was kids. Did Izzie have any problems that you know of? Anyone bothering her?"

Michelle nodded vigorously, eager to share. "She has an ex-husband who wasn't happy when she left him. He's a piece of work. Spends most evenings at the bar and then ends up on her doorstep drunk as a skunk. That's one of the reasons she . . . was moving into the Fresh Start house."

She choked up on the last sentence just as the kettle began to squeal.

Suspecting her friend wanted the space to take a few deep breaths, Aury didn't ask any more questions while Michelle jumped up to finish preparing the tea.

Scott was trying to catch Aury's eye, but she pretended not to notice. She was afraid something in her expression would betray just how much she understood the victim's plight.

Aury and Scott murmured their thanks as Michelle placed two steaming mugs of water in front of each of them.

"Earl Grey or chamomile?"

"Sorry?" Aury blinked away the mirage of her former disastrous relationship.

"For the tea." Michelle held two boxes in her hand. "I didn't know what each of you would prefer, so I left it up to a cup-by-cup basis."

"Oh . . . chamomile, please." Aury wasn't much of a tea drinker. Her vice of choice had always been coffee.

Michelle handed her a little packet and turned to Scott.

"Earl Grey." Scott produced the kind of reassuring smile Aury wished she could muster right now as Michelle passed him the bag. "Thank you. It's one of my favorites."

First Aury assumed the statement was part of Scott's usual kindness, but the delight in his eyes was genuine. Since when did Scott have favorite teas? Aury couldn't remember ever seeing him drink it. They usually had coffee together. Did he drink it only when she wasn't around, or was he just being nice?

The thought nettled her more than it should have, burrowing in alongside the other stressors pounding the inside of Aury's brain.

"Do you think Izzie's ex-husband knew she was moving into Fresh Start?" Scott took a little sip from his steaming cup, pausing for a second to inhale the aroma.

Surprise favorites or not, Scott was getting them back on track, for which Aury was immensely grateful. She had to focus. There were more than her little anxieties at stake here.

"I would hope not," Michelle mused. "But . . . it's a definite possibility. Though moving out is the first step, it takes a while longer to break old habits. Many of the Fresh Start ladies struggle with keeping their former partners out of the loop on their lives, no matter how bad things between them once were. You know how these things go."

Only too well.

Aury took a sip of tea to be polite. "Did you tell the police about Izzie's ex-husband?"

Michelle's cup stopped partway to her lips. "Of course."

Aury could have sworn she caught a glint in Michelle's eyes.

Michelle lowered her tea back to the saucer without drinking. "They said they would track him down."

Scott frowned. "How long do you think that will take?"

"A layabout like him?" Michelle snorted. "Please. No doubt they're closing in already."

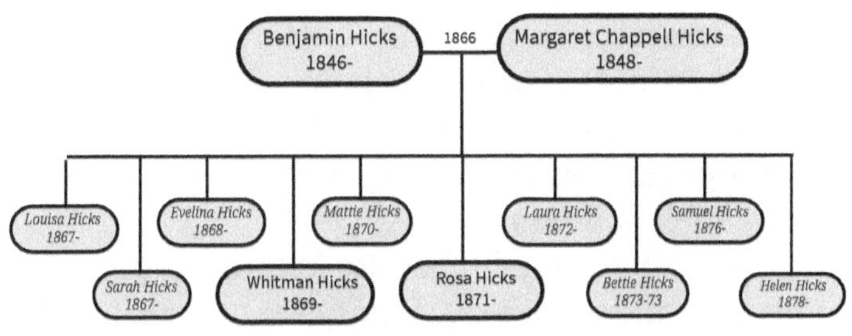

Chapter 7

Spring 1880

Margaret stood on the front porch and watched her husband load the last of their belongings into the wagon. She didn't like the idea of Talmadge Freeman moving into their house, but it was a reality she had to accept. Tears threatened to sting her eyes, but she refused to let them fall. God had never failed them, and He wasn't about to start now. She clung to faith as a lifeline in the face of uncertainty. She believed that every challenge was a step in God's intricate plan—even if the path remained obscured. This new adventure was part of His plan.

"Come on, Mama." Rosa tugged at Margaret's hand. "Pa said I get to sit up front this time. He might even let me hold the reins."

Margaret allowed the eight-year-old to help her down the steps. Child Number Ten wasn't due for another three months, but with every pregnancy, it felt like she got bigger faster.

"Aren't you excited for Southampton, Mama? They have a railroad! We're going to be able to watch the trains go right through town." Rosa kept up a steady stream of questions and comments. "And won't it be fun to have Sunday dinners with Grandaddy and Nana? We won't have to do all the cooking and cleaning now. Pa says Nana makes the best corn chowder ever."

As Rosa prattled on, Margaret let her ruminations drift back to early Sunday dinners with her in-laws. Although she was a wonderful woman, Nana sure could make Margaret feel inadequate when it came to being a wife. The first year living under the same roof was claustrophobic. That was the primary reason they had made their way to Surry. Leaving had allowed her and Benjamin to grow closer and establish their own ways to bring up their children.

Now, with Benjamin's parents getting on in years, his father needed him to take over the acres of farmland that he had been tending. Margaret listened often as Benjamin spoke with excitement about the chance to implement many of the latest farming techniques he had been studying. He felt that planting the same crops year after year caused the soil to be depleted quicker. He wanted to rotate the planting every three years, circulating between peanuts, soybeans, and grain.

Two years ago, she and Benjamin scraped together enough money to buy the house and farmland they had been living on for nine years. So many memories of her young ones were tied to this house. She wasn't ready to let it go.

Benjamin convinced her that the increased acreage on his father's Southampton land would allow him to experiment with farming techniques at a lower risk if one crop didn't take. Plus they would still have income from the property they rented out in Surry to keep them afloat.

Rosa handed Margaret off to Benjamin and ran to claim a seat near the horses.

Margaret glanced longingly back at the house. "Do you really think Talmadge will be able to keep up on his payments?"

Benjamin took her hand and walked her to the waiting wagons. "I'll give him five years. He claims he needs more space to grow his new crop and work out the kinks of the contraption he's been putting together. I want to support anyone who's willing to put forth the work . . . I'm just not sure he's cut out to be an inventor. He wants to make a quick buck rather than look at the bigger picture."

Benjamin helped Margaret onto the bench of the second wagon. She smiled at the large cushion placed on the seat for her benefit.

"Nothing but the best for my queen." Benjamin kissed her hand. He addressed their eldest daughter holding the reins. "You take care of this precious cargo. You hear me?"

His daughter rolled her eyes but added a smile. "Yes, sir."

Whitman handed his mother a squawking baby. "I think she's getting hungry."

This little one was always hungry, but nothing gave Margaret more fulfillment than tending to her babies. She counted heads one more time as everyone found a seat. Nine. All accounted for.

The trip to Southampton would take two days at least. Benjamin and their eldest son had made the trip many times already, transferring most of their belongings to their new home, not far from her in-laws. Margaret hoped her small bladder wouldn't add too many stops along the way.

Benjamin settled the other children into the back of his wagon. Whitman and Rosa sat on the bench beside him.

Snapping the reins, Benjamin called out, "To our next great adventure!"

"To adventure!" the children echoed.

Chapter 8

Present day

Aury took comfort in the familiar sights and fragrances of Gran's kitchen. From the quilted table runner that changed with the seasons or Gran's mood to Aury's middle school artwork framed and hanging on the wall, this was Aury's happy place. The smell of cinnamon hung in the air, and she inhaled deeply. When she visited in the mornings, she could count on a delicious pastry or cookies. In the evenings, the kitchen usually smelled of sizzling garlic and onions. In this kitchen, Aury's worries always seemed manageable.

After picking up her car and taking a long, hot shower, Aury had come to her grandmother's. Scott had to wait at Eastover to accept a delivery, but Aury wanted to make sure to tell Gran before she heard about the attack on the news.

"That's just awful. That poor woman." Gran put a scone on Aury's plate and slipped two onto her own. "What are you going to do about it?"

"I'm not going to do anything. This is a job for the police." Aury took a big bite, savoring the sweet icing.

"Pah." Gran bit into the orange-glazed pastry. "We didn't read all those Nancy Drew books together for no reason. The sooner this killer is caught, the sooner we can all rest easier. Lord knows the police can use all the help they can get."

"I'm sure they would beg to differ. Besides, I have enough on my plate. I need to sort through all the donations I've been getting for the crafters' cottage and see what I still need to buy." Aury closed her eyes and massaged her temples. The stress of the day was catching up with her.

"Did you ever find out what Michelle wanted to give you?" Gran slid a bottle of ibuprofen across the table to her granddaughter.

Aury took one of the pills with her coffee. As she stared into her mug, her mind drifted briefly to Scott and his tea drinking. *Who was he drinking tea with?*

Stop it! You're being paranoid. She pushed the thought away. "More canvases, some old canning jars, and plenty of paint brushes. She said she'd bring them by once the police released the house as a crime scene."

"I used to can with my mother. I should dig out some of her old recipes. Maybe we can find a better use for those jars besides cleaning paint brushes. In the meantime, I think you should do some research on that David fellow. Why is he sticking his nose into things?"

Aury almost choked on her scone. "You mean the way you want me to? He at least has some connection to the house. I don't."

Gran popped the rest of the pastry into her mouth, but her smirk still broke through.

"I'm more curious about the ex-husband, to be honest." Aury stirred creamer into her coffee. Wasn't the spouse always the first suspect? Or the ex? "If Izzie was afraid of him, he must be a piece of work. I wonder what he gains from her death. Michelle said they didn't have any children, and if she was moving into the Fresh Start house, she must not have much money."

"Maybe there's a life insurance policy." Gran licked the sugar from her fingers, then wiped them on a napkin.

"I'm sure the police are looking into that angle. Maybe Izzie knew something the ex didn't want revealed." Aury stood and took the pad of paper that was sitting by the phone back to the table.

Gran tapped the pad. "That's it. Channel your inner Nancy Drew."

"Let's think this through. One option is Izzie was the target; the other is that the target was Michelle, and the killer made a mistake." Aury scribbled on the pad.

"Who would want to kill Michelle? She runs a nonprofit, for goodness sakes." Gran's mouth quirked in a mischievous grin. "Unless she leads a secret double life."

A chuckle escaped Aury. "That's it. No more mystery novels for you. You're clouding the facts with your imagination."

Gran's eyes twinkled.

Aury rested back in her seat, finally feeling the tension ebb. Her grandmother could always make her smile. She wondered if she should talk to Gran about her concerns with getting remarried. But then again, Gran was Scott's number one fan.

"Or Fresh Start was the target." Gran's comment brought Aury back to the topic.

"Good point." Aury jotted that down. "Who would want to shut down Fresh Start?"

"You said Brandon Paris was obnoxious. He just recently came sniffing around, didn't he? Would he benefit if it closed?"

"I wouldn't think so. Less work maybe. Fresh Start is a nonprofit, so Michelle doesn't really own the house. It wouldn't go to anyone in her family if she died." Aury drummed the pen on the table.

"What about Penny's family? She's a wonderful woman. We crossed paths often at various Women's Club of Williamsburg events. But you said her nephew was spouting off at the station." Gran wiped the crumbs from the table into her hand, then dumped them on her plate.

"Willard. David Willard." Aury wrote it down. "He came across as too stuffy to move to Surry. It's more likely he wants to sell the house and pocket the profit. I'll bet Hamilton Moore would snatch it up in a heartbeat."

Gran wrinkled her nose. "That man is a snake. He doesn't care about the feel of the town. He's all about the money."

Aury sketched a few dollar signs on the paper in various sizes. "If Penny wanted to sell the house, she could have sold directly to Moore."

"So she didn't need the money. Maybe Willard does."

Money was a big motivator. Was the property worth killing over? Aury blew out a breath. "But would she give the house to her nephew if Fresh Start fell through?"

"She might. She and Christopher never had kids of their own. Willard might be her closest relation." Gran carried her plate to the sink and rinsed it.

Aury took a note to see exactly how they were related. "If he wanted her money, wouldn't it make more sense to kill Mrs. Warren? Not some random person in her house?"

"Could be he was being patient, waiting for Penny to die, but now he's getting the feeling his inheritance isn't as locked up as he thought."

Aury struggled to follow the what-ifs they were conjuring up. She read her list, doodling question marks on the page. "I should probably learn a little more about Izzie. She's from Surry. That's why she was moving here."

Gran waved her hand at the paper. "Find out where she was working. Maybe she uncovered a criminal plot, and it's got nothing to do with the house."

Aury chuckled. "This is Surry we're talking about."

Gran crossed her thin arms and tilted her head. "But the nuclear power plant is in Surry. Who knows what they could be covering up."

Chapter 9

Aury couldn't sleep. Her conversation with Gran raised more questions; Aury had to get answers. That was how she dealt with stress: through action.

Under the low glow of the kitchen counter lights, she made herself a cup of hot chocolate. The scent of peppermint and cocoa fortified her as she settled in front of her computer at the table. Smoothing out the crinkled paper with the notes she'd jotted down earlier, she opened various social media avenues and started typing. Brandon's account quickly popped up. Open to the public with no security settings. *Figures,* she thought.

Aury scrolled through selfie after selfie of Brandon hamming for the camera, sometimes posing with hand gestures he obviously thought made him look cool. His wardrobe seemed to consist mainly of hard rock band t-shirts and jeans at least three sizes too big for him. Perhaps no one had taught him how to shave, as his facial grooming was haphazard at best. The blond scruff he sported made his face appear grubby and young rather than almost thirty, as Michelle had told her.

A flash of metal recurred in many pictures. When Aury enlarged one of them, a two-inch pendant shaped like a sailboat stood out against his black t-shirt. If it was real gold, it was worth a pretty penny.

Scanning through more photos, Aury noted that Brandon had stopped wearing it a few months ago. It was very prominent in the older photos, which made its absence more obvious in recent posts. The chain was gone too. On a sticky, she scribbled the last date he wore it in the photos.

She studied the dates more closely. He had many more posts per day before the chain disappeared than he did afterward. When she hit a button, her printer whirred out a close-up of Brandon's face and shoulders, the pendant in full display.

Next, Aury clicked back to her search engine, typing in David's name. Nothing on social media, but there was one hit on the employee page of a small investment firm in New Jersey. In the photo, David was about ten years younger and twenty pounds lighter. He had a little more hair back then. Aury printed the photo anyway.

She jumped back to the home page. The latest update was a few years ago, so she searched for the name of the company.

She mumbled the headline to herself, "Lexon Financial Declares Bankruptcy. Leaves Investors Ruined."

Aury skimmed the details, then printed the article. She didn't find any other mentions of David Willard on the internet, so no new fancy job earning him a place in a company's hierarchy. If Willard was out of a job, that could be driving a need for money. Maybe he was counting on his aunt's fortune, and her donation to Fresh Start had him nervous.

Hamilton Moore's connection to the Warren house was nonexistent at this point, but he was easy to gather information on. His company website lauded his many accomplishments, but social media was overflowing with criticisms and complaints. A lawsuit was pending over workplace conditions that allegedly violated labor laws. Aury added that to her growing pile of research.

Another person in financial trouble?

When she searched for Izzie Clayton, the only thing to pop up was a local article about her murder. There was nothing on social media that was open to the public. She appeared to be a very careful and low-key person. There was no mention of her ex-husband in the article, and Aury cursed herself for not asking Michelle his name earlier. Without a name, she couldn't find information on him.

Anyone who read crime novels knew the ex or spouse was the most likely culprit, but for some reason, Aury's mind didn't want to entertain that idea. Izzie shouldn't have lost her life just as she was finding her freedom. There was no justice in it.

She glanced at her watch. It was close to midnight. Aury decided to give sleep another try. Quietly opening the bedroom door so as not to wake Scott, she was surprised to find him sitting up in bed, making notes on a drawing.

"Oh, I thought you were asleep." Aury kicked her slippers off and propped the pillows so she could sit beside him.

He hastily folded the pages and tucked them into a bag beside the bed.

"What are you working on?" She tried not to sound accusatory, but she couldn't ignore the sick feeling in her stomach. A warning that something wasn't right?

"Nothing important. Just jotting down ideas while I was thinking of them." He pulled back her side of the quilt, so she could slide her feet under. "You couldn't sleep either? Are you doing okay?"

Her spine went rigid. She didn't want to have this conversation again, but then she checked herself. It was a fair question. After all, she wasn't the only one up late. She pushed her wariness aside. This was the man she had promised to spend the rest of her life with. Snuggling in beside him, she laid her head on his bare chest.

Scott stroked her hair as he held her. "I have to admit it scares me to think how that could have been you." His voice caught. "What if you had gotten there earlier and surprised the killer?"

Aury's heart skipped a beat. She couldn't deny that the thought had also crossed her mind. She squeezed him tight. "Let's just be thankful I didn't."

Wanting to change the topic, she decided to fill him in on her sleuthing. "Gran thought it would be interesting to learn a little more about some of the people we met today. I was looking for any mentions of them on the internet."

"She *would* encourage you."

Even though his tone was soft, once again, Aury's defenses were up. She stiffened in his arms. No one said anything bad about her grandmother.

Scott huffed a small laugh. "What did you find?"

Aury forced herself to relax. Scott was a huge fan of Gran; he didn't mean it as a negative comment. Why was it so difficult for her to get past this sensitivity to every small thing?

She filled him in on the little she had uncovered.

He quietly absorbed the information. "David Willard does come across as a little desperate. Maybe he's hurting for money."

"Enough to kill for it?" Aury winced at her callous tone.

Scott shrugged. "Of course, if Penny Warren has enough money to give away a house, wouldn't she help a nephew who was down on his luck? Maybe he feels cheated out of something he thought should be his."

"Unless she had bailed him out before and has given up on him." Aury thought that tracked with his demeanor.

Shifting slightly beside her and tucking the quilt around her, Scott asked, "Why did you look up Hamilton Moore? He doesn't have a connection to any of this."

She waited until he settled again before placing her head back on his chest. "That was a side quest based on the idea that the house could somehow be turned into profit for either Willard or Brandon. Moore would be the logical one to sell to."

"You think Brandon has money trouble too?" As if understanding had suddenly come to him, Scott nodded. "Ah, that's why the interest in Brandon's necklace."

Aury shrugged. "It's just a feeling. I mean, why suddenly stop wearing something he was obviously attached to?"

"Are you going to ask him about it?"

"Not him, but maybe Michelle knows why he doesn't wear it anymore." She drummed her fingers against his stomach as she contemplated how she could bring it up casually in conversation.

"What did you learn about Michelle?"

Aury tilted her head to get a better look at his face. "Why would I look up Michelle?"

"You checked out all those other people. Are you immediately ruling her out because she's your friend?"

"Of course." But he had a good point. Her lips thinned as she thought about it. She had only known Michelle for a year, since they'd moved to Surry. Maybe there was something in her past Aury should be aware of.

That was the terrible thing about investigations. When digging for the truth, she ran the risk of overturning a lot of other dirt.

Chapter 10

"Michelle, you didn't have to come out here. I would have stopped by." Aury wiped her hands on her paint-speckled jeans as she approached Michelle's van.

She was taking advantage of the seventy-degree weather to air out the cottage. The door was propped open, and a fan hummed in the background.

"That didn't work out so well last time, did it? Besides, I was running errands." Michelle climbed out and walked to the doors at the back of the van.

Aury followed her. "Did the cops release the house already?"

"Last night. Everything but the room . . ." Michelle took a deep breath before clearing her throat. "They don't want me working on the second floor, but they said I can still clean up outside and on the first floor. They took lots of pictures, but the place is such a mess, it would be hard to tell if things had been disturbed. I can't imagine what a thief thought he could get."

"Does Lieutenant Elliott think it was a robbery?" Aury knew she was more interested than she should have been, but she couldn't rest easy until this crime was solved.

Michelle pressed her lips into a tight line. "Elliott's not telling me much."

"What about Izzie's ex-husband? Did you know him?"

"The cops tracked him down, but they didn't arrest him. I saw him at the diner, acting the grieving husband to anyone who would listen." Michelle shook her head. "I don't know what to think. He's a scumbag, for sure."

"I guess if it was him, that would make everyone else feel safer. I mean, then it's not like there's a madman on the loose." Aury ended her sentence abruptly, suddenly worried her reasoning had sounded too crass given the circumstances.

But if Michelle was uncomfortable, she didn't let on. "Then maybe everything will get back to normal soon. Izzie's service is in a few days. She doesn't have any family, and her ex isn't stepping up, so the ladies from Fresh Start are pulling something together."

Aury felt a pinch on her heart as she thought of her own lack of family. Gran was all she had. Once Gran was gone, who would be holding the black umbrellas and listening to Aury's eulogy? Would Scott be the one to speak for her? She swallowed a lump in her throat. "Let me know if we can help in any way."

"Thanks. I'll keep that in mind." Michelle opened the back door. "Let's get rid of this stuff first. You can have whatever you think is useful. The rest is going to the dump."

Aury poked through the items, pulling out anything she thought she could repurpose—an old tarp, glass jars, flower vases, and empty wooden picture frames. Creative ideas flew through her brain with every object she picked up. At this rate, Michelle wouldn't have anything left to take to the dump.

She studied Michelle's haggard face. "This is a lot. Please don't tell me you're taking care of it on your own."

Michelle rested her hands on her ample hips. "That good-for-nothing nephew of mine was supposed to help me get everything loaded. As usual, he didn't show up. Thomas Freeman from next door is such a sweetie. He offered to help, but by then I was almost done. There's a young boy working at the dump who will unload it for me, so I'm set. The hard part is done."

Aury considered a large piece of glass but thought better of it. Learning how to paint on glass was on her wish list, but she had more than enough material to work with. When she needed more, perhaps she would make a trip to the dump to dig up more treasures. She smiled to herself when she thought how Scott would tease her endlessly.

She wiped heavy dust off a wooden kitchen chair. The paint flaked away with it. "Have you heard any more from Willard? Penny's relation?"

"That guy from the station? He's quite a piece of work, isn't he? He came by the house. Tried to barge his way in like he owned the place, but I wasn't having any of that. I began by talking to him politely, but I finally had to threaten to call the police if he didn't leave."

"You're kidding! The nerve of that guy." An image of her ex flashed in her mind: angry, standing in Gran's front yard in the middle of the night, bellowing for Aury to come out. Gran wasn't the type to suffer fools; she turned the garden hose on him.

Michelle was still talking. "I tried to call Penny, but she's out of the country on vacation. My lawyer says I don't have anything to worry about. Willard doesn't have a claim because Penny owns the house outright."

Their discussion was interrupted by a sudden crashing through the brush behind the cottage. A large rabbit shot from the woods, followed closely by Treasure's dark form. It resembled a game of tag more than anything sinister.

"Treasure!" Aury called.

The puppy hesitated and almost tripped over her large paws.

"To me." Aury had little hope that the black Labrador would respond to her command, so she was pleasantly surprised when the pup gave up the chase and loped to her side.

Aury bent down to scratch behind Treasure's ears. She pulled burrs and dead leaves that somehow stuck to the short fur. "Looks like we'll have to brush you out again. I swear you do this for the attention."

Michelle laughed. "She's a beauty. It looks like her training's paying off."

Aury glanced up at Michelle while she continued to comb through Treasure's coat. "I'm not sure if she's being trained or if I am."

Treasure had given Aury a sense of permanence when Scott presented the pup to her. That was when their house together felt like a home.

Scott emerged from the path through the woods. He pushed a wheelbarrow full of yard tools, sweat marking the t-shirt pulled tight across his broad muscles. "There she is. I swear, I can't keep up with that dog. Hey, Michelle. How are things going getting the Fresh Start house open?"

This question induced a heavy sigh from the older woman. "Slow progress. A few of the ladies who were scheduled to move in are rethinking it. They don't feel safe. Some of them are getting out of bad relationships, like Izzie. They don't want their exes to get any ideas. I need to get the security system up and running sooner than I thought."

"If someone wants to get to you, cameras won't stop them." Aury's hand instinctively covered her mouth when she realized she had spoken the words out loud.

Scott shot Aury a sympathetic glance. To Michelle, he said, "Something is better than nothing. I know a guy who can hook you up. Just say the word."

Michelle looked at her quizzically, but Aury dropped her head and re-doubled her efforts on Treasure's grooming.

Scott stuck his head in the van. "Oh, is that a sawhorse?"

"Take it, please. I need all this stuff to go." Michelle sagged against the bumper.

As Scott dug through the pile, Aury watched him. Her chest tightened as her love for him expanded. He knew about her relationship with Todd and was patient when its effect on her reared its ugly head.

Scott was the opposite of her ex in so many ways. That was why the idea he was hiding something from her hurt so much.

But she wasn't the same woman she'd once been. No, Aury had become quite the detective. If some horrible history was about to repeat itself, she had every intention of seeing it coming.

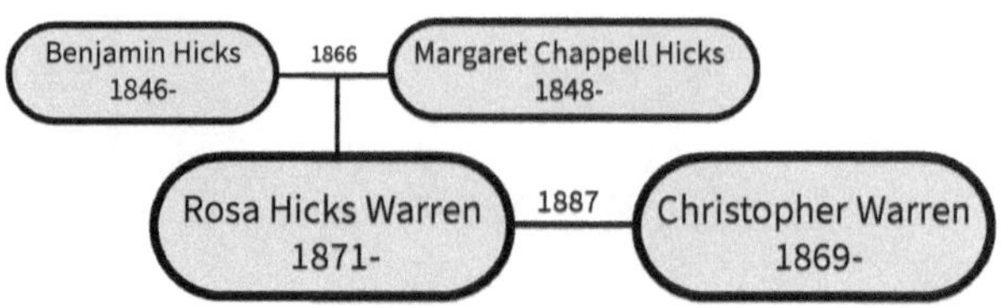

Chapter 11

Late Winter 1888

Christopher Warren extended his large, weathered hand to Talmadge Freeman. "I hope there're no hard feelings."

Freeman looked at the hand with disgust before his eyes tracked across the front of the regal house. "Why would I have hard feelings about you putting my family out on the street? All because you married the rich man's daughter."

"C'mon now, don't be like that." Christopher dropped his hand. "It's not my fault you couldn't pay the rent. Benjamin gave you three years past the original agreement, and it's not like you are without a home. He leased you the house next door."

"A house half the size."

"With rent that's also less than half. If you don't like it, you can always find someplace else to lay your head."

"Bah." Freeman stormed down the street.

Rosa Hicks Warren took her husband's elbow. "He's not going to make a very good neighbor."

"He'll get over it eventually or move on. We'll stay on our side of the fence." Christopher guided her to the front door. Before she could step over the threshold, he swept her into his arms.

She tried to catch her wide-brimmed hat before it fell to the porch. Unsuccessful, she gave up and laced her hands behind his neck. "You do realize I've been here before, right?"

"Only as Rosa Hicks. Not as Mrs. Christopher Warren. This is our home now." Pride swelled his chest.

She kissed him deeply.

Christopher's head swam, and he had to pull back to catch his breath. He carried her into the house. "You keep that up, and we'll fill this place as fast as your parents did."

She jumped from his arms. Picking up her skirt, she dashed playfully down the hall and through the kitchen.

He caught her on the wide back porch that overlooked the fields. The sun caught the white of her teeth, making them gleam brilliantly against the dark brown of her face. The sight of her left Christopher breathless. He was the luckiest man in Virginia. After sliding his arms around her waist, they rocked in companionable silence for a few moments.

Turning, she wrapped her arms around his neck. He gazed into her amber eyes. The extra fleck of dark brown in her right iris felt like something special only for him. One had to be close to see it, and no one else would ever get as close to her as he did.

She tilted her head and pressed herself closer to him. "You know Pa doesn't expect you to keep up with him. He never stops."

"I've been working for your pa for years. I know exactly what he expects. That's all well and good, because he taught me everything I know about farmin'. We'll be fine." He spun her to face the field again. Picking up her wrist, he used her arm as a pointer to indicate the coppery soil to the right. "We'll put soybeans there."

He redirected her to the left acreage. "Cotton there. We'll see how they do and make adjustments."

Her shoulders rose and fell. "But we always grew peanuts here. Even Mr. Freeman's been growing peanuts."

"And that's why Freeman couldn't pay his rent. He's been planting the same crop for the past eight years. Each yield is smaller than the last. I think your pa's onto something. Rotating the crops keeps the soil rich. It's working for him in Southampton." Christopher kissed her temple. His body vibrated with excitement. They were given a wonderful opportunity, and he wasn't about to disappoint the great Benjamin Hicks.

She glanced over her shoulder at him. "And then? I know farming isn't your first passion."

"You are, my lovely." Kissing her again, he couldn't have dreamed of a better partner. His life was blessed, and he would do anything in his power to make his wife happy.

Rosa rested the back of her head against his chest. "Okay. I'll accept that. But what else have you and Pa been scheming?"

He squeezed her close, then let her go to lead her to the porch swing. "We've been talking about what comes next after farming. It's good and right to feed the community, but what if we could sell our produce farther away than the river? The railroad can carry goods across the country. We need to be able to package our harvest so it can travel easily."

He sat and pulled her down beside him. "Someday our descendants will look back at this farmland and know it all started here."

Chapter 12

Present day

Aury wandered through Karmine's art studio, studying the sketches and pastel drawings tacked on standing easels scattered throughout the large, open space.

Karmine held a canvas up where the special lighting in her studio would enhance the colors. "These are lovely. You've come a long way in your painting."

Aury laughed. "Oh, no, these aren't mine. I'm sticking with basic landscapes and crazy animals for now. Someone gave them to me to reuse the canvases. I wanted to get your opinion before painting over them."

Karmine was an art instructor whom Aury had taken many classes from. Her infectious teaching style had inspired Aury to try different things with her creativity outside of quilting.

While Karmine taught in Richmond for Virginia Commonwealth University to pay the bills, she spent as much time as she could working with young children in underfunded school districts. Aury had gone along to help during a few of these sessions and remained in awe of Karmine's ability to reach people with her art.

"Don't sell yourself short. A few years ago, you weren't painting at all. And now your colorful characters are hanging up in restaurants around town." Karmine studied the painting closer. "You didn't find a hidden Rembrandt or anything, but I'll bet the work was done in the late nineteenth century, maybe the early 1900s. The paint isn't high quality. Maybe homemade. See where the layer has flaked off here?"

Aury squinted at the area the artist indicated. "If you say so." She stepped back. "Do you think they're worth keeping?"

The beads in her hair clinked together as Karmine picked up a second canvas, tilting it this way and that. "They're interesting. Not monetarily, but maybe as an example for your crafters' cottage. How's that going?"

When Aury had the idea for the cottage, Karmine was the first one she reached out to. Well, after Gran and Scott, of course. The ladies had planned and brainstormed over wine for hours until Aury was convinced this was something she could pull off. Karmine offered to help Aury with the summer program for local children.

"Scott put in skylights, and it gives the whole cottage a different look. Now he's considering adding them to some of the other buildings on the property. He thinks it'll cut down on electricity bills if people don't need lights during the day."

"That's a wonderful idea. I can't wait to see it." Karmine propped the two canvases up next to each other on easels. "If you give me some time, I'd like to test this paint to see what it's made of. It could be a fun challenge to recreate."

The saying "watching paint dry" immediately sprang to Aury's mind, but she held her tongue. "Sounds interesting. Help yourself."

Karmine's eagerness to examine the paintings more closely was evident by the way she had to tear her gaze from them. "I'm glad you came by. I have a few canvases for your cottage. They aren't the highest quality; someone gave them to me as a gift, and I don't want them to go to waste."

She slipped into the backroom and came out with a handful of blank canvases ranging from 12x16 inches to 24x36 inches.

Aury took them gratefully. "This is wonderful. Thanks."

Karmine escorted Aury to her car and opened the door. Aury placed the canvases on the floor of the backseat and covered them with an old blanket she had used to wrap the paintings.

Waving goodbye, Aury left Karmine and set out for the quilt shop. She promised herself it would be a quick stop. She needed a little more trim to finish the curtains in the kitchen.

The wind had picked up, and the tang of rain was in the air. Aury took in the dark clouds, praying it would hold until she got off the ferry.

She loved coming into Williamsburg. It still had the small-town ambiance she appreciated but with many more amenities than Surry. A pang of disappointment hit her when she sighted the for-rent sign on the old pancake house Gran had taken her to on many occasions. Todd hated breakfast for dinner, so Aury and Gran had turned it into their special place.

As she pulled into the quilt store parking lot, Ralene stepped outside, staring at the sky.

"Are you doing valet parking now?" Aury asked.

The store owner crossed her arms, still distracted by the clouds. "I would if I thought it would bring in more customers. What brings you back so soon?"

"I'm about a half yard short on that green I got to trim the kitchen curtains. Thought I'd grab it while I was in town."

With a final glance at the weather, Ralene followed her into the shop. "You better hurry home. That ferry's going to be a bumpy ride. Let me grab that material for you."

Aury found herself stroking the powder-blue flannel with ducks and ships. A new bolt was wedged in beside it; this one was sage green with the same ducks and ships. Removing it from the shelf, she added it to the cutting table. "I'll take four yards of this too."

Ralene beamed.

"And if you tell Gran, I swear I'll never come here again."

Back in her car, Aury couldn't help herself from pulling out the green fabric again. The soft, fuzzy finish would make a great backing for a baby blanket. She placed it on her lap as she drove.

The line for the ferry was long. Obviously she wasn't the only one trying to cross ahead of the rain. Hers was the last car loaded, and she breathed a sigh of relief. Instead of getting out as she usually did, she rolled down her windows and sat in the car. With her eyes closed, she listened to the seagulls call to one another and the waves slapping against the boat.

The ferry bumping the dock jolted her awake. Glancing around self-consciously, she was relieved no one had seen her. She couldn't remember the last time she had taken a nap, but she sure needed it.

As she waited for her turn to file off, she realized, with everything that had happened, she forgot to ask Alan about the fight on the ferry Linda had witnessed. She'd place a large bet that one of the men was David.

And with his mouth, she'd go so far as to say he started the fight.

Chapter 13

"Miss St. Clair, isn't it?"

Aury looked up from her paperwork when she heard Elliott's voice.

"Spending a little too much time at the police station, aren't you?" His smile was bright, but his eyes were dark and serious.

"Not by choice. My car was broken into." Aury pointed at the papers. "I'm filing a report for the insurance company."

Now his smile disappeared. "Was anything taken?"

"Nothing. I don't keep anything valuable in my car."

"Where were you?" He crossed his arms and scrutinized her.

"At the grocery store."

"How did they get in?"

Aury put the pen down, curiosity piqued by his questioning. "Don't you think this is a little below your pay grade? You have a killer to catch, remember?"

He nodded. "And you are the one who found the victim. Maybe the killer thinks you found something else as well."

Aury's eyes grew larger. She hadn't considered that. She forced herself to recall the details of her day. "I was running errands. I went to the hardware store to pick up a few things, then to the art store for paint and brushes for the crafters' cottage. I drove to Williamsburg to meet with an artist friend to ask her questions about the paintings Michelle gave me."

She tapped the pen absentmindedly on the counter as she rattled things off. "I stopped at the quilt store for a few things, then took the ferry back. The grocery store was supposed to be my last stop before heading home. When I came out, the driver's window had been shattered. I wasn't far from here, so thought I should get this paperwork done right away. I haven't even called Scott yet."

Not that she knew *why* she hadn't called Scott yet. She had plenty of time on the drive to the station, but he already seemed to think she was fragile. Running to him over a broken car window felt like surrender. A surrender of what, Aury wasn't sure.

"Did you have the paintings with you?" Elliott asked.

"No, I only took a few with me, and I left them with my friend. They aren't valuable though. Michelle had them appraised before she gave me the canvases to repurpose."

"Then why were you taking them to an artist?"

"The technique interested me. The paintings look like they were done by the same artist. It's the perspective I find fascinating." Aury thought of the collection, showing so much and so little at the same time. There was something mysterious about their deliberate incompleteness. "I can't really explain it. It's like you're looking through a window, spying on the scene."

Elliott nodded, but Aury got the impression he was being polite more than anything.

"I know nothing about art myself," he admitted a moment later. "I'd have to find someone who does."

Aury turned back to her paperwork. "I'm sure it's not that serious, Lieutenant. Really, they weren't worth much."

A scuffle at the outer doorway drew their attention.

"This is ridiculous! Hasn't my family been through enough?" Brandon caught sight of Aury. "This is your doing, isn't it? I don't know why Aunty Michelle puts up with you. You're just nosing around for a handout."

"Project much?" Aury mumbled under her breath.

Elliott chuckled. "We're bringing Brandon Paris in for further questioning. We received a call about him trying to sell off some antiques. It's a small town. Folks here know what happened at Fresh Start and want to help where they can. We've been getting all kinds of tips about anything out of the ordinary."

"But he's Michelle's nephew. Maybe he's doing it for her."

Elliott pointedly looked from Brandon back to Aury with one eyebrow cocked.

She grinned; she hadn't really believed it even as the words were leaving her mouth. "Okay, but did you at least ask Michelle?"

"She didn't authorize any sales, nor did she offer any alternative explanations for the sales. I get the sense she's tired of her nephew's schemes." Elliott addressed the patrolman who was escorting Brandon, "Take him to interview room two."

"Where's my lawyer? I haven't had my phone call yet."

Brandon continued complaining as the door closed behind him, Elliott following.

Aury signed the final document and left the station. She sent Scott a text to meet her at the local dealership.

The clouds weren't as ominous on this side of the river, but rain was still threatening in the near future. She drove to the local dealership. After filling out more paperwork, she unloaded her groceries and sat on the bench in front of the repair shop waiting for Scott.

She texted Gran about the car and then scrolled through emails on her phone.

Ten minutes later, Scott pulled up in the pickup. He jumped out and pulled her into a hug. "Are you okay?"

Ah. The headlining question again, starring the same crease in his brow.

"I'm fine. Just tired." Aury slipped from his hold.

Scott picked up the grocery bags and loaded them behind the seats. "Is there anything in here that needs to be refrigerated?"

"Nope." She slid into the passenger side of the truck.

"Let's go to the diner." Scott buckled in. "I don't want to cook."

Aury sighed. "Me neither. I could go for some comfort food."

"By comfort food, do you mean Mel's apple pie and cinnamon ice cream?" He grinned like a small boy who was getting away with something.

Her eyes finally met his. "You really know me."

And it was true; Scott had taken the time to absorb everything Aury had revealed to him. If only that was an exhaustive list. She rested her head on the side window and closed her eyes.

Scott changed the radio station a few times. "How long is the car supposed to take?"

"A few days."

"I would think they should be able to replace glass pretty quickly. What's the holdup?"

"Don't know."

"Did you call the insurance company?"

"Yes."

Perhaps Scott picked up on her short answers, because he let them finish the drive to the diner unfettered by more questions.

Aury had no good reason for *not* discussing the day's excitement with Scott. Other than Gran, he was her closest confidant. Why, then, did each one of his concerned expressions look like a scene from a movie she'd already seen and despised?

Soon they were nestled in a red vinyl booth in the back of the most popular eatery in town, and the miracle that was Mel's cooking managed to push everything else from Aury's mind.

By the time Aury finished her food and pushed the plate away, she was feeling more like herself. "Lieutenant Elliott thinks the break-in could be connected to Izzie's murder."

"How so?" His eyebrows drew together.

"I'm not sure. He suggested the killer may think I have something to implicate them."

"Or you have something they want." Scott used his bread to sop up the last of his gravy.

"But all I have from the house is some old junk Michelle was throwing out. Miss Penny didn't think it was worth keeping." Aury used her fingers to count off the items she had besides the old canvases. "Canning jars, paintbrushes, picture frames, clear glass vases, and a few wooden chairs."

Scott stacked his empty plate on Aury's. "Maybe the killer knows something we don't, or they think you have more than you do."

The front door banged open, followed by the sweet whiff of rain.

Scott tilted out of his seat to get a better look. "Not one of your favorite people."

Aury turned to see Brandon strutting toward them. She sat back and closed her eyes; the relaxation she had enjoyed over dinner evaporated. "The neighbor helped Michelle with the last load, but Brandon packed the canvases into Michelle's van the first time. Besides, he's been in and out of that house. He would know what she gave me. Lieutenant Elliott says he's been selling off items from the house without Michelle's permission."

Brandon plopped down on a stool at the counter. With elbows on the surface, he hung his head and clasped his hands behind his neck.

Regarding him carefully, Aury shook her head in disgust at the dingy underwear sticking out above his low-riding jeans. As Brandon reached for the menu, the discoloration on his knuckles stood out. Aury squinted, trying to bring it more in focus.

"What are you looking at?" Scott made room on the table for the waitress to put down their pie.

Aury peered around the waitress at Brandon. "Does his right hand look bruised to you?"

Scott smiled a thanks at the waitress and glanced Brandon's way. "Can't tell from here. Eat your ice cream before it melts."

She dug into the dessert, savoring the cold cinnamon in the dairy against the warm gooeyness of the apple pie. "Oh yeah, this is what I needed."

Between mouthfuls, she asked, "How's the work on the trail coming?"

Scott wiped his mouth. "After that last big rain, some of the topsoil washed away. We'll have to bring in more to fill the holes."

"Where do you go to get dirt?"

"Well, it's a dirty business." Scott drummed a ba-da-bump on the table.

Aury rolled her eyes. Then her mind drifted while he came up with a serious answer to her question. She chewed slowly, her mind wandering back to what Scott said earlier.

Without meaning to, she spoke out loud. "Why would the killer think I know anything? I wasn't even there very long. The paramedics showed up, and I left."

He chuckled. "I knew you weren't really interested in dirt."

She gave a sheepish smile. "I'm sorry. I am. Okay, not really in dirt, but in your work on the trail, yes." She closed her eyes and pinched her lips together. "I just can't shake this feeling that I should know something. That there's a clue sitting there, waiting for me to pick it up."

"It'll probably come to you when you stop trying. It works for me." Scott used his fork to snag a bite of pie from Aury's plate.

She pulled it away from him playfully, shoveling the last few bites into her mouth.

When they finished, Scott took the bill to the cashier to pay. Aury sauntered over to Brandon still seated at the counter.

She extended her hand to shake. "We haven't been properly introduced. I'm Aury St Clair."

Automatically, Brandon took her hand.

So he does have some manners hidden in there somewhere.

"I know who you are. I suggest you stay away from Aunty Michelle."

Spoke too soon.

"And I suggest you help her out more. She's overworking herself. Didn't she bring you in to help fix up that old house?"

Brandon yanked his hand back, but not before Aury got a good look at the dark circles around his knuckles.

"Mind your own business." He swiveled back to his plate on the counter.

"You have a good day too." Aury made her voice as chipper and sweet as possible.

When she met Scott at the door, he opened an umbrella over her head for their dash to the truck. His expression was half-suspicion, half-pride. "What are you up to?"

Chapter 14

Scott started the pickup while Aury got Lieutenant Elliott on the phone. "You're on speaker phone with me and Scott. We just ran into Brandon at the diner. When you talked to him, did you notice the marks on his right hand?"

"Yes, but there were no bruises on Izzie."

An image of Izzie on the floor popped into her head. She pushed it away. "Did he say where he got them?"

"Working at the house with his aunt. Said he banged them moving furniture." Elliott shuffled papers.

"I seriously doubt that. He shirks work whenever he can. Poor Michelle has been doing practically everything by herself. I do have another theory though."

"I'm listening."

Elliott didn't sound like he was on the edge of his seat, but he didn't seem as irritated as he had been with the likes of Freeman and Brandon, which heartened Aury.

"Did you see David's face? He's got a black eye." Somehow, Aury felt this was important, but she wasn't sure why.

"I noticed that. He said it happened before he got to town. 'Ran into a door.' Besides, it wasn't fresh when he came into the station the day of Izzie's murder."

The impatience in his voice forced Aury to get to the point. "That door's name might be Brandon. Did you hear about the fight on the ferry?"

He hmphed without answering her question. Aury took that as a signal for her to go on.

She filled him in. "I'm not sure what the fight was about, but it would account for both injuries."

Elliott was silent, but Aury heard him writing.

"Thanks. It might not have anything to do with the murder, but it would answer some questions."

Scott glanced at Aury and nodded. "Like whether David and Brandon knew each other before this incident."

"And well enough to get in a fight. I'll look into it."

She rushed to get her question in before he disconnected. "Did you find Izzie's ex?"

There was a pregnant pause before Elliott answered. "You're well informed, aren't you?"

A small laugh escaped Scott's lips. "Wait until you get to know her better. Nothing will surprise you."

Aury rolled her eyes. "Does that mean you found him?"

Elliott coughed. "I'll share a little since you're sharing with me, and I don't want you hunting down the information on your own. Victor Clayton lives in Hampton, works as a handyman for a rental company. Says he was on a job at the time, but no one can corroborate it. His boss says the work was completed though." The sound of pages being turned came across the speaker clearly. "Prior Army. Honorably discharged. He's in debt but didn't gain anything from Izzie's death except he gets to stop paying alimony. That would have stopped anyway once she moved into Fresh Start. He was only required to help pay her rent."

"One last question." Aury knew she was pushing her luck.

Elliot sighed.

"Where did Izzie work?"

"She worked for the county tourism board. Customer service for folks looking to explore the area."

It was Aury's turn to sigh. "Thanks."

She clicked off. "So much for knowing secrets at the powerplant."

Scott shook his head. "You amaze me. You can't help but get involved, can you?"

"I get that from my grandmother." Aury grinned.

"Maybe some of it." Scott put the pickup in drive, and they headed for Eastover. "But I'm pretty sure at least part of this madness is all you."

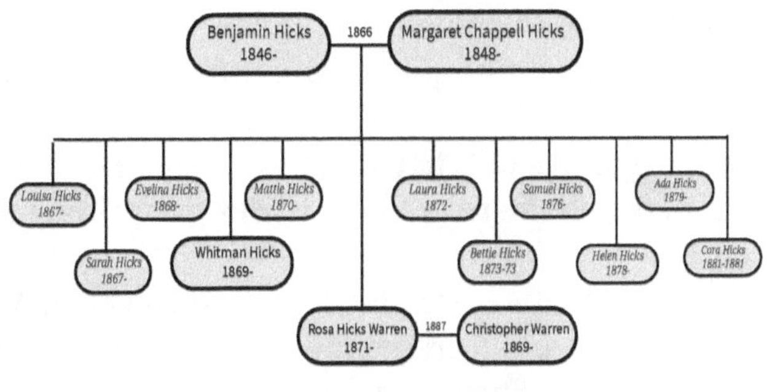

Chapter 15

Spring 1894

Margaret Hicks held the kerosene lantern up high. "Are you out here tinkering again? You need to get inside and wash up for supper."

"I'm almost done. Just gotta tighten down this bolt." Benjamin swore when his hand slipped. He waved it in the air as if it were on fire.

She stepped closer to examine it. No blood. "Uh huh. Heard that one before. It's getting too dark in here. Get yourself inside."

Benjamin wiped his hands on an already oily rag, then tossed it on top of the plow he'd been fighting with. "There's got to be a better way to pull up them peanuts. I'm sick of wasting time messing with this monstrosity each season."

His wife tapped his temple with her index finger. "Get those wheels spinning. You'll come up with something."

He took her hand in his, interlacing their fingers. "Woman, you know exactly what to say to me." He pulled her closer. "I have some ideas, all right."

"Hush, you." She gave him a playful shove as the color rose in her cheeks.

Benjamin's eyes lit up. "Did you hear about that new-fangled machine they got for people to ride around in? It runs off liquid rather than being horse-drawn."

"The ladies were talking about it in the shop. The mayor might be getting one." She guided him through the door of the barn.

Benjamin guffawed. "That's because his horse is struggling to carry him. Surely there are better uses than riding around to be seen."

The song of the cicadas split the night, like tiny tambourines rattling to a crescendo before cutting off, just to start the cycle over. When Margaret was a little girl, she had nightmares that this was the sound of snakes, looking for a way between the logs of their two-room cabin.

Bringing her attention back to Benjamin, Margaret recognized his silence. He got this way when he was stepping through a puzzle. "What are you devising now?"

He kissed her hand. "Do you suppose whatever liquid they use to make those automobiles go could work to drive this peanut picker?"

"If you have anything to say about it, sure enough."

They moseyed hand in hand toward the house. The sun was setting over acres of dark, rich soil. He filled his lungs. "Ain't that a pretty sight? I never get tired of that view. Could look at it forever."

"I prefer when it gets to the leafy green stage. Then at least we know there's something under there. Right now, who's to say how much you gonna get out of all that hard work?"

"The Lord ain't let us down yet."

Chapter 16

Present day

Aury offered a selection of plastic templates for Michelle to choose from. "I thought one of these patterns would look great painted with sage green and lilac to accent the dining area."

Michelle picked through the choices, holding up one and then the other against the wall of the Warren house. "This is super sweet. You really don't have to go out of your way to help me with this project."

"It's the least I can do. You're working so hard to get this place going." Aury shrugged. "Besides, it gives me a chance to play with a different art project."

Michelle handed her a template with vines and ripe bunches of grapes. "This one."

"That's my favorite too." Aury pointed to a spot high on the wall. "I was thinking above those windows and maybe bringing the vines down in the corner."

"I love it!"

A noise from the living room stopped the ladies' conversation.

At first, Aury thought she might be imagining things, but the intense look of concentration on Michelle's face matched her own. After a few minutes of straining her ears, Aury laughed self-consciously and whispered, "You heard that too, right?"

Michelle's lips were thin white lines. She nodded curtly, still silent.

Aury tried to decide what they should do when the silence was interrupted by something scraping across the wood floor.

Before Aury could suggest their next action, Michelle dropped the templates onto the dining table and stormed into the living room.

A man wearing a leather jacket stood with his hands on the back of a sofa, looking at the painting over the mantel.

"What are you doing here?" Michelle demanded. "Do I need to call the cops?"

The couch screeched on the hardwood as it slid out from under his hands. He spun to face the women.

The self-important man from the police station.

He regarded the women, then pulled himself up straighter. "Sorry. The door was unlocked."

"And that somehow gave you permission to come in uninvited?" Aury crossed her arms.

Dismissing her question, Willard focused on Michelle. "I'm glad to run into you again actually. I need to apologize for my behavior when we met at the police station. I was just a bit shaken."

"Not nearly as much as I was." Michelle's voice was calm and cold.

Aury had never seen this side of her friend. It was a little scary. Still, Willard deserved it.

Willard spread his arms, palms up. "This place is special to my wife. When she was a girl, she spent many summers here with her great-aunt Penny. We were more than a little surprised to hear that Penny donated it without asking the family."

Aury wasn't buying this guy's explanation for a second. "Why would she have to ask the family when it's her house?"

He still didn't look at Aury and spoke directly to Michelle. "Just common courtesy, I would think. Put yourself in my wife's shoes. She's told me so many stories about this place, I feel like I've been here before. I wanted to see it for myself."

When Michelle's face softened, Aury sensed the older woman's kind-hearted nature overruling her logical response to the ridiculous excuse Willard provided.

"I haven't heard an apology yet." Aury wasn't going to play nice with him.

Michelle touched Aury's arm but addressed Willard. "Well, you should have knocked, is all. I don't mind you looking around a bit, but I've got work to do."

As if to emphasize her point, Michelle marched back to the dining room.

Aury caught Willard's mouth twist into a quick smirk before he sobered his expression.

Anger built inside her. "If this house was so near and dear to your wife's heart, I can't imagine she would be very happy if you sold it to Moore so he could tear it down to build another strip mall."

Willard's face snapped toward her as if he had been slapped.

It was Aury's turn to smirk. She'd finally gotten his attention. "Mrs. Warren must know her family better than you think."

Before he had a chance to reply, Aury went on. She couldn't help herself. "Your eye's looking better. How did you say you got that shiner?"

His hand went reflexively to his face. "I didn't."

"Ferry boats on the James River appear to be getting dangerous these days. Hope you at least got your shot in."

Willard's pretense at niceties dropped, and he openly scowled. "I'm not sure what you have against me, Miss St. Clair, but I suggest you stay out of my business."

"We look out for each other here."

"That didn't work out so well for the dead girl, did it?"

Aury's jaw dropped. The audacity of this man!

"Time for you to go." Michelle spoke from the doorway, all traces of softness gone.

Willard threw a glare at Aury and stomped from the room.

The ladies followed him to make sure he left the property. On the wide front porch, Willard came to an abrupt halt when he almost ran into Thomas Freeman.

The neighbor looked past Willard to Michelle. "Is everything okay here, Michelle?"

"It's fine. He was just leaving," she said.

"That's a good idea." Freeman puffed out his chest as if he were protecting the ladies.

Aury almost laughed at the thought of the slight sixty-something-year-old standing up to a forty-something man who was at least six inches and fifty pounds bigger than he was.

Willard got in Freeman's face. "Don't act all high and mighty. I know the game you're playing, and it's not going to work."

Aury gave the older man credit. He didn't back down.

"You're the only one playing games here. Don't you have other people to harass?"

Willard cocked his head toward Michelle. "Does she know you were trying to get your hands on this house? You were pushing pretty hard to get your way. That's one of the things that turned Aunt Penny against your offer."

"Thomas?" Michelle's unspoken question came through loud and clear in that one word.

He dismissed her concern with a wave. "Of course I put in a bid. I didn't want someone like this," he indicated Willard, "living next door. I was protecting the neighborhood."

Willard snorted. "Came across as entitled, if you ask me, old man."

Freeman crossed his arms and stood taller. "No one asked you. Penny made her choice. Now it's time to get behind Michelle and Fresh Start."

"Keep telling yourself that, but I got your number." Willard was practically snarling.

"Get off my property, Mr. Willard." Michelle was done with their posturing.

"It's not yours quite yet." Willard pushed past Freeman, shouldering him out of the way unnecessarily.

Once he had cleared the sidewalk and climbed into his car, Michelle let out a whoosh of air. "What a dreadful man."

Aury stroked her friend's arm. "You were a lot nicer than I would have been."

Michelle gave a tight smile. "Oh, well, sometimes nice doesn't work."

As if remembering her manners, Michelle introduced Aury to Thomas.

This was the man from the neighborhood watch who had pointed the finger at Brandon after Izzie's murder. Aury wondered if Michelle knew that.

He extended a well-manicured brown hand. "You must be the young lady who is setting up the crafters' cottage. There's quite a buzz about the idea. I think you'll do well."

Aury shook his hand, detecting the pungent odor of whiskey that she associated with her ex-husband. She forced her face not to give away the repulsion she felt. "That's good to hear. People have been generous in helping me get it off the ground."

"When will you open to the public?"

The question made her realize she hadn't officially set a date. Doing some quick calculations, she replied, "This time next month. It'll be great to have it open to make Christmas decorations."

Freeman returned his attention to Michelle, grasping her forearm gently. "Are you okay?"

She covered his hand with her own. "I'm fine. I'll be so relieved when the closing goes through and I know there's no action Willard can take to mess up this donation. The women and families of Fresh Start are counting on having a place to live."

Willard's words were still plaguing Aury. "What would make you entitled, Mr. Freeman?"

He shook his head. "He was trying to stir up trouble. Don't give it another thought."

That answer only fueled the embers of the many angles spinning inside Aury's mind.

"Did you need something, Thomas?" Michelle asked.

"I was going to the hardware store. Thought I'd see if you wanted to ride with me. We can pick out the new security system you want to install." A wide smile split his wrinkled face.

Aury imagined him as quite the ladies' man in his youth.

Michelle glanced at Aury.

"I'll just grab my templates before I go." Aury hesitated, not sure if Mr. Freeman driving after drinking was such a good idea.

As she took quick measurements of the dining room to determine how much paint she would need, she tried to think of a way to politely keep Michelle out of a vehicle with Freeman behind the wheel.

When she approached the closed screen door, she heard Freeman and Michelle speaking.

Freeman's deep voice carried easily, although he was talking in hushed tones. "It might be a good idea to give me a spare key in case you get locked out or you need me to let in a repairman when you aren't home."

"I don't think that would go over well with the ladies who will be living here. I won't even give Brandon a key." The exasperation in her tone told Aury this wasn't the first time Michelle had answered this particular request. "We'll be fine. Thanks for the offer though."

"Maybe at least until the others move in?"

Aury pushed the screen open. "Michelle, I can take you to the hardware store. You can show me what color the drapes will be and help me pick out the accent colors."

Thomas frowned at her. "You were on your way out. Don't you have somewhere to be?"

"I have to make a quick stop, but it's on the way to the hardware store, and it'll give me a chance to show Michelle the dressers I found at the second-hand store."

Michelle gave her a curious glance. "Thanks anyway, Thomas. Aury and I can pick out the system. I'll just grab my keys and lock up."

She ducked into the house.

Aury and Thomas stood in awkward silence for a few moments, as she played over the interaction with Willard.

Finally, Aury broke away from her reflection. "You've lived here a long time, haven't you?"

Thomas stood straighter and nodded. "Grew up in the same house I own now. It was my father's and his father's before that."

"Wow. That's impressive. Must be nice to have solid roots somewhere. We moved around a lot when I was growing up."

"Folks don't appreciate the importance of heritage."

The screen door slammed closed.

"I'm ready," Michelle announced.

They said their goodbyes and walked to Aury's car.

Michelle moved in close to Aury. "What's this about dressers? You know I'm reusing what was left in the house."

Aury checked over her shoulder to see Freeman drifting up his front steps. "He's been drinking. Besides, I didn't like the way he was pressuring you about the key."

"He was pretty insistent about that, wasn't he? I wonder why." Michelle fell silent for a few steps.

Aury struggled to come up with an answer.

Michelle continued, "Oh, he's just a nice old man with nothing much to do. He's looking for something to give his day more meaning. He got hurt on the job at the nuclear power plant, so he can't work, but his settlement barely gives him enough to get by. That's hardly fair."

"Still, doesn't he have kids or someone else he can hover over?"

Michelle shot a furtive glance toward Freeman's house. "I think he has a few kids, but I've never seen them around. His wife passed years ago. He's been very helpful cleaning up around the house, at least as much as he can. Certainly more so than Brandon."

"Have you heard from your nephew lately?" Aury wondered if he had filled his aunt in on his discussion with Lieutenant Elliott. She didn't want to be the one to break it to her.

She shook her head. "He was supposed to come by yesterday, but he said he had a job interview."

Or an interview at the police station. Aury kept that thought to herself.

As they approached the pickup, Aury clicked the remote to unlock the doors. "Well, I hope he gets it."

Michelle sighed heavily. "I'm not holding my breath."

After dinner, Scott and Aury sat quietly next to the firepit, drinking a glass of wine from Songscape Winery. Aury had fond memories of their trip to the Finger Lakes—the almost-being-murdered part aside, of course.

Scott refilled their glasses. "Did Michelle like the paint template you picked out for the dining room?"

"Yeah, she did." Aury shifted in her seat. "But something weird is going on. While I was there, Mrs. Warren's nephew showed up like he owned the place. We found him in the living room."

"And I'm sure you and Michelle quickly showed him the door." Scott beamed at her.

Aury melted at that smile. Tonight had been wonderful. Scott had surprised her with spareribs on the grill, and their conversation had flowed effortlessly, like it used to. The small fire in the pit staved off the chill in the evening air. Treasure curled up on Aury's feet, keeping them toasty.

"We got rid of him, but why is he sniffing around? I don't believe for a second that he's just visiting a special place from his wife's past. If that was the case, why wouldn't she be here?" She thought about taking Scott back to her childhood home.

Her parents' deaths were still too painful, but maybe someday. She certainly couldn't imagine Scott going there on his own.

"What other reason would he have? Do you think he wants to buy the house from Michelle?" A yawn escaped from Scott, although he tried to cover it.

"If so, he's going about it all wrong. Not that she would consider it anyway. She'll never get such a generous offer again." Aury spun the wine glass slowly between her hands. "He was probably hoping his wife would inherit the house, and they could sell it to that slimy developer."

Scott sat up, shaking off the sleepiness. "Which developer?"

"Moore is better," Aury said in an icy, sarcastic tone.

"Why would the developer want that house?"

She threw her hands up. "Who knows. Gran said he's tearing down older homes in Williamsburg and putting up ugly office buildings and strip malls."

He poked at the wood. A log rolled off the top of the pyre, sending sparks dancing toward the sky. "Well, you have to admit, some of those old houses are eyesores and safety risks. Many don't even have central air or heat."

"That doesn't mean we need more rental space that sits vacant. Williamsburg has had empty buildings on the market for years."

Scott tossed his stick into the flames and sat back. "It may not be as cut and dried as that. Houses need to be updated."

"Well, why does he have to replace them with commercial property? Why not starter homes?" Aury realized her voice had been getting steadily louder, so she dropped the volume. "Not those mini-mansions either. I mean affordable homes for the people who work in Williamsburg."

Scott dipped his chin and attempted a laugh, but it came out strained. "You sound more like Liza every day.

Aury took his hand. "I'm sorry. I know you're the engineer, and I'm probably not saying anything you haven't already dealt with. It just infuriates me to think of all the young people who move away because they can't afford Williamsburg prices. Did you ever notice how many restaurants are understaffed? I hear it's the same in the hotel industry. That's taking a toll on the tourist industry."

He sighed. "Some of it is simply economics. Did you sell your house at a loss when you moved here?"

Aury bristled. Giving up her house had been a tender topic for months before she finally sold it. Apparently the scab was still healing, because her insecurities were ripping through again. "No, but I also didn't try to fleece the buyer."

"Is that what Moore is doing?"

Aury's outrage froze in an instant. She wasn't sure of the answer.

Scott went on; this time, *his* volume increased slightly. "So is your hatred of Moore because he's a businessman? Or because he's renovating old buildings, or because young people can't afford to live in an upscale area like Williamsburg? Sounds like you haven't decided what to be angry about."

He tossed a stick in the fire and got up. "I'll take Treasure for a walk."

Hearing her name, the puppy jumped to her feet and dashed after Scott.

Aury watched them disappear into the darkness.

Chapter 17

Aury puttered about the house. After her discussion with Scott last night, she didn't sleep well. He was already gone when she rolled out of bed to get ready for Izzie's funeral. She kept rehashing their conversation in her head. Things had been going so well, then they went off the rails. Now her mood was as dark as her clothing.

Gran picked Aury up thirty minutes before the funeral was expected to start. "I caught the ferry a little early this morning. I didn't want to be late."

Aury got into the car and smoothed the wrinkles in her black skirt so they wouldn't set.

"Thanks for driving. I should have my car back tomorrow." Aury was anxious to leave the house before Scott came back. Gran would easily pick up on the tension, and this wasn't something she wanted to talk to Gran about.

The tulle on Gran's black hat brushed against the car's ceiling when she turned to look for traffic before pulling out of the Eastover property. "I'd rather not go to these things alone anyway. It's too sad."

Aury appreciated the real reason Gran offered to go with her today. The last funeral Aury had attended was for her parents. She and Gran had depended on each other for the weeks that followed. Any reminder of their loss was bound to provoke severe emotions, and Aury was thankful Gran was willing to put herself through that for her granddaughter's sake.

"There's another one of those blasted bumper stickers." Gran pointed at the silver car in front of her. Its sticker seemed a little more worn than most; the "r" in "Moore is Better" had been almost totally scratched out, and the blue color was fading.

"That's the Volvo from the ferry." Aury squinted at the car. "I wonder if he has some connection to the developer."

Aury didn't want to admit Scott was right when it came to her dislike of Moore. Was she only going off what Gran had told her? Was the developer as bad as Gran made him out to be? Aury was missing something. A small, vindictive part of her would like to prove Scott wrong or at least validate her opinions as right.

Gran stepped on the gas. "Let's see where he goes."

Aury glanced at her watch. They had plenty of time. "Don't get too close."

After a few turns and several stop signs, the Volvo pulled into a shopping center sporting many "going out of business" signs. Liza parked in front of one of the few stores still open and cracked the car window. A tall, dark-haired man got out of his car a few stores down from where they waited.

Aury grabbed Gran's arm. "That's him. That's the man I saw on the ferry."

"Yep, that's Hamilton Moore."

Aury imagined that, if it wasn't so unladylike, Gran would have spit on the parking lot after saying his name.

"He looks a lot older than his website photo. I expected him to be in his late twenties." Aury angled toward her grandmother to get a better look out the driver's window.

Gran snorted. "He's vain as well as greedy. Probably using a very old picture. He's fifty if he's a day."

Moore balanced against the hood of his car and lit a cigarette. He'd only taken a few puffs before another car pulled in next to his.

"That's Penny's nephew—David Willard," Aury whispered, although the men couldn't hear her at this distance.

Willard's suit was rumpled, and his tie was loose around his neck. Moore didn't react as Willard approached him. In fact, he barely spoke; Willard did most of the talking.

The longer the conversation went on, the more animated Willard became. His hands moved along with his mouth, but the words didn't reach Gran's car.

Aury strained to read their lips, but it wasn't easy with no context to go on.

Moore shook his head. His mouth barely moved with the reply.

Willard swore. That word was easy to make out, even if his volume hadn't increased dramatically.

He was practically begging now, palms together in a sign of prayer. "I need more time."

Gran shot Aury a look. Those words were as clear as a bell.

Moore mumbled something, then tossed his cigarette onto the pavement before crushing it under his boot. When he pushed himself off the car, Willard stumbled back a few steps. Moore climbed behind the wheel and closed the door.

"It'll work. He'll come through. I know it." The words were loud enough to penetrate Moore's closed car window. "Thank you."

After Moore pulled out, Willard paced frantically on the sidewalk, three or four steps either way. Without warning, he spun and punched the plate-glass window of the closed shop.

Aury and Gran jumped in their seats.

Cracks shot out from the impact point as the glass fractured but didn't shatter.

Willard shook his hand and swore loudly. He looked around, but the ladies averted their eyes just in time, becoming engrossed in something on the seat between them.

When his car started, Aury risked a look. "He's lucky that was safety glass with some give. Regular glass would have cut him up good."

Gran checked her hat in the mirror. "We better get to the funeral."

"I wonder *who* will come through for Willard?" Aury stared out the window as Gran drove but only saw the interaction between the two men replaying. "It has to have something to do with the house, right? Else why would Willard be talking to a developer?"

"Is that house zoned for commercial? Is it even an area Moore would be interested in?"

Aury made a mental note to look up the zoning restrictions.

At the church, Gran parked, and they hurried into the building. It wasn't packed, but there were more people than Aury expected, considering Izzie had no family, and she had only recently moved back to Surry. Most were probably people drawn by the sensation of a murder in their town.

Sliding into a seat in the back, Aury studied the people in the pews in front of her. Michelle was in the front row with several other women, most in their thirties, if Aury had to guess. They had to be the other Fresh Start future residents.

She spotted Lieutenant Elliott when he turned to look her way. They nodded to each other.

A man with greasy blond hair sniffled loudly from the second row. He buried his face in his hands.

Gran elbowed Aury. "Think that's the ex?"

She nodded. "Bet you're right. Victor Clayton."

The organ's first notes of "Amazing Grace" rang out, and the congregants stood. The blond wiped his nose with the back of his hand and rose, holding on to the pew in front of him.

As they sang the familiar song, Aury looked for Brandon. The least he could do was be there for his aunt today. But no, she didn't see him. Michelle's neighbor Thomas was a few rows ahead of Aury. He sang along without the need of a hymnal.

Michelle gave the eulogy. It was nice to learn more about Izzie, rather than to think of her just as a murder victim. She had gone to Surry County High School, where she was a point guard for the basketball team. She had left for Army basic training right after graduation.

Michelle didn't mention Izzie's marriage or her ex-husband. Aury read between the lines and surmised Izzie met Clayton while they were in the service. Michelle didn't mention the reasons that brought Izzie to Fresh Start but did praise her for her willingness to lend a hand whenever necessary.

Aury knew Michelle still blamed herself for Izzie's death. The guilt was written all over her tear-streaked face.

After the service, they filed outside and gathered in the cool autumn air. Izzie was cremated, so there would be no graveside service. Aury guided Gran between the groups clustered around until they were within feet of Clayton.

He was still sniffling as he accepted condolences from people who obviously didn't know Izzie well. If it wasn't for him, she probably wouldn't have needed Fresh Start. He told anyone who would listen that he and Izzie were reconciling.

Aury couldn't help herself. Tacking on a look of faux sympathy, she approached Clayton with Gran at her side. "I'm sorry for your loss."

She didn't extend her hand. He had repeatedly wiped his nose with that hand, and no amount of acting could get her past the revulsion she felt looking at him.

"Thank you. She was the love of my life." Again with the tears.

"If you were so in love, why was she moving into Fresh Start?" Gran's tone was no nonsense.

Aury had heard that tone a time or two.

Clayton shook his head vehemently. "She wasn't. She was coming home."

Gran sniffed.

"Izzie just hadn't got around to tellin' that old woman who runs the place that she didn't need her. She felt bad, so she wanted to help out until it got up and running. That's all."

When Aury didn't soften, he went on. "Do you know where they put her things? The cops won't let me have them, when, by all rights, they're mine. I'm her next of kin. She didn't have no one else. Some of those things are sentimental."

Aury's eyes swept the crowd, seeking escape now that she had confirmed for herself that Clayton was a dirtbag. Elliott stood nearby. He wasn't looking at them, but he was obviously listening to the conversation.

She decided to make things easier for the police officer. "What things are you looking for? Maybe I can ask Michelle if she knows where Izzie kept her belongings."

"You know, just things." Clayton shrugged one shoulder.

Gran glared at him. "Like her hairbrush? Or maybe her dresses? I don't think they'd fit you."

He turned his back to Gran and focused on Aury. "Things that would have meant something to her . . . like her jewelry. Or the purse I got her for Christmas."

"Or the cash inside it, more likely," Gran muttered.

He reached out to take Aury's arm, and she flinched. He dropped his hands to his sides. "I just want what's rightfully mine. Something to remember my Izzie by."

Shooting a look at Elliott, Aury caught his tight smile in profile. Deciding she had aided the police lieutenant enough for one day, she brought the conversation to a close.

"I'll ask around. That's all I can do." Aury took Gran's arm. "Let's go. I want to meet up with Scott."

Gran dropped Aury at Eastover. Treasure met her at the door.

Aury caught the puppy's face in her palms. "Hey, girl. What are you doing inside? It's a beautiful day."

Treasure danced around, anxious to be running. Aury let her slip out the front door and went to her room to change. Anxious to doff the depressing black from the funeral, she slipped into comfortable jeans and her brightest flannel shirt. Her first instinct was to pull her hair back into her usual messy bun, but she changed her mind. It wasn't right to dismiss all thoughts of Izzie so easily.

When she emerged from the cottage, Treasure bounded up to her with a ball in her mouth. Aury took the gift, tossed it far across the field, and strolled toward the beach path where Scott said he was clearing trees.

The game went on for the trek across the property. Treasure showed no signs of slowing. As they hiked the trail,

Aury didn't hear the expected buzzing of the chainsaw or even the whump of an ax hitting wood. The stump grinder was just off the path covered by a blue tarp.

She reached the river without any sign that Scott had been there that day. He hadn't gone with her to the funeral because he wanted to finish with the grinder and get it returned as soon as possible. Where could he be?

Aury backtracked up the path and drifted to the crafters' cottage. Treasure disappeared into the brush.

A new screen door was fastened in place, just awaiting a coat of paint. Aury slipped inside and was thrilled to see the new backdoor also in place. She unlocked it and propped it open as she inspected the screen. A nice breeze circulated through the cottage between the two open doors. A grin split her face as she surveyed her space. It was like a dream come true. Natural light poured in through the doors and the skylights above. Light fixtures hung from the ceiling along the outside walls of the large open room. Aury had ordered color-rending bulbs specially made to mimic the sun's full-spectrum light.

She couldn't wait to share this space with other artists.

Digging through paint cans stacked in the corner, she selected an outdoor green paint and set to work. The hardest part was keeping Treasure's nose out of the can.

It was dinner time when she finished. After cleaning up, Aury dropped Treasure at the house before hiking to the dining hall. They had several guests visiting this week, so Alan would be pulling out all the stops.

Aury sauntered through the hall, stopping to chat with guests as she went. She saw no sign of Scott, so she filled her tray and sat in the backroom off the kitchen to eat. While welcoming guests was readily appreciated, Aury didn't want them to get the impression they had to talk to her. They were there to relax and spend time with the people they came with, not her.

When Alan finished serving, he brought his tray and joined her.

"The screen doors look great. Thank you." Aury wiped her mouth.

"No problem. The doors were delivered first thing. We knocked them out in no time." Alan ate quickly. "Good thing 'cause I had to take the missus to a doctor's appointment this afternoon. Just a routine checkup, but she feels better when I'm there."

"Oh, I thought you and Scott were grinding stumps this afternoon."

"He said he'd get to it. We can finish up tomorrow if need be." He shoveled in his last forkful and jumped to his feet. "Gotta get cleaning. I want to be home for the football game."

Aury pushed food around on her plate, having lost her appetite. Where had Scott been all day if he wasn't working the trail? Refusing to let her imagination run wild, she pushed the thought away.

She carried her tray to the dishwashing station. Pulling an apron from a nearby hook, she hung it around her neck and started the conveyor belt that took the dirty dishes from the dining room to the wash racks. Her hands moved without having to engage her mind as she automatically scraped plates and loaded one rack after the other, then slid them through the industrial dishwasher.

Alan popped his head in. "You didn't have to do that, but it's appreciated."

"Why don't you take off? You've got a game to get to. I'll lock up." Part of her knew she was still avoiding Scott.

By the time she got back to the house, it was late. The bedside lamp glowed softly, but Scott was fast asleep.

Maybe he was avoiding her too.

Chapter 18

Scott was gone when Aury got up the next morning. He had left the coffee pot ready to brew, so she pushed the button and set about her morning tasks. After showering and dressing, she checked the online bookings for Eastover and returned emails. She placed orders with their various vendors based on Alan's upcoming menus. The rest of the morning was dedicated to creating social media posts for the following week.

A soft tap of the car horn caught her attention. Scott had arrived to take her to collect her car. She picked up the file folder containing the information she had gathered so far on the people possibly involved with Fresh Start and went outside to meet him.

A gust of wind tangled her hair around her face as she jumped in the truck. "I think fall is exerting herself. I'll have to get out the leaf mulcher soon."

Scott put the truck in gear. "Are you going to see Liza after you get your car?"

She nodded. "We're having lunch, then I may go see Linda. I want to confirm a hunch."

He glanced at her sideways. "Are you getting into something?"

"Nothing you wouldn't approve of. Besides, Linda's longarming Gran's bed quilt. Gran's not interested in hand quilting anymore. It takes too long."

He chuckled. "Your grandmother doesn't need to worry about time. She'll outlive us all."

Aury smiled her agreement, and they fell into an amicable silence. Then her mind began to race. Gran had lots of time. Aury had lots of time. She wasn't in a hurry to get remarried. Why wasn't she in a hurry? Didn't she want to spend the rest of her life with Scott?

Why wasn't *he* in a hurry? Wasn't he excited about spending the rest of his life with her?

This line of thinking was unproductive. She needed to think about something else. The first thing to pop into her head was the funeral yesterday.

She warred over whether to question him about where he had been instead of going with her, but she didn't want to come across as controlling. Her inner curiosity won. "How's the work on the path to the beach going?"

He cleared his throat. "I let it go too long. There's a lot to cut back, but it should be ready if you still want to decorate it for the holidays."

"You worked on it yesterday, didn't you?" She flexed and unflexed the folder in her hands.

Scott glanced out the side window, then back at the road. "Yeah, but it's slow going."

This time, it was Aury's turn to stare out the side window. Why was he lying to her? She was going to have to confront him about it eventually. She began picking apart their most recent conversations. Was there a clue she was overlooking?

Oh, listen to me now. She had fallen into investigator mode. Her grandmother was getting to her. She pushed those broodings to the back of her mind.

When Scott dropped her at the dealership, he kissed her cheek. "Try to be back for dinner. I'm barbecuing, and I'd like you to make your famous potato salad."

"You mean Gran's famous salad. It's her recipe."

She waved as he pulled out, but he didn't seem to notice. She went inside to pay the bill.

After accepting the keys, she looked at her watch. She could still swing by Michelle's before she needed to be in Williamsburg. After shooting off a quick text to Linda, she got in her car.

Michelle was loading items into her van when Aury pulled up. She grabbed the folder from the front seat before getting out.

"Glad you got your car window fixed so quickly," Michelle said.

"News travels fast around here, doesn't it?"

"Small town. You get used to it. Someday you may even be grateful for it." Michelle jumped as if struck by lightning. "Oh my! You haven't heard yet, have you?"

"Heard what?"

"David Willard was killed last night!"

"What? How?" Aury's mind instantly spun to the scene between Willard and Moore outside the closed-up shop.

Michelle shrugged. "I don't know any details."

"How did you find out?"

"That police lieutenant came to see me. Willard made it pretty obvious that he wasn't happy with Fresh Start, so the lieutenant needed to check my alibi. That was easy; I was here with a few other women, scrubbing and painting. Actually, I think he really wanted to warn me in case the press came sniffing around. He was very nice."

"I can't believe it. I just saw Willard yesterday." Aury covered her mouth.

"Maybe the police will come talk to you next."

Aury flinched. "That has to be unusual. Two deaths in Surry so close together? And you knew them both. How are you handling it?"

Michelle's shoulders slumped, but she shook it off quickly. "Bad things happen. You can't let them slow you down. Working keeps me sane."

Aury's mind darted in several directions at once. It must have shown on her face.

Michelle tapped Aury's hand holding the folder to get her attention. "Don't worry yourself. Did you need something?"

"It's nothing important." Aury was fairly certain this wasn't the right time to quiz Michelle about her nephew.

Michelle put her palm out. "Show me what you've got."

Sheepishly, Aury pulled out the picture of Brandon. "I wanted to show it to a friend of mine. She thinks she might have seen Brandon before but didn't know his name. I found this on social media to see if we were talking about the same guy."

"Does he owe her money? Wouldn't surprise me."

Aury chuckled. "No, nothing like that."

"This is such a silly picture. Why do young people always have to make faces at the camera?" She handed it back to Aury. "But you've met Brandon. You know that's him. What did you need from me?"

"It was more of a curious thing really." Aury pointed to the sailboat around Brandon's neck. "This is a beautiful necklace. Do you recognize it?"

"Sure do. He inherited that from his father. I think Jeremiah received it as a prize from a sailing regatta. He loved being on the water." Her eyes sparkled when she spoke of Brandon's father.

"Were you close with Jeremiah?" Aury asked.

"Very. Jeremiah's father was my only brother, which actually makes Brandon my great-nephew. My brother and I spent a lot of time together, and I vacationed with his family every spring. My nieces and nephews often came to stay with me during their summer breaks. I didn't have kids of my own, so I enjoyed spoiling them." She smiled wanly.

"Did something happen to Brandon's father? You look sad."

Michelle sighed as if pushing her nostalgia away. "He died in a freak accident. He was trying to help someone whose boat had capsized. Jeremiah pulled the man out of the water, but my nephew's legs got tangled in the lines, and he was pulled under when the other boat went down."

"That's horrible." Aury touched Michelle's arm lightly.

Michelle wiped her eyes. "To make matters worse, Brandon started acting out in school soon after. He was in the seventh grade, as I recall. That boy had more detentions than anyone I ever met. His mother was beside herself, and I don't blame her. She remarried a few years later. Brandon's stepfather didn't cut him any slack. At the time, I thought a firm hand was what he needed."

She fell silent, lost in memories. "I'm sorry to go on about my family like that."

"I don't mind. I'm a good listener whenever you need one," Aury assured her.

Michelle shook off her blue mood. "Why were you asking about the sailboat pendant?"

"It caught my eye because it's so unique. In his early social media posts, Brandon wore it all the time. In his most recent ones, it's gone."

Michelle swore under her breath. "I knew he was up to something. Probably pawned it. I can't believe he would stoop so low."

Aury had a sinking feeling in her stomach. If Brandon's money trouble was serious, perhaps that would be motive to get his hands on the house somehow. "I saw him at the diner the other day. Did he happen to mention to you how he hurt his hand?"

"He said he was helping a friend haul logs, and he smashed it. I knew that was a load of baloney."

"Why?"

"Brandon help someone? No way. Maybe if he was being paid, and if someone was there to supervise him the whole time. I'm giving him free room and board while he gets on his feet. All I asked was that he help me get this house ready. He showed up a few times early on, but now he always has one excuse or another. Says he's looking for work, but I've heard that line before."

Aury shifted her stance. She wasn't sure if she should fill Michelle in on Brandon's fight with David.

"Spit it out. I can see you want to say something," Michelle said.

Aury took a deep breath, then let it out quickly, rushing her words. "I think Brandon was fighting with David Willard on the ferry."

Michelle's eyes widened. "Why would they know each other?"

Aury shrugged.

This time, Michelle's eyes narrowed to slits as she glared at Aury. "What are you implying?"

Aury held her hands up. "I'm not implying anything. I thought you should know."

The older woman shook her head emphatically. "That doesn't make sense."

"Do you have any idea what they might have been fighting over?"

Michelle stood up straighter and thrust her chin out. "Brandon might not be the greatest help around here, but my nephew didn't raise a killer!"

Aury recognized the end of the conversation, so she didn't say it out loud, but privately she thought, *No one ever does.*

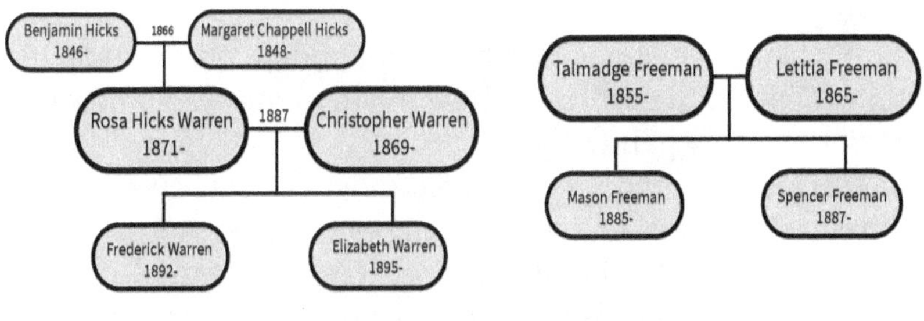

Chapter 19

Winter 1897

Rosa Warren's mouth fell open as she gazed around the bedroom. "You do such beautiful work, Letitia."

"Thank you. I'm mighty grateful for this chance. I'm not used to such a big space to paint." Letitia Freeman stepped back and dropped her paintbrush into a bucket. She wiped her hands on a rag, head tilting as she studied her art.

Rosa stepped closer to the wall, imagining her son lining up the stuffed animals his grandma Margaret made for him. "Frederick will be so excited. He talks about how he's going to live in the jungle and hunt wild beasts when he grows up." She dropped her voice conspiratorially. "I think he'd be more likely to befriend every last one."

"Well, nothing in this here painting will hurt him none." Letitia pointed to a tree. "And I'm goin' put a little ole monkey right there to watch over him."

Rosa clapped her hands together as she bounced on her toes.

"And what's going on in here?" Benjamin Hicks's booming voice cut through their chatter.

"Oh, Pa, you're early." She embraced him warmly.

Christopher entered the room behind them. "Benjamin, I put your bag in the room at the end of the hall."

Rosa slipped her arm around her husband's waist. "Look what a stunning job Letitia is doing on Frederick's room.

It'll be a surprise for him when he's ready to move out of the nursery."

Christopher shook his head but didn't try to hide his smile. "You spoil that child. How much money did you waste on all this fancy paint?"

Letitia flustered. "Sir, I mixed most all of it myself. Used things right out of the garden or the woods nearby."

Christopher held up his hands. "It's fine, Letitia. I'm just poking fun at this wife of mine. You've done a wonderful job. You won't hear a complaint from me."

Benjamin stroked his chin.

Rosa's gaze shifted to Benjamin. Her father was up to something. She knew the look. "Pa, what are you thinking on over there?"

He didn't answer her question directly. "Letitia, I've got a special project for you, if you're willing."

The painter's dark cheeks turned darker. "I'm always happy to help you out, Mr. Hicks. You know that."

"Well, this wouldn't be just a favor. I'm willing to pay for your time. I would like to commission you to paint a number of canvases for me." Benjamin explained the project in detail.

"I never done nothing like that before. Not sures I can." The young woman regarded the wall as if the answer were hidden in the jungle.

"Oh, Letitia, you're a great painter!" Rosa bubbled over in excitement. "It will be marvelous."

Benjamin gave the painter an encouraging nod. "You are extremely talented. I have every confidence in you. You just take your time. Let me know what you need, and I'll have it delivered to your house directly."

Letitia inclined her head. "You're generous, Mr. Hicks. I won't let you down."

He held out an elbow to his daughter. "We better go rescue your mother from those little rascals of yours."

Rosa took his arm. "Are you kidding? Ma won't let them out of her sight now that she's here. She complains they grow too fast in between visits."

"And she'd be right, as always." Benjamin spoke over his shoulder to his son-in-law. "We've got some paperwork to do after supper. Think you could lend me a hand?"

"Of course. Whitman and his family will be by in time for dessert." Christopher picked up the bucket of supplies Letitia had been painting with.

Benjamin winked at his daughter. "Oh, so they let him out of that fancy office to visit his old man, eh? Glad to hear it."

Rosa patted his arm. "Not everyone can be a farmer, Pa. Else who would eat everything you grow?"

"You mean who would suck up my earnings, making me pay to push papers around?" He gave a small chuckle. "Nah, you know I'm proud of him. I'm proud of all y'all. Every last one of you has turned into an upright citizen. Couldn't ask for nothing better."

Chapter 20

Present day

Liza was waiting when Aury appeared in the kitchen door. Her latest quilt top and backing were folded neatly into a large cloth bag.

She gave Aury a quick hug. "I figured you'd be in a hurry today, just getting your car back and all. Let's grab lunch on the way."

Over lunch, Aury poured out her story of upsetting Michelle. "I feel awful. Michelle has been nothing but nice. She does so many great things for the community."

"You didn't accuse her of murder, Aury." Gran bit into a fry. "Or Brandon, for that matter."

Aury twirled the straw in her drink. "I know, but no one wants to think their relative could hurt someone."

"Well, I had an uncle who scared people by just lookin' at them. That came in handy when boys thought to pick on me at school."

Aury smiled at Gran's attempt to cheer her up. "I don't have proof about Brandon. I'm guessing."

"So let's gather more information." Gran wiped her hands on the paper napkin and tossed it onto her plate. "First stop, let's finish what you started when you thought it was a simple fight on the ferry."

Aury drove to Linda's house while they tossed theories back and forth.

"Who was on that list of yours?" Gran asked. "Who would benefit from Izzie's death?"

"The only possibility is her ex-husband, Victor Clayton, but I'm not sure it would be worth killing over. Lieutenant Elliott said the ex wouldn't get any money. He'd doesn't have to pay alimony anymore, but that would stop when she moved into Fresh Start."

"Hmmmm. Doesn't sound like much of a motive. Okay, what if the killer thought it was Michelle?" Gran's eyes were closed, and her head rested against the seat.

Aury still hadn't done any research on Michelle as Scott had suggested. It made her feel guilty to look into her friend's past that way. She could only go with her observations. "Michelle seems to live frugally. Her house is nice but not grand or anything. She does a lot of charity work. Her brother already passed. She has nieces and nephews but sounds like Brandon is the only one who ever comes around."

"Does Michelle have a will?"

"How would I know?" Aury shot her grandmother a look, but Gran's eyes were still closed in concentration.

"Should find out. Could be important." Gran was in her zone now. "Now about Dave Willard. Did he have any connection to Izzie? Or to Michelle?"

"Not that I know of. Doesn't sound like he would have crossed paths with Izzie for any reason unless it was at Fresh Start. Same with Michelle. She said she never heard of him until he showed up snooping around."

Gran's eyes flew open. "Then that's probably your answer. Their murders have something to do with that house."

"But maybe the deaths weren't connected." Aury didn't want to jump to any conclusion. She had been doing that too much lately.

"Right." Gran gave her the side-eye. "Two unconnected deaths in one small town. Don't you read detective books anymore?"

When they arrived at Linda's, she oohed and awed over Gran's quilt top. "This is one of your best designs yet."

"You don't have to butter me up. You know I'm leaving it for you to longarm." Gran ran her hand across the fabric. "I was thinking about a variegated thread. Let's look at some designs."

After the ladies picked out a quilting template and the thread, they folded up the top and put it back in the bag. The moment was so cheerful, Aury almost left the photos in her bag, so reluctant to ruin it. But two people were dead. There was a lot more at stake than a cheery moment.

"I have something I want to show you." Aury pulled out the pictures of David and Brandon she had printed from the internet. "Do you recognize either of these people?"

Linda peered at the pages. She gave Aury an incredulous look. "How did you figure out who was fighting on the ferry?"

"So this is them?" Aury's heart quickened.

"Yep." Linda handed the pages back. "What made you care enough to go looking for them?"

"I've had recent dealings with this guy." She held up Brandon's picture. "I just had a hunch."

Linda walked them to the door. "They didn't seem to be guys you want to tangle with. Better off keeping your distance."

Aury indicated Willard's picture. "This guy is dead."

Linda stopped in her tracks. "Are you kidding me? You must be kidding. That's insane!"

Gran shook her head. "She's not joking. So I recommend you stay away from the other guy."

When they were back in the car, Aury sighed. "So much for clearing Brandon's name. Seems like there might be a motive we don't know about."

"Just because he fought with Willard doesn't mean he killed him. It just means they knew each other."

"Neither one was from around here. Why would they know each other?" Frustration was giving Aury a headache. She rubbed her temples before starting the car.

"Unless the connection is Fresh Start . . . again."

"But Michelle doesn't own the house. It was donated to Fresh Start. If something happened to her, the house wouldn't go to Brandon."

"Where would it go?" Gran asked.

Aury started the car. "I assume it would stay with the Fresh Start Foundation, and another director would be appointed."

"This necklace you mentioned, what was that all about?" Gran tapped her chin.

"I was trying to guess what Brandon and Willard could be fighting about. Money is a common topic, right?" She frowned. "Brandon doesn't have a job, and he's been picked up for selling off items that didn't belong to him." Aury was warming to her theory.

Gran nodded. "The fact that he had a very special necklace and now doesn't might indicate money trouble."

"Or it might be that he gave it to a special someone. Nothing nefarious."

"Let's not get ahead of ourselves. We'll follow the clues. That's what they always say on TV." Gran crossed her hands in her lap as if she'd just provided an indisputable expert opinion on the matter.

Television-trained sleuthing aside, Aury was already on to the next step. "When was the last time you went to a pawn shop?"

Gran's eyes glimmered. "Can't say as I've ever been to one. Sounds like fun."

Using a picture of the sailboat pendant in the image search feature on her cellphone, Aury quickly got a hit on a pawn shop that regularly posted items for sale. It was in Newport News, the next town over from Williamsburg. They had plenty of time to make it before it closed for the day.

The door chimed when Aury and Gran stepped into the stale, warm air of the shop. Gran wrinkled her nose. "They could do with some air freshener."

A man appeared from the back room. "Can I help you, ladies?"

Aury held up her cellphone. "Do you still have this?"

He squinted at the screen. "Sure do. And it's a fine piece. Pure gold."

He reached into the glass case near the cash register and pulled out a black felt necklace display. The chain and pendant shone brightly, even in the dim light.

Gran picked up the pendant and weighed it in her hand. "Nice try. At most, this is gold-plated."

The owner scowled before trying to hide it behind a fake smile. "You must be mistaken. This here's fine craftsmanship."

"This is a cheap trophy made by the hundreds for some local charity race." Gran leaned into the man's personal space. "Don't try to pull one over on me. I've been around longer than you have."

"Come on, Gran. It's not what I was looking for." Aury took Gran's arm, and they headed toward the door.

"Wait. I must have been thinking of another piece that already sold. You may be right about this one. Let me look up the details." The man typed quickly into a laptop on the counter. "Ah, yeah. Here it is. You were right. Gold-plated. I can give it to you for a good price."

Gran countered his offer with fifty percent of the price he named.

He chuckled and slid the necklace back into the case.

The ladies turned to leave again.

They made it to the door before the man cleared his throat. "I feel real bad about my mistake about the gold. How's about we split the difference?"

Gran glanced at Aury, who nodded slightly.

"Only if you include the information on who sold you the pendant. I want to make sure it wasn't stolen." Gran waited with her arms crossed.

The owner feigned indignation. "I would never buy stolen property."

"Then you won't mind providing the info. You don't have to disclose what you paid for it. I don't care about that. I just don't want the police coming after us." Gran drifted back to the counter.

The man relaxed his shoulders and blew out a breath that stank of stale tobacco. After hitting a few keys, the printer spit out a single sheet, which he handed to Gran.

Aury scanned it. Brandon Paris was the previous owner. She pulled out her credit card. "We'll take it."

Gran hooted after they left the shop. "That was more fun than I've had in ages."

Aury put her arm around Gran and gave her a squeeze. "You're the best. I need to take you with me for all my negotiations."

"I love this sleuthing."

Aury had to agree. "It is pretty satisfying."

"You were always great at puzzles. It's how your mind works. That's why you're good at quilting too, you know."

Aury raised one eyebrow.

"Don't look at me like that. It's true. The measuring, cutting, fitting pieces together—that's your math brain. The color combinations and attention to detail—that's the other half of your brain. You exercise both on a regular basis." Gran opened the car door and climbed in.

"That must be what's kept you so sharp. I guess I'll keep it up." Aury smiled as she slid behind the wheel.

"What's your next step? Are you going to see Lieutenant Elliott?"

Aury nodded. "I think he'll want to know what we found."

"What about Michelle? Will you tell her first?"

Aury thought about it. "I don't think so. It may not have anything to do with Willard or Izzie, and I don't want to upset her unnecessarily."

"What's the connection between Willard and Brandon? Could they have been fighting about money?"

"But what could Willard have to do with Brandon's finances?" Aury sighed.

"From what you told me, sounds like Brandon would be looking to make a quick buck wherever possible."

Aury turned in her seat to look directly at Gran. "So was he working for Willard?"

Chapter 21

A few hours later, Aury found herself at the police station again, sitting in Elliott's office. "Michelle told me Brandon was supposed to be helping her the day Izzie was killed. She was late getting back to the house because she was making a trip to the dump that Brandon said he was going to do."

"She told me the same thing. We still haven't been able to corroborate where he was. Says he was at home alone." Elliott tilted forward in his chair.

"Well, I have a theory about that."

"Of course you do." Elliott couldn't hide the amusement in his voice.

Aury pulled out the sailboat pendant. "I found this at a pawn shop in Williamsburg."

He took the clear bag and examined the necklace. "So?"

"This belonged to Brandon. His dad gave it to him, and Brandon wore it all the time." She handed him the copy of the receipt the pawnshop owner had given her. "Until he pawned it."

Elliott read the page, zeroing in on the date. "This is the date of Izzie's murder."

"Brandon had to be in deep to pawn his dad's necklace. He must owe serious money to someone he didn't want to tell his aunt about."

"Thanks for bringing this to our attention." Elliott slipped the paper into a folder on his desk. "But don't get your hopes up. This doesn't prove anything."

"What do you mean? It proves he was at the pawn shop!"

"But did you look at the timestamp? He could have still made it back to the house and killed Izzie before you found her."

Aury blew out a confused breath. "I wonder why he didn't try to use this as an alibi. Why won't he tell you where he was?"

"I'm not sure he realizes what kind of trouble he's in." Elliott sat back.

"You don't suspect him for Willard's death too, do you?"

Elliott raised his eyebrows. "You heard about that, huh?"

Honestly, why did that surprise him? Aury shot the lieutenant a candid look. "Of course I did. How did he die?"

Elliott's sigh was heavier than ever this time. Two strange deaths within a week of each other in the same small town had to be stressful for local law enforcement. Quite the escalation from petty theft and property tax violations.

"I suppose everyone will know before long." Elliott shuffled papers on his desk. "The maid found his body in his hotel room when she went to clean. We don't have an official cause of death yet."

"Was it murder, or could it have been a heart attack or something?" Aury prayed it was anything besides murder.

"All I can say is we think there might have been someone else there at the time."

"But—"

He cut her off. "Please, no more questions for now. I shouldn't have told you as much as I did."

"Then you should probably know Gran and I saw David Willard and Hamilton Moore talking earlier in the day." Aury took a bit of satisfaction in the way the lieutenant's posture perked up with interest once again.

"You did? What time?"

"Just before the funeral."

"Did you hear what they talked about?"

"No, we couldn't get close enough."

"Are you trying to tell me you sought them out?"

Aury twisted uncomfortably in her seat. "Not really. Well, sort of. We saw Moore's car and followed out of curiosity. Gran and I heard he was looking to do a land grab in Surry like he's been doing in Williamsburg. We thought maybe he was scouting a possible location, and we were curious."

The police officer hung his head. "It wouldn't do me any good to warn you to restrain yourself from investigating, would it? Or light stalking, for that matter?"

She grinned. "Not really." She switched to a more serious tone. "Willard showed up a few minutes later. He was mad. Well, at first he was begging, then after Moore left, Willard got mad."

"How do you know he was begging?"

Aury put her hands in front of her, palms together. "I think it's an international sign. We did hear him raise his voice at one point. He said he needed more time. Then he said, 'He'll come through. I know it.' Or something like that."

Elliott wrote Willard's words on a pad. "Do I need to tell you to stay away from Moore?"

Aury smiled her sweetest smile. "If it would make you feel better, go right ahead."

After dinner, Aury called for Treasure. The overgrown puppy bounded into the room.

"Wanna go for a walk, girl?" Aury scratched behind her ears as Treasure's tail wagged furiously.

"Can't it wait until morning?" Scott was sitting in front of the TV, a laptop open in front of him.

While they ate, they had talked about the Willard murder and Aury's meeting with Elliott. Then the conversation fizzled.

"I won't be long. I have this silly painting idea in my head that needs to make it to the canvas before it drives me crazy." She pulled on her William and Mary hoodie and held the door open for Treasure to lead the way.

The dog disappeared in the dark but, moments later, circled back to check on her human. Then, with a happy pant, Treasure galloped away again. Aury stuffed her hands into the pocket of her sweatshirt. She lifted her eyes to the night sky and luxuriated in the pinpricks of light that broke the velvety canopy.

Away from the manmade lights of town, the night sky at Eastover was brilliant with stars. Aury picked out Orion lying on his side and followed the glowing spots on his belt to locate Sirus, the brightest star in the sky. Along with quilting, Gran had taught Aury a lot about stars and constellations. When she was troubled, taking in the vastness of the solar system allowed Aury to put her problems in perspective.

As she neared the crafters' cottage, she called for Treasure in a hushed voice so she didn't bother the Eastover guests staying nearby. The dog trotted up beside her and pushed through the door as soon as Aury opened it.

Aury took in the scent of the paint and wood before flicking on the lights. It was beginning to smell more like a working cottage than the musty funk of a shut-up building. Pleased, she tossed a work apron over her neck and tied the cord. She crossed her fingers before turning on the new faucet. Alan and Scott had only installed the water lines earlier that day. The tap spit and bucked a few times before providing cool, clean water. Aury sighed in satisfaction and filled a jar for her brushes. Funny how the little things can make such a difference.

This cottage was turning into her private refuge. Giving up her house in Williamsburg to move in with Scott had been an adjustment. She had to admit there were times when she wanted to watch silly romcoms and eat ice cream without worrying about what someone else would think. Not that Scott would necessarily care, but she didn't want to take any chances.

After taking a blank, prepped canvas from a stack against the wall, Aury placed it on an easel. She started with a quick sketch, trying to place items in the scene appropriately. When she finished with the pencil, she squeezed acrylic colors onto the paint board, ready for mixing and creating.

Aury pulled out her phone and zoomed in on the photo she had taken of one of the paintings she got from Michelle. The perspective was so captivating. Once her brush hit the paint, she absorbed herself in the process. Many times, she used a splotchy rag to wipe off excess paint when she felt the picture wasn't shaping up to match her vision. Then she would start over, covering her mistakes with different hues and brushstrokes.

Her eyelids were drooping, and she was losing focus. *Time to call it a night.*

Standing, Aury stretched her arms high above her head, then bent at the waist to touch her toes. As she straightened and reached for her paintbrushes, a loud snap sounded from outside. Straining to hear anything more, she fixated on the door.

When the muffled sound of something being dragged was followed by a louder crash, she searched for a place to hide. As quietly as she could, she made her way to the back of the building and slipped into the space where the bathroom would eventually go. Spying a piece of a two-by-four leaning against the wall, she snagged it and clutched its wooden corners with white knuckles. Aury pressed herself into the corner. *Please let this be my imagination. Please.*

For a moment, she envisioned herself sprawled in a pool of blood—Scott finding her cold, dead body. She shook herself out of the trance, determined to fight back. She lifted the board to her shoulder.

The handle creaked as it turned, and the outer door opened with a groan.

"We need to oil these hinges."

At the sound of Scott's voice, Aury released the breath she was holding.

"Aury? Are you in here?" Concern tainted his words now.

Shaking slightly, she stepped out of her hiding spot.

"What are you doing back there? You know it'll be a few more days before the commode gets delivered." He stopped laughing when he saw her face.

"What happened? What's wrong?" He rushed to her, encircling her in his arms. With her face buried in his shirt, her sheepish chuckle was barely heard.

"I'm fine," she finally managed. "I just got spooked."

Scott rubbed her back. "I'm sorry. I tried calling, but you didn't pick up. I figured you must have fallen asleep out here."

She released him and moved to her easel, where she had left her phone. "It's dead. I must have left it on too long studying this picture."

He joined her beside the painting. "Wow! It's really coming along. I love how you can't see the whole person in the foreground."

"I know, right? That's what I loved about the paintings Michelle gave me, so I wanted to recreate it with my own twist. The perspective makes you feel like you're standing inside the scene."

Treasure nosed her way in between them.

"Some watchdog. You didn't even bark." Aury gave the dog's head a good scratch anyway.

"To be fair, it was only me. She's been trained not to bark at us or the people who're around all the time." Scott patted Treasure's side. "You were here just in case, weren't you, girl?"

Treasure licked his hand.

"Let me drop these brushes in clean water, and we can get out of here." Aury dumped the used water down the drain and refilled the jar from the faucet.

"That's a great use for those old jars. Are they from Michelle too?"

"Yep. She gave me cases of them." Aury rinsed the brushes quickly before dropping them into the jar. Before they stepped out into the night air, she flicked off the overhead light. She closed the door behind her, testing to make sure it locked.

At Scott's raised eyebrow, Aury said, "You can't be too careful in Surry."

Chapter 22

Aury arrived at the police station early the next morning. "This was your lead, so I'm breaking more than a few rules to let you listen in. Don't go telling everyone." Elliott led her into a darkened room with a window displaying four white walls, a table, and two chairs. "I might have more questions for you after. Wait in here, and I'll come back for you. Don't touch anything."

In no time, Elliott ushered Brandon into the other room and gestured for him to take a seat. They were carrying cups of coffee and chatting about nothing in particular. Brandon was trying his best to turn on his swagger, but he wasn't fooling Aury. Surely Elliott wasn't falling for it.

Brandon took in the room with darting glances. "This room doesn't look the same as the one I was in before. Is this an interrogation room?"

Elliott let a short chuckle escape. "Not when we aren't interrogating people. Sometimes it's just a quiet room away from the hubbub of the office."

The younger man relaxed slightly at that and sat. "Why did I need to come down here?"

"I thought you'd prefer that to me showing up at your aunt's in a police car. No sense stirring up the gossip chain. Am I right?" Elliott dropped a folder on the table and sat.

"Go ahead then. What's so important?" Brandon's attempt to take control fell flat. His lowered voice was a little too forced as he scratched at the stubble on his chin.

Elliott made a show of looking at the pages in the folder. "You told us you hurt your hand helping out your aunt."

"So? What of it?"

"David Willard has a black eye."

"I don't know the guy."

Elliott placed the picture of Willard in front of Brandon. "You sure about that?"

Brandon gave it a cursory look. "Yep. Don't know him."

"We have a witness who saw you fighting on the ferry. Ring a bell?"

Brandon angled his body toward the door. "Oh, that guy."

"So would you like to change your statement?" Elliott was nonchalant.

"Yeah. I didn't know his name, that's all."

"But you also didn't hurt your hand helping your aunt. You hurt it on this man's face." Elliott tapped Willard's photo.

"Why? Is he pressing charges or something? He started it. I was minding my own business."

"I'm sure you were. Let's start over. When was the first time you met Mr. Willard?"

The surly man sat back in his chair and crossed his arms over his chest. Aury thought his attempt to act cool and in control came across like a little boy preparing to throw a tantrum.

"Dude came up to me at the Fresh Start house, asking questions about Aunty Michelle. I told him to buzz off."

"What kind of questions?"

"Bunch of stuff about the house and Aunty Michelle's nonprofit. Like how she knew Mrs. Warren. Wanted to know how much the house appraised for, what she was doing with the items inside, and the like."

Elliott jotted down something in his folder. "What did you tell him?"

Brandon shrugged. "I don't know anything about Mrs. Warren or the value of the house. I figured it couldn't be worth much. Why else would someone give it away?"

"And the items?"

He shrugged again. "Like I said, I told him to buzz off."

"But it got you thinking about all the stuff your aunt was giving away, didn't it?"

"A bit." Brandon sat forward, resting his forearms on the table. "If she was giving it away, I assumed she wouldn't mind me having some things. After all, most of it was going to the junkyard or to that woman at that camp."

"We'll come back to that. You were telling me about how you met Willard."

"Like I said, he came to the Warren house."

"And that's where you punched him?" Elliott didn't look up from his note-taking.

"No, man. A few days later, he got in my face."

"This was on the ferry?"

Brandon nodded. "I wasn't doing nothing but chillin'. Then he started running his mouth. It's one thing to say things about me, but when he started in on Aunty Michelle, I clocked him. That shut him up."

"What did he say about your aunt?"

"Said she was a gold digger and that she was selling off valuable things from the house to make a quick buck. That's not my aunt's style."

"But it's your style, isn't it?" Elliott slowly raised his head to look at the man.

Brandon visibly tensed.

"You already admitted you took things from the house to sell," Elliott said.

"Well, that's different."

"Maybe a few lamps? Some small furniture pieces you didn't think she would notice?" Elliott referred to his notes, but Aury doubted he really needed to. This had to be for show.

Brandon squirmed in his chair. "Aunty Michelle doesn't mind helping me out. Besides, those rejects were headed to the junkyard."

"Were they? Sounds like Michelle was planning on using those pieces when she opened Fresh Start."

"She didn't mention that to me. How was I supposed to know?" The petulant little boy was back.

"If you helped out like you were expected to, you would," Aury muttered to the empty room.

Elliott dropped it and moved on. "What happened after you hit him?"

Brandon sat back again, trying to relax. "Nothing. The ferry docked, so we got back into our cars and went our separate ways."

"And you didn't have any dealings with him after that?"

"No, and if he said I did, he's lying."

"Why were you on the ferry?"

Elliott's question caught Brandon off guard. "What do you mean?"

"Why were you going to Williamsburg? Do you have family or friends there? I thought you were new to the area." Elliott sipped from his coffee cup.

"Is it a crime to leave Surry once in a while? Not a lot happening around here." Brandon's defenses were back up.

"Just seems like you've been spending a lot of time on the other side of the river."

"Yeah, I got some friends."

"Do you want to share their names?"

"No, why would I?"

"Where were you when Izzie was killed?"

Brandon jumped to his feet, knocking the chair back. "I thought we were talking about this Willard guy. Why are you bringing up the dead chick?"

"Just thought these friends of yours might be able to give you an alibi for the time of Izzie's death."

His eyes narrowed. "Why would I need an alibi?"

"Everyone connected needs an alibi."

"I wasn't with them."

"Where were you?" Elliott stayed cool as he peppered questions.

Brandon's chin jutted out. "I don't remember."

"But you know you weren't with them?"

Brandon stared sullenly at the door.

"Maybe you were pawning the necklace your father left you when he died." Elliott slid the receipt across the table where it balanced on the edge.

Brandon snatched it before it could fall. He read the paper and sank back into his seat. "Yeah, so? It was mine to sell."

"Strikes me like a special kind of low to hawk something from your dead father. How much money do you owe?"

Brandon's eyes snapped up to Elliott's.

Elliott went on, "You must be in deep to let this go. How much did you get for it?"

Wadding up the paper, Brandon snapped, "It's none of your business."

This time Elliott shrugged. "No skin off my nose, but I'd think twice about borrowing money from your friends."

"Selling my stuff isn't a crime."

"Killing David Willard is."

Brandon's mouth opened then closed again. "Killing? Willard is dead?"

Lieutenant Elliott placed a photo on the table in front of Brandon.

Brandon turned away. "I didn't have nothing to do with that."

"In the same way you didn't even know him?"

"No, man, I'm telling you. I could never hurt anyone."

"I'd like to believe you, but the murder weapon tells a different story. Do you recognize this?" Another picture was placed on top of the first.

Brandon's face blanched. Aury thought he might be sick.

Elliott tapped the photo. "If I ask Michelle, will she be able to tell me where it came from?"

"Don't tell Aunty Michelle. Please. Yes, I took it from the Warren house, but she was giving things away left and right. I doubt she even missed it."

"How did it end up in my crime scene?"

Brandon gulped. "I gave it to Willard."

"Why?"

"I owed him money."

"How did you end up owing David Willard money?"

"You aren't going to tell Aunty Michelle, are you?"

Elliott didn't bother responding.

Brandon gripped his fingers behind his head, tucked his chin, and rocked in his seat. After thirty seconds of this, he lifted his gaze and dropped his hands. "Willard paid me to talk Aunty Michelle into giving up the house. I wasn't making any progress, so he wanted his money back. I'd already spent it."

Brandon pointed at the picture. "This statue has to be worth a lot of money. It was solid and really heavy. I found it locked inside a cabinet in the living room."

"What did Willard say?"

Brandon shook his head. "He said he'd hold it for collateral, but he wanted the cash. I was trying to come up with it."

Elliott cocked his head and crossed his arms. "You can see why this doesn't look good for you, right?"

"What do you mean? I told you what happened."

"You owed Willard money that you didn't have. With Willard dead, there goes your debt."

Brandon jumped to his feet again. This time his chair toppled over. "No way! You aren't pinning this on me! I want my lawyer."

"You aren't under arrest. You're free to go."

Brandon hesitated as if he had heard wrong. Then he found his voice. "I'm outta here."

The police officer let him go. Elliott took his time straightening out the crumpled receipt and placing it back in his folder. A few seconds after he departed the room, the door next to Aury opened, bright light spilling in from the hall.

Aury took in Elliott's smug look. "Wow, you're good. I never want to be on the other end of one of your investigations."

Elliott smiled. "I hope you never are."

"How did you know he was spending a lot of time outside Surry?"

"I didn't. It was a hunch. But he's right. It isn't a crime to sell his own things, and his aunt doesn't want to press charges against him for stealing from the house."

Aury leaned against the wall. "Now what?"

"I'm waiting for the autopsy report on Willard. Brandon has a motive for wanting him dead, and his fingerprints were on the statue."

"But he explained why his fingerprints were on it. That doesn't mean anything." Aury's mind raced as she tried to come up with another explanation.

"We're still looking into it."

"What about Izzie?"

Elliott held his palm out. "Even if he didn't kill Izzie, there's a chance his *friends* came looking for someone he cared about. Izzie could have been in the wrong place at the wrong time."

An image of Izzie lying prone on the floor in a puddle of her blood resurfaced in Aury's mind.

Wrong place at the wrong time was quite the understatement.

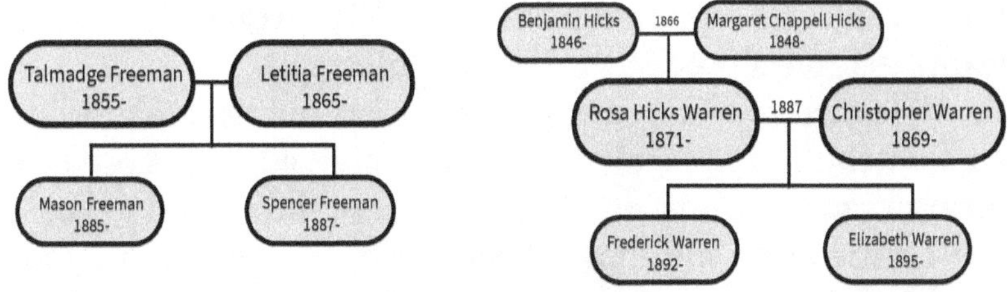

Chapter 23

Summer 1900

Letitia Freeman stood and stretched. "That's the last of it. I'll be needing your help cutting 'em down to framing size."

Talmadge towered in the doorway leading out to the porch. His sour mood was sucking the joy she felt at completing the project. This stage of it, at least.

The large canvas was stretched across a rickety frame leaning against the back wall of their house. When Letitia stepped back to scrutinize her work, the floorboards creaked, and she almost lost her footing on a loose plank.

Her husband scoffed, and the odor of cheap hooch hit her, turning her stomach.

He spit over the porch railing. "I don't know why you spent so much time on a project for that man."

Catching herself on the banister that also wasn't very stable, she straightened up and wiped her hands together. "He pays me well for my time."

Letitia couldn't very well tell her husband that they needed the money to pay their debt at the grocer's. Besides, being paid to do something she loved was fulfillment beyond anything she had experienced as a farmer's wife.

"What a way to waste money—on some stupid piece of canvas that you're gonna chop into pieces anyway." He rolled his shoulders and stood straighter. "Senseless."

She bristled at his words, and tears stung her eyes. "I don't think my talents are a waste of money. Mr. Hicks sees that, even if you don't. Besides, I think it's wonderful that he wants to leave a precious gift to his children."

"He throws money away on this crap, but he don't forgive an old debt." Talmadge's words had a hard edge that brooked no argument. He pushed off the doorway and turned to go.

Letitia knew she should keep her mouth closed. No good would come from quarreling with her husband. He didn't have a nice word to say about anybody. She was so tired of hearing the same speech about how wronged he felt. He repeated his lies about helping to invent the peanut picker so often, she was afraid he had begun to believe them.

When she overheard their eldest son complaining to his friends how his father was kicked out of the bigger house even after he shared all his invention ideas with Mr. Hicks, she put her foot down. It had gone on long enough. She tried to explain their situation to their son and received a blackened eye for her efforts when Talmadge heard about it.

The Hicks family had been good to them. They were more than fair to give Talmadge a second chance to make something of himself as a farmer. When that didn't work out for him, Benjamin Hicks paid him as a hired hand, with a bonus at harvest time. Not many employers would be that generous.

No, Benjamin Hicks was a good man and fair to boot. Letitia's husband could learn a thing or two from him.

Trying to keep the derision from her voice, she asked, "Didn't you say you're about paid up? That's something to be thankful for."

Talmadge spun toward her, and Letitia flinched.

"You think I should be grateful to a man who sits on his high horse in another town, directing how I work on land I used to own?" His face contorted with rage. "Next you'll be sayin' I didn't have no part of that gadget he uses in the field. The same one he's using to take away my job, same as he did my house."

Letitia suspected her husband had no idea how the peanut picker worked. He had never even heard of it until a few years ago when Benjamin asked Talmadge to come to Vicksville to help during the harvest.

If Talmadge had any useful ideas, Benjamin wouldn't be the type of man to steal them. He had helped many farmers perfect their tools in his blacksmith shop. That was one of the reasons he was so well respected.

Talmadge, on the other hand, spent too much time running his mouth at the local pub and not enough time in the fields.

When the men gathered to bring in the harvest that year, Margaret Hicks had welcomed Letitia and her kids into her home. It was a much-needed respite for Letitia. It also gave her a chance to see the peanut picker up close and complete sketches for the painting she was working on.

When they first arrived, Benjamin had been making last-minute adjustments to the monstrosity. It was so funny-looking, Letitia couldn't imagine how it could move, let alone help with the picking. When the inventor cranked it up, it made an awful racket, and white smoke billowed from the top pipe.

All the children gathered around cheered as the contraption inched its way forward, slowly picking up speed. That scene was cemented into her brain and had made it to the canvas.

Chapter 24

Present day

Aury dragged her feet as she headed toward the beach trail, dreading the idea that Scott might not be there. When she got close, Treasure charged toward her, stick between her teeth. She tossed it for the pup to chase.

Halfway down the trail, Scott and Alan were setting four-by-four, treated wood alongside the trail.

A sense of relief washed over Aury, followed by guilt for feeling that way. "Looks great."

Most of the trail had been outlined by the wooden beams. Aury surveyed the foliage from the trail to the trees beyond. "Do you think this will help control the underbrush?"

Scott brightened when he saw her, and Aury's heart skipped a beat. *He seems happy to see me. That's a good sign, right?*

"We're hoping it will keep hikers on the path. When they stray on this hill, they're more likely to sprain an ankle or get poison ivy."

"It also has the added benefit of slowing down erosion." Alan stomped on the wood, ensuring it was settled.

"How did it go with Elliott?" Scott asked.

"He let me watch when he interviewed Brandon. I can't believe that man is related to Michelle. They have nothing in common." Aury used the wood as a balance beam, seeing how far she could go up the trail without falling off.

Scott snuck up behind her and tickled her sides.

She fell into his arms giggling. This was her Scott, the one she was madly in love with.

He squeezed her tight before releasing her. "What did you learn?"

"Brandon seemed surprised about Willard's death. I don't think he did it, but the murder weapon was something he took from the Warren house."

Alan let out a long, low whistle. "That doesn't sound good."

"I know. Poor Michelle." Aury's mood dipped. "But I'm sure there are other suspects. I just need to gather more information."

"Do you hear yourself?" Scott's gaze was intent on her face. "I don't think trying to track down a killer is the safest use of your time."

She returned his look with a stubborn one of her own. "I said gather information, not confront suspects in a dark alley."

Scott opened his mouth to speak but closed it, turning to pick up the shovel instead. Aury watched him for a few minutes in silence before leaving them to work on the path. Was Scott's comment controlling or concern?

When she returned to the house, she opened her laptop to get a jump on the employee scheduling for the next month. Her mind kept racing, and she found she was making mistakes because she couldn't focus. Ice cream would solve her problem.

She checked the freezer with sad results. Grabbing her keys, she felt like she was on a mission as she headed to the store. Cookies and cream or peanut butter cup should be the toughest decision she made today.

When Hamilton Moore departed the peanut store next door to the ice cream parlor, Aury's thoughts jumped back to her conversation with Scott. *Well, this wasn't a dark alley.*

"Mr. Moore, isn't it?" Aury pasted on a smile and extended her hand.

He responded with an equally fake smile and a handshake. "Nice to meet you . . ." he trailed off, giving Aury the chance to fill in the blank.

She skipped past that expectation. "I understand you're the developer who's interested in buying the Warren house."

He pulled his hand back. "I'm always interested in acquiring good properties."

"It *is* a lovely property, isn't it? I hear it's being turned into a home for women who are trying to get a fresh start on life. That's quite the noble endeavor. But you probably wouldn't understand doing something so selfless for the community. Not profitable enough for someone like you." Aury never dropped her smile.

Moore shook his head and tried to skirt around her.

She sidestepped into his path. "Did you ever take a look inside the house? See what they're doing there?"

He sighed. "Listen, miss, I'm not sure what you want me to say. Yes, I was interested in buying the property. I made an offer, but it was rejected. I have better things to do than lose sleep over one business deal."

"I understand Brandon Paris was trying to work things out for you. Through David Willard, perhaps?"

His face paled, but he recovered quickly. "I don't discuss my business dealings with strangers, particularly ones who accost me on the sidewalk."

This time, she let him push past her.

Gotcha.

Chapter 25

Aury paced back and forth across her small living room. Her laptop sat open on the table, calling to her. After running into Moore last night, she knew she should do her due diligence and research Michelle's past as Scott had recommended.

The tightness in her chest suggested that her heart and mind weren't in agreement. Michelle had been nothing but nice to Aury when she moved here. She was the first one to invite Aury for ladies' night out and to bring donations for the crafters' cottage. Michelle started an organization to help woman get out of tough situations. How could she be anything but good?

Plopping down in the kitchen chair, Aury gave a weary sigh and ignored the lump in her throat. The cursor blinked at her. If she didn't get this over with, she wouldn't be able to get any work done.

She took a fortifying sip of coffee and opened a browser. Stories about the establishment of Fresh Start were the only things that popped up under Michelle's name. According to one of the early interviews, Michelle was originally from Georgia but had lived in Surry since 1985. She had worked at the local hospital, then as a home healthcare worker before establishing Fresh Start.

Aury read over the articles again, more slowly this time. When asked why she founded Fresh Start, Michelle only said everyone should have a place to go. A shiver went down

Aury's spine. Throughout the articles, Michelle answered that question the same every time. Aury couldn't help but wonder if there was more to Michelle's story.

Further searches showed no social media, at least not under her name. Fresh Start had a page, but the postings were sparse and only told of events and ways to donate to the cause. Michelle was never pictured in any of them.

Switching tactics, Aury entered the words Georgia and 1980, along with Michelle's name into the search bar. Nothing.

She took out the year, and an article about Jeremiah Paris's boating accident was listed. He was touted as a hero, and Michelle was listed as family when they mentioned who he was survived by.

Another obituary also popped up where Michelle was recorded as family. Her brother died of cancer five years ago.

The timing could be coincidence, but Aury flipped back to the establishment of Fresh Start. The date was six months after Michelle's brother died.

Aury closed her laptop. She was meeting Gran and couldn't waste any more time on this. At least nothing negative popped up. The only way to get to know Michelle better was to talk to her directly.

After parking on the ferry, Aury got out to enjoy the crisp air. Standing at the back of the boat, she tracked the seagulls riding the air currents. The foam churned up by the engines inspired the idea for a quilt pattern. Aury studied the details closely, so she could jot them down. The bump against the pier brought her out of her musings, and she returned to the car.

Her grandmother was waiting outside her house when Aury arrived. Gran stood in the garden, a bunch of weeds in her gloved fist. She dropped them in a nearby bucket along with her gloves and straightened her wide-brimmed hat. "Beautiful day, isn't it?"

Aury's heart lightened when she saw her grandmother. Gran never let things get her down, and she taught Aury resilience. She felt better just being around her. "Are you in the mood to go to the library after lunch?"

"Two of my favorite things—food and books. Do you really need to ask?"

Over lunch, Aury caught Gran up on her talk with Lieutenant Elliott and Brandon's interview.

"So what are we looking for at the library?" Gran finished her salad and wiped her mouth.

"I'm curious about the Warren house. It's been around for a long time, but no one remembers much about its history."

Gran gave Aury a knowing look. "Do you think it has something to do with these murders?"

Aury shrugged one shoulder. "There's still the possibility Izzie was killed by her ex, and Willard's death was a coincidence, but it feels like a stretch that there's no connection."

"And the only connection you see is the house. I understand."

"Or Michelle could be the connection, but she didn't know Willard well. His connection is with Mrs. Warren." *Until he was caught in the lie, Brandon said he didn't know Willard either,* a nagging voice in her head reminded her.

Gran pushed herself to her feet. "Let's get going. Those books won't read themselves."

A short drive later, Gran and Aury were occupying a table in the Williamsburg Regional Library on Scotland Street. Stacks of books lay haphazardly across the surface. Gran's sticky notes marked pages in various volumes.

Aury opened another book. "There's so much history here, I'm getting sidetracked on our quest."

"It's fascinating, I'll say that. That whole tract of land was once a plantation, but after the Civil War, the emancipation of the enslaved people created a shortage of manpower. Many of the plantations went under, and the property was split up. A lot of it was bought up by a collective of Black families. They farmed it using sharecroppers." Gran took off her reading glasses and dangled them between her fingers. "I always thought sharecropping was just another way to enslave people without calling it slavery."

Aury pulled out her notes. "Even before 1860, over a third of the Black people in Surry County were already free. Many owned farmland and businesses. Listen to this. 'In 1887, Goodman Brown, an African American from Surry, was elected to the House of Delegates representing Surry and Prince George Counties.' Apparently he owned a huge farm growing peanuts and corn."

"Did you find anything specific about the Warren house?" Gran shuffled the books, making room for a larger volume.

"Mrs. Penny Warren told Michelle that her in-laws inherited the house in 1945. When they wanted to move south, they passed the house to their son, Penny's husband. When I searched online for the Warren family in 1945, it brought up a lot of hits. There are quite a few in the area."

Gran propped her elbows on the table. "Didn't they make their money in peanuts?"

"Yep. The Warren Peanut Company was established in 1898 by Christopher Warren. They started small, when peanuts were first grown as a commercial crop, so they were well ahead of anyone else. Now they have country stores all over Virginia, and they ship worldwide."

"So Penny's husband was a Warren through that line?" Gran tapped on the table with her index finger. "That explains why she can afford to donate her house to Fresh Start."

Aury nodded. "I think so. I'll also reach out to Mrs. Warren to see if she knows anything else about the history of the house. I wonder if she's still out of town."

"She's been gone a while, hasn't she?"

"Michelle said she was out of the country on vacation. I'm not sure when she's coming back." Aury glanced around at the piles of books. "We should make a trip to Richmond to visit the Library of Virginia and look at the land tax books to see if we can figure out how the property was broken up."

Gran opened another volume. "Ah, the smell of microfiche. I can't wait. I'll bring my Post-it Notes."

Chapter 26

When Aury parked in front of the Warren house the next morning, Michelle was standing on the front porch talking to her nephew. Brandon's eyes flared against Aury, then he slunk into the house.

She climbed the steps. "I see Brandon's helping you again."

Michelle grimaced. "Not by choice. I need him to keep his nose clean. I told him until this all blows over, I'm to know where he is at all times. We ride to work together, he does what I tell him to do, and we go home together. He's really not a bad worker when he stays focused."

"I'm glad you're getting the extra help." Aury shuffled from one foot to the other.

"Lieutenant Elliott came by." Michelle folded her arms in front of her. "He said you were trying to help clear Brandon. Thank you for that."

"I feel horrible for upsetting you. I never meant to." Aury's stomach had been in knots since her fight with Michelle.

"Honestly, I think I was more upset with myself that, for a moment, I entertained the possibility at all." Michelle cleared her throat, and her chin quivered slightly. "Of course, he may be in trouble anyway for breaking the conditions of his parole. He's in serious debt because he's been gambling. But I don't think he could hurt a soul." Her wide, pleading eyes sought Aury's.

"What will happen to him?"

"I'm not sure, but I certainly can't bail him out. I put everything I had into this place." Michelle nodded at the house.

Aury's heart sped up, but she tried not to let it show. This was the opening she'd been hoping for. "I've been meaning to ask you, why did you start Fresh Start?"

"Everyone needs a place to live."

That same old line. "Yes, but why you? Why is this mission so near and dear to you?"

Michelle lowered her head slightly and scrutinized Aury. "You are really direct, aren't you?"

Aury gave a one-shoulder shrug. "I'm a curious person. I like learning about people."

Michelle huffed out a breath and stood straighter. "Five years ago, my brother died. Nothing suspicious, if that's what you're going to ask next. It was cancer."

The tightness is her chest made Aury avert her gaze.

Michelle went on, "He left me a chunk of money, and I wanted to do something good with it. I'd been working in the hospital system and saw the needs of some of the people who came through the emergency room."

"I'm sure your brother would be proud of what you've done." Aury's voice was soft.

A sharp sound that wasn't quite laughter escaped Michelle's lips. "He'd say it was about time."

Aury decided it was best to let that go for the time being. She produced the sailboat pendant. "I have something for you."

Michelle took one look at it, and tears formed in her eyes. Holding it almost reverently, she kissed the gold. "Where did you find it?"

"Pawn shop in Newport News. I suggest not letting Brandon know you have it."

"Definitely not. I'll put it in a safe place. Or maybe I'll wear it myself. It'll be like keeping my nephew Jeremiah close. He had a good heart, like my brother." She gave Aury a quick hug. "There's no way Brandon will get his hands on it again."

When Freeman emerged from the house carrying two boxes, Michelle wiped her eyes.

He looked at her sideways. "Are you okay, Michelle?"

She tapped his arm. "I'm fine. These are happy tears."

He put the boxes in the back of the van. "I think that's all for this trip."

"Mr. Freeman." Aury nodded at him by way of a greeting.

"Ah, Miss St. Clair. How are things going with the crafters' cottage? I understand Michelle has taken a few loads of donations to Eastover."

"And I'm ready for another one." Michelle slapped the side of the van. "I was hoping to unload some stuff today."

Aury hesitated. "I'm sorry. I'm on my way to see Gran. I just stopped by to give you the pendant."

"I can take it by, if that would help," Thomas offered. "Just tell me what you want, and I can leave it for you."

"I don't want you to go to any trouble." Aury waved off the suggestion. Casually, she stepped closer to him, searching for any signs that he had been drinking.

"Thomas already offered to drive things to the dump for me. Your place isn't that far out of the way, and it would save me a separate trip." The dark circles under Michelle's eyes displayed the pressure she was under. Getting this house ready, finding a dead body, and keeping her great-nephew out of jail would exact a toll on anyone.

Aury didn't pick up the stench of alcohol, and Freeman's eyes weren't glassy. "Well then, that would be great. I'll let Alan know to unlock the door."

She rummaged through the van and pointed out a few items she thought she might be able to repurpose: an old bookshelf that could use some love, two more wooden chairs, and yet another box of glass jars.

Brandon carried another bin from the house and placed it in the van. His gaze slid over Aury, but he kept silent. A perpetual scowl seemed to darken his features.

Michelle handed Thomas her van keys. "You're a lifesaver. Thanks for all the help today."

"Happy to help out where I can."

Michelle gave Brandon the once-over. "Thomas, why don't you take Brandon with you? He can help unload."

Brandon's eyes blazed brightly for a second but then went back to flat. He didn't speak and kept his face neutral as he hitched up his sagging pants.

Thomas cleared his throat and jerked his head toward the van. "Let's get on the road."

Aury's curiosity sparked as she watched the exchange. Shouldn't Brandon be more grateful to Michelle? She seemed to be his life preserver. "I need to go too. Gran and I are going to Richmond. But I'll be over soon to paint in the dining room."

She gave Michelle a quick hug, glad they were back to normal. Maybe after this research trip, she would put together a historic booklet about the Warren house as a keepsake for Fresh Start.

Aury sat in her favorite overstuffed armchair reading over the notes she and Gran had put together on the house that afternoon. Light glowed softly from the lamp beside her, while the rest of the house remained dark.

At the slow creak of the screen door, Aury held her breath. Treasure sat up from her place at Aury's feet, nose twitching as she prepared for an intruder.

The knob on the main door turned with excruciating care. Aury's heart beat fast in her chest, but Treasure still didn't move.

When the door finally opened a crack, Treasure charged the door.

Aury jumped to feet, grabbing the table lamp, thinking how unsubstantial it felt in her grasp.

Instead of hearing barks of warning from Treasure, Aury recognized the merry jingle of the dog's collar as she danced around Scott, waiting for him to take off his boots.

Aury put the lamp back and tried to appear unruffled, although her pulse pounded in her ears.

Scott lifted his chin. "You're still awake. I thought you would have gone to bed by now."

Was he trying to avoid her by waiting until after she was asleep to come home? Aury cleared her throat. "No, I've been reading."

He plopped down on the couch and let Treasure scramble into his lap. "What's so interesting?"

She filled him in on her trip to Richmond with her grandmother. "Gran even found some black-and-white photographs of the house on the microfiche that will be perfect in the booklet we're putting together for Fresh Start. We printed a few, but I'll have to figure out how to clean up these copies. They aren't the greatest."

Scott picked up a photo of several farmers leaning against an odd-looking machine. The Warren house was prominent in the background. "What's this?"

"The caption in the microfiche listed it as a gas-powered peanut picking machine, invented in 1890 by Benjamin Hicks."

"How can that thing pick peanuts?" Scott tossed the photo back onto Aury's stack of papers.

"You got me. Hicks filed a patent on it in 1901." She rifled through the stack and handed him another grainy photo. This was clearly the Warren house but not quite as large as it was today. Some additions must have been added later. A couple with nine children posed on the front porch.

Aury kept talking as he studied the photo. "We studied the land tax books."

"That must have been riveting." Scott's mouth quirked into a half-smile.

She ignored him. "Christopher Warren received the house in 1888 as a wedding present from his in-laws when he married Rosa Hicks."

"As in peanut-picker Hicks?"

"One and the same. The Hicks's family history was even more interesting. Benjamin Hicks was born into slavery in Courtland, Virginia, but three years later, emancipation freed his family." Aury checked her notes to get the facts right. "When he grew up, he was a sharecropper like his father. He did blacksmithing on the side to save up enough money to buy his own land."

"That's impressive." Scott squinted closely at the man in the photo.

"He farmed peanuts, apparently a huge crop in this area."

"Hence the invention of the gas-powered peanut picker," Scott finished for her.

"Hicks and his wife, Margaret, had eleven children. They moved back to Vicksville, Virginia, in 1880. I already told you the rest." Aury stacked her papers together and closed her notebook.

Scott handed her the last photo. "You and Liza never cease to amaze me. And all this to create a brochure for Fresh Start?"

"You have to admit, it makes a great backdrop for a program designed to help women make something of themselves. Hicks's rise from being enslaved to being a patent holder is inspiring. He was known for constantly improving farming techniques and methods. Always tinkering." Aury stood and stretched.

Scott also rose to his feet, displacing Treasure. "Speaking of tinkering, I need to get some sleep so I can tackle the trail again tomorrow."

Aury reached out to kiss him goodnight, but he had already turned away.

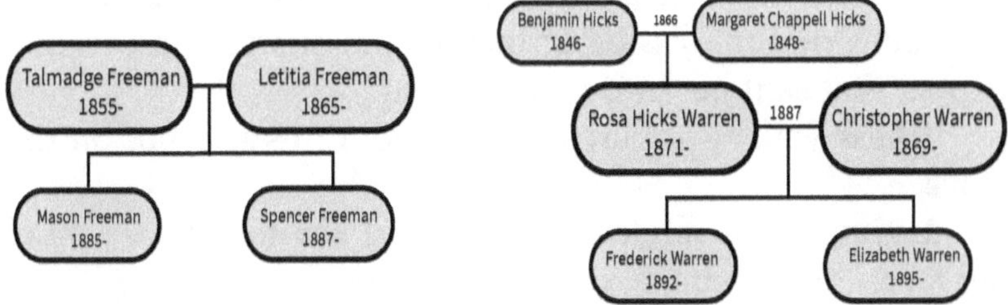

Chapter 27

Fall 1904

L etitia and Rosa sat on the back porch of the Warren house shucking corn. Their children played a convoluted game of tag in the yard. Letitia couldn't begin to understand the rules as the kids kept changing them.

"I love this weather. It's cool enough to be outside without being eaten up by mosquitos." Letitia tossed the outer peelings into a bucket and ripped away the next layer.

"I hope we get a little more rain for the peanut harvest. It's been awfully dry this year." Rosa shook the clingy corn silk from her fingers. "My pa's pondering an idea on how to irrigate the fields. He's been corresponding with several farmers in Colorado."

"I wish my husband had half the gumption of your father." Letitia slapped her hand over her mouth. A lump rose in her throat as she looked around to see if anyone had overheard. "I'm sorry. Please don't go tellin' anyone I said that."

Rosa chuckled and shook her head. "I would never. Honestly, I have no idea where Pa comes up with these things. I would say his tinkering was an excuse to seek the quiet of the barn, but he drags my brothers and sisters out there with him."

The women carried the shucked corn to the cast iron kettle in the yard hanging above a low fire. They slid the cobs into the pot, being careful not to get splashed by the scalding water. When that task was complete, Letitia followed Rosa inside.

A storm of aromas assaulted her senses. Letitia thought the chili powder was the strongest, but it was the cayenne pepper that sent her into a sneezing fit.

"Bless you." Rosa crossed the room to stir a pot on the stove.

Letitia's eyes blinked rapidly, and she fought to school her face. "My goodness, what are you cooking?"

The sweet melody of Rosa's laughter filled the kitchen. "Not me. That's Christopher's concoction you smell. It overrides anything I do."

One side of the kitchen was roped off with paper signs hanging along the line in various places. Letitia tilted one so she could read it. "'No crossing or risk the punishment of the coop'? What's this all about?"

Rosa's eyes danced around the many pots and bowls spread across the counter. "That's Christopher's not-so-subtle way of telling the kids to stay away from his experiments. Frederick ate a particularly spicy peanut last week, and his face turned beet red. I think Christopher took that as a sign that he added too much pepper."

"So these are recipes for the peanuts he's cooking up in that factory?" Letitia perused the pages of notes next to each bowl. Precise ingredients were penned in a careful hand, down to the field where the peanuts came from and any spices that were locally sourced.

Rosa wagged her index finger and stressed the first word. "Potential recipes. Now that the factory is taking on regular orders to ship the boiled and salted peanuts across the country, Christopher wants to figure out how to increase the demand."

Letitia recognized the sharp pain in her midsection for the envy that it was. Her husband couldn't think past his next break, let alone plan for expansion. But she loved to hear about Christopher and Rosa's successes. It restored her faith that hard-working people did exist and were rewarded. She just hoped Talmadge hadn't ruined their sons' potential with his laziness.

"I'm glad to hear the factory is doing so well." Letitia's heart quickened when she saw the artwork on the wall. "You have one of my paintings!"

"We each have one." Rosa straightened the frame. "Pa wants us to remember how fortunate we are, and that we are a part of a greater whole. He said there's something extra special in these paintings, so we'd remember what we get from working hard. I'm glad he let you keep one too."

Letitia blushed, but she couldn't stop the wide smile from splitting her face. "He was very kind. That was probably the most special thing I ever painted."

"Pa is very sentimental, though he covers it up well with his no-nonsense business approach. He's tried to drill the seriousness into my brothers, but I think my sisters and I inherited more of his drive than they did."

Letitia stared at the painting affectionately. "Well, it's a wonderful thing he has done for your family."

"Same with you." Rosa took both Letitia's hands in hers. "I know these paintings will keep our family close for generations to come."

Chapter 28

Present day

Aury woke up full of energy after a replenishing day spent with her grandmother. She hit the grocery store before it got busy, and then she spent the afternoon doing bookkeeping for the property.

Next she pulled up their list of ongoing and proposed projects. They were meeting with Alan at the end of the week to prioritize for the future. There were many lofty ideas, including building a new bathhouse closer to the camping sites and clearing the scrub from the area behind the crafters' cottage to add an archery range and maybe even a ropes course. Aury was leaning toward refurbishing the cabins that were closer to the scout camp next door. They were in bad shape, so she and Scott needed to decide whether to tear them down or see if they could be salvaged.

Stretching, she stood and pulled sheets of paper from the printer. She placed them on the counter and called for Treasure. The click of her nails on the wooden floor announced the pup's arrival.

"Time to walk." Aury opened the door, and the dog bolted into the field.

The sky was darkening as the sun fell behind the trees. Aury breathed in the cool, clean scent and smiled. It was going to rain soon. The humidity made her hair frizz, so she pulled it back in a loose ponytail as she walked. With her official work done, she wanted to work on her painting for a while. Something about the technique was eluding her, like an itch she couldn't scratch. At the same time, she enjoyed the challenge of mastering something new.

The rubbery odor of fresh paint hit her as she approached the crafters' cottage. She touched the wood on the screen door and was pleased to find no sticky residue. The paint had set well. Thankfully it dried before the rain had a chance to make a mess of it.

She flicked on the overhead lights and soaked up the ambiance. Being in this room fulfilled a part of her she didn't realize she had been missing. Quilting was her first crafting love, but being able to branch out and explore different artistic traits gave her a sense of accomplishment, even when she wasn't good at some of them. It was the love of creating.

Another trip to the secondhand store would provide enough tables to set up the sewing and quilting area. Large bulletin boards stood against the wall where they had been since they were delivered. This would be where she advertised the options for campers to try different skills while on retreats at Eastover. She took a mental note to hang one on the outside of the cabin under glass.

Time to treat herself. Aury filled an old canning jar with water for her paintbrushes and carried it to the easel she had been working on. Her painting wasn't there. In its place was a landscape Michelle had donated from the Warren house, but it wasn't even the sample she had been referencing.

She flipped through the canvases leaning in the corner but couldn't find her work in progress. It seemed like a few others were missing too, but she couldn't say which ones off the top of her head.

Frustrated, she locked up the cottage. Calling for Treasure to follow, she strode to the beach trail where Alan was packing tools into the golf cart.

"I thought you'd be gone by now. Won't your wife be worried?" Aury handed Alan a shovel she plucked from the edge of the path.

Alan shook his head. "She's at a book club with her sister. She won't even know I'm gone. I didn't feel like going home to an empty house."

Alan's need for company had grown as his children had married and left the area. Aury was grateful he enjoyed their friendship enough to hang around, even when he wasn't working.

"You should come up to the house for a drink before you go." Aury examined the trail. "You guys have done a great job here. Are you about done?"

"All the big stuff is finished. Just doing a bit of cleaning. The path is safe and usable though. That's what's important." He climbed in behind the wheel.

Aury's mind immediately plotted out the trees she would use to hang the Christmas lights. Maybe if the lights worked out well, they could stay up year-round. She'd have to talk to Scott about it. Her attention snapped back to the reason she came down to the trail. "Hey, did you happen to move some paintings from the crafters' cottage? I'm looking for one in particular."

"Not me. Haven't been in there since I unlocked it for that Freeman fella."

Aury recalled the old chairs stacked neatly in one corner, so Mr. Freeman had come by. She couldn't dream of a reason he would take old canvases, but she would ask next time she saw him. "Have you seen Scott?"

"Said he was going to hang your bulletin boards. He's probably at the crafters' cottage."

Aury frowned.

"I'll drop this in the shed and stop by for a quick minute. Wanna ride?" Alan started the motor.

"No, I'll walk. Thanks. See you in a few."

After the golf cart was out of earshot, Aury pulled out her cell phone. "Hey, Scott, did you take any canvases from the cottage?"

"No, why?"

"I wanted to hang a few to add color to the room, but I can't find them."

"I thought you took some to your painter friend in Williamsburg."

"I took some but not all. The one I was working on the other night isn't there either."

"Did you ask Alan? I can't imagine why he would have moved them, but no one else would have a reason to be in there."

A strange squeal came through the connection. "Where are you, anyway?"

After a heartbeat too long, Scott replied, "I'm on the trail. Finishing up though."

"See you at home soon?" Aury tried to keep her imagination in check. There had to be a good explanation for this lie.

"Yep. Should be back in about five minutes."

Aury hung up and stormed down the trail, Treasure hot on her heels.

Back at the main house, Aury mixed up a pitcher of Pimm's and ginger ale. She sliced apples and oranges and added them to the drink. By the time she carried the tray with glasses and the pitcher to the patio, Alan was ambling up.

They sat around the firepit, and Alan pulled out his phone to share the latest pictures of his grandbabies. They were each on their second drink when Scott finally strode out of the dark. Treasure ran out to meet him.

Aury poured him a drink. "That was longer than five minutes."

Scott took a long swig. "I had to make one extra stop. Sorry about that."

She was itching to call him out on his lie about being on the beach trail but didn't want to drag Alan into the middle of anything. While she normally enjoyed Alan's company, she was anxious for him to leave. On the other hand, she wasn't sure she wanted to hear what Scott would tell her.

"Isn't that right, Aury?"

Her head snapped up, and she locked eyes with Scott. She had lost the thread of the conversation.

He laughed and covered her hand with his.

"You must be getting tired. I'll get going." Alan placed his glass on the tray and stood. "Thanks for keeping an old man company."

They stood with him.

"You're family, and family's always welcome." Scott shook his hand. "See you in the morning."

The silence hung between Scott and Aury after the older man wasn't there to keep up the conversation. Scott poked at the fire with a stick.

Aury twisted her engagement ring around her finger. "I'll help Alan in the morning. Then I'll make a deposit at the bank before meeting Michelle at Fresh Start. Don't forget you said you would come help move furniture."

"I'll meet you around eleven."

The silence became unbearable. Aury stood and carried the tray inside while Scott ensured the small fire was out.

She rehearsed what she would say to him while she put the glasses in the dishwasher and wiped off the counter.

The screen door slammed when Scott entered. "I'm beat. I'm going to grab a shower and hit the rack."

Before she had a chance to respond, he was through the kitchen and into the bedroom, closing the door behind him.

Chapter 29

Once again, Scott was gone when Aury rolled out of bed the next morning.

When she had slipped into bed, Scott's arms found her as naturally as if they had been together for decades rather than a few years. She couldn't bring herself to say anything that would upset that feeling. That didn't mean she hadn't lain awake a good part of the night thinking up plausible scenarios for Scott's strange behavior.

Was he seeing someone else? Was he bored with her already?

Aury refused to let those negative misgivings interfere with her morning. She had things to do, and worrying about her relationship wasn't getting things done. The sunshine streaming through the window helped to lift her sour mood.

As soon as she could steal away, she collected Treasure and headed into town.

After running a multitude of errands, she pulled in behind Michelle's van at Fresh Start. She led Treasure to the fenced-in backyard where she could explore while Aury helped Michelle.

Brandon was trimming weeds along the fence line. The headset he wore must have been playing music, because he was singing along but not very well.

"Good morning," Michelle called from the back porch. "Want some coffee?"

"No thanks. Had my fill. I'm excited to get started in the dining room." Aury followed Michelle inside the large, brightly lit kitchen.

Freeman was sitting at the round oak table in the corner. He stood when he saw her, but his bloodshot eyes strayed past her as he spoke. "Nice to see you again, Miss St. Clair. Hope all is going well with your project."

"Mr. Freeman, what a nice surprise." Aury's words didn't mask the wariness in her voice. She still thought he was a bit over-ingratiating toward Michelle but couldn't put her finger on why it bothered her.

He lowered himself back into his seat, picking up the string of the tea bag and tugging it a few times to stir the liquid in his mug.

"Thanks again for dropping those things off at the cottage." Aury grappled with the best way to bring up the missing paintings. Direct was her usual approach, but she wasn't sure how he would respond to that. She tried for a lighthearted chuckle. "Sorry I left things in such a mess. It's pretty crowded in there. I seem to have misplaced some paintings already."

His eyes narrowed, losing their dull appearance. "What are you accusing me of, Miss St. Clair?"

She was taken aback at his quick shift to a defensive tone. She held up her hands in surrender. "Nothing at all. You stacked the chairs neatly inside, so I wondered if maybe you had to move things around to make room for the donations."

He sniffed indignantly. "I'm not in the habit of rearranging items belonging to other people. Next time I'm helping Michelle, I'll make sure to leave any items for you outside in the elements."

Michelle didn't appear to notice the chill between her guests. She hustled Aury through to the dining room. "Everything is coming together so nicely. I can't wait for the final touches."

Aury inhaled deeply. "New carpet?"

"They finished installing it yesterday, and the mattresses were delivered this morning. The best news of all—we're officially closing on the house this week." Her smile faltered. "Miss Penny came back for her nephew's funeral."

Aury wondered when it would be appropriate to reach out to Mrs. Warren. She should probably wait until after the funeral, out of respect, but Aury really wanted to ask her some questions about the house.

To Michelle, she said, "Concentrate on all the lives you'll positively impact when Fresh Start opens."

Michelle gave Aury a grateful smile. "Thanks. Thomas and I are tackling the basement next. Who knows what hidden treasures we'll find. Do you need anything to get started?"

She spread her supplies on a tarp already laid out on the floor. "Do you have a ladder I can use?"

"Of course. It's on the second floor. Do you want me to grab it?"

Aury was already heading toward the steps. "I'll get it."

She paused halfway up.

Michelle must have sensed her hesitation. "The police got anything they were going to get, so they let me back in the room. Did you know you can hire companies to come in and clean up after a crime like that? They came down from Richmond. I had them strip the carpet and scrub everything. They even painted the walls."

A shudder ran through Aury, but she continued up. Outside the door where she had found Izzie, she paused. The clean-up crew had done a good job. There were no telltale signs anything bad had happened in there. She continued down the hall until she spotted the ladder in one of the bedrooms and hauled it out. She remembered one of the doors being locked on her first visit. Out of curiosity, she tried the handle. Still locked.

She carried the ladder down the stairs and set it up in the dining room. When Michelle came in, Aury asked, "Am I allowed to know what's behind the locked door upstairs?"

"I can't believe I haven't shown you yet. Come see." Michelle grabbed Aury's hand and practically dragged her up the stairs. Then she pulled a key from a string around her neck. "This will be my office eventually. I didn't want anyone in here messing it up."

She unlocked the door to reveal an oasis of color. Large murals covered all four walls from floor to ceiling.

Aury stepped into the center and spun in a slow circle, trying to take it all in. The jungle scene was so realistic, she would have sworn the temperature had risen fifty degrees. "This is amazing. Who did it?"

Michelle's smile split her face. "Miss Penny doesn't know. She said it's been like this for as long as she can remember. She thought it was overwhelming, so she never used this room, but she couldn't bring herself to paint over it. Isn't it glorious?"

Aury touched the monkey hiding beneath the banana leaves. "I can't believe it. I feel like I'm in the jungle."

"I know, right? Do you think you can help me pick out curtains that will match the theme without distracting from the painting?"

Upon closer inspection, the paint was chipped in places and sun-faded in others. "Of course. You might also want to have my painter friend Karmine look at these murals. She could date the painting and then touch up some of the colors using the right medium from the era."

"What a wonderful idea! Let her know for me, will you? It's not pressing, but I would like to know more about the artist."

The front doorbell rang, and Michelle left to answer it.

Aury walked slowly around the room, taking in the minute details. She pulled out her cellphone and snapped a few pictures to send to Karmine.

"Wow!"

She turned at the sound of Scott's voice. "Gorgeous, isn't it?"

"I'll say." He strode into the room and stood next to her.

Aury chuckled to herself as he turned in a slow circle, the same way she had.

She opened her mouth to speak, but a rage-filled shout cut across her thoughts like a shot.

Chapter 30

"It's your fault my wife is dead!" Clayton had his grimy finger in Michelle's face.

She slapped his hand away. "You get off my property this instant!"

Aury and Scott took up a place behind Michelle in the entry hall.

Clayton's eyes shifted from the older woman to Scott. A flicker of hesitation crossed his face. With much less vigor, he addressed Michelle again. "I'm going to sue you for everything you have! I'll be the one tossing you out soon enough."

He stomped through the doorway, slamming the door behind him.

Aury concentrated on controlling her breathing. So this was the menacing side of her ex that Izzie was afraid of, not the simpering fool he acted during the funeral. Aury had been on the receiving end of many tirades like this during her first marriage.

Michelle collapsed against Aury, her whole body shaking.

Aury led her into the living room and lowered her onto the well-worn couch. Scott arrived moments later with a tall glass of water.

Michelle took a deep drink before she spoke. "That man has no right!"

"Of course not," Aury assured her. "He's all bluster. He's only looking for a way to make money off Izzie's death."

"But what if the killer *was* after me and took Izzie instead?" Michelle's lips trembled, and tears pooled in her eyes.

Scott put a hand on her shoulder. "Only the killer is to blame for Izzie's death. You can't let that guy get to you."

"Brandon thinks I should give up Fresh Start. He says no one will want to live where there's been a murder." Michelle dabbed her eyes with a tissue from the end table.

Aury patted her knee. "Since when have you cared what Brandon has to say?"

Michelle released a small laugh at that. "Good point. He's a bit useless, to be honest."

"That's right!" Aury peered closely at Michelle's face. "Are you feeling better? Do you want to go home?"

Michelle shook her head and slapped her hands to her knees. "No, I'm good. I'm not letting that bully derail my plans for the day."

Aury stood and put her hand out for Michelle. "Then let's get moving. We have to get this place ready for the women who are counting on you."

Michelle's knees creaked as she stood. "I'm so glad Miss Penny put her trust in me. I'd hate to see what would have happened to this beautiful house if she had sold it to that revolting developer."

Scott gave a boyish grin. "C'mon now, Michelle. Not all developers are bad. I've worked for many over the years."

"Hopefully not one like Hamilton Moore! He came sniffing around when I was meeting with Miss Penny. Slippery as a snake, I say. She was none too impressed either."

"Do you know what he planned for the house?" Aury asked.

Michelle shook her head. "No, but this area is zoned for commercial and residential. Not a big leap to think he would tear it down to make more empty strip malls. I think he offered to buy Thomas's house next door too. No thank you!"

Scott cleared his throat and flashed Michelle an overly bright smile. "You had furniture you wanted moved?"

While Michelle decided on what pieces needed to go where, Aury and Scott followed her directions. They finished in no time, and Scott departed to get back to Eastover.

Aury finished wiping down the last of the furniture. The hint of lemon in the polish tickled her nose. She stretched her back and took in the original sitting parlor. It wasn't very large, but Michelle had made it cozy with plump cushions in a variety of colors. A treasure trove of toys rested in a corner, waiting for their house guests.

Aury went to work in the dining room. She traced the grapevines onto the wall using the templates and applied the first coats of paint before she climbed down to survey her work.

Michelle's arrival was preceded by the fragrance of cinnamon and nutmeg. "I know you'll be getting ready to leave soon, but I was wondering if I could bother you for one last favor? I'd do it myself, but I'm waiting on the building inspector to come by."

"Of course. Anything." She dropped her paintbrush into a bucket.

"Would you mind taking this over to Thomas for me? He's been such a big help. I want to thank him. Of course, there's another pumpkin bread waiting in the kitchen for you too." Michelle winked.

Aury's stomach rumbled. She took the covered dish from Michelle. "I'd be happy to."

As she walked across the lawn, dark storm clouds moved swiftly in the sky. Aury glanced at them. She should still be able to make it home before the rain started. Anything too heavy still tended to cause rivulets in the unpaved road running through Eastover. They really needed to move paving that road higher on the to-do list.

She used her elbow to ring the doorbell of Mr. Freeman's house. Moments later, the door swung wide, and his smiling face greeted her.

Inwardly, Aury sighed in relief. After their last run-in, she wasn't sure what kind of reception she would get from the older man. "I come bearing a gift from Michelle."

He took a whiff. "Hmmm. I'm detecting pumpkin, if my nose doesn't deceive me."

"It doesn't." Aury smiled back.

He held the screen door open. "Come on in. I just put on coffee. Would you like some?"

"Sure. Why not?" She stepped through the door and handed the dish to Freeman.

"I'll put this in the kitchen, then we can sit on the porch. I love watching the storm clouds."

Aury stood obediently for a few moments, but then something in the sitting room caught her attention. With her latest obsession of painting, she was always drawn in when she spotted a canvas. This was a landscape of a lush, green crop with plants that grew low to the ground. Stepping closer, she noted the wood frame with a light stain that brought out the colors of the field in the painting. This was definitely a better color choice than the dark wood frames on the ones Michelle gave her. She might have to consider reframing one of hers to show artists the difference the right frame makes.

She admired the brushstrokes and variety of shades, wishing her paintings had the depth of this one. Sighing, she turned to take in the rest of the room. It was cozy with worn furniture that made her want to curl up with a book and a glass of wine. A crocheted blanket in fall colors lay neatly across the back of the couch. Aury ran her hand along the pattern, feeling the knots and ridges. She wondered if Mr. Freeman could crochet or if his wife might have made it. She realized she knew very little about him, including whether he was married or not.

An old, leather-bound journal rested on the end table next to the couch. The cover was embossed with the name "Freeman" in an elegant scroll. It didn't match the no-nonsense vibe Aury got from the older man. He didn't appear to be the type to indulge in an expensive journal. A gift, perhaps.

More pictures in frames covered the mantel. Aury stepped closer to look for a wedding photo among them. Nothing including an obvious wedding dress, but one photo may have been a young Mr. Freeman with a slight woman wearing a Sunday hat with a veil. They were both smiling as if someone had made them laugh.

Aury grinned back at them as she moved on to the next photo. A small, black-and-white photograph rested among many others printed in color. She picked it up and tilted it toward the open curtains so the light would catch it better. Her breath caught as she recognized the composition of the photo. Several men leaned against a large, boxy machine. This picture was the same as the one on the microfiche or at least eerily close.

Maybe Mr. Freeman's ancestor was one of these men.

From the doorway, the older gentleman cleared his throat loudly. "Were you looking for something in particular, Miss St. Clair?"

Aury caught the ice in his tone. She placed the photo back on the mantel. "Are these relatives of yours?"

"Probably a number of them. Back then, everyone was related to everyone in Surry." The tray holding two coffee cups rattled in his hands. "I just remembered I have to be somewhere shortly. We'll have to reschedule our coffee for a later date."

Taking the not-so-subtle hint, Aury moved toward the door, but not without one last look at the living room. She couldn't shake the feeling there was something she was missing.

But Mr. Freeman ushered her out with surprising efficiency, so Aury was forced to content herself with one final sweep while he put the tray down.

"Well, I hope you have a nice day," he said, hand on his front door. "Come back another time, and we'll have that coffee for sure."

"Of course," Aury said, though it was clear as day the man was lying. This was one invitation with a permanent raincheck. The real question was why.

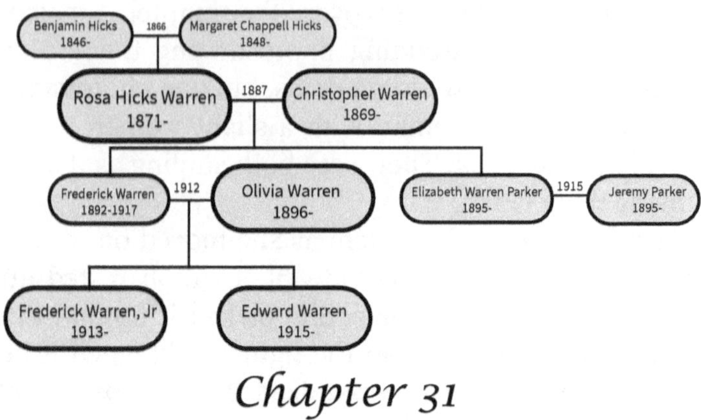

Chapter 31

Summer 1917

Rosa stood on the front porch, gazing forlornly down the dirt path. A wind gust ruffled her long black skirt. When it settled, she didn't have the energy to correct the pleats. She toyed with the wedding ring on her left hand. This should never happen.

A dust cloud rose in the distance, announcing the arrival of her permanent house guests.

"Christopher?" She didn't bother turning her head. She knew he would be close; he always was these days.

The screen door opened and closed quietly. Christopher's hand went protectively around Rosa's waist.

Two horses connected to an open wagon came to a stop in front of where Christopher and Rosa stood. The driver hopped down and chocked the wheels before lending his hand to a small woman, veiled and dressed in black.

Rosa didn't think her heart was capable of this much pain. As she descended the steps to fold the waif into her embrace, Christopher assisted the driver. The children leapt into their grandpa's waiting arms. He squeezed them tight before placing them on the ground, then turned his attention to unloading the bags and crates from the wagon.

Rosa did her best to hold back the tears. Having her grandchildren there lifted her spirits slightly. She knelt down, allowing them to run into the shelter of her arms. At two and four, the boys reminded Rosa so much of her darling Frederick at those ages. Tears streamed down her face, even as she tried to put on a smile for the sake of the children.

When they squirmed, Christopher snuck up behind them and tickled their sides until they were squealing with delight.

As the wagon pulled away, Rosa stood and took Olivia's hand. They watched Christopher chase the kids around the yard.

"Would you like tea?" Rosa finally asked.

Olivia nodded, and the ladies retreated to the warm kitchen.

Rosa filled the kettle while Olivia pulled mugs from the cupboard.

"How are the boys handling the change?" Rosa put the pot on the stove.

The younger woman shrugged. "They're excited to visit their grandparents. Little Freddy thinks Daddy will join us after the war, even though I never gave him that impression. It's a knife to my heart when he pretends with his friends to be a soldier like his father. Edward is happy no matter where he is." She stifled a sob. "What will they do without their father?"

"They're young and a lot more resilient than we are. They'll bounce back quickly as they form new memories here." Rosa's eyes landed on the painting hanging above the table. The greens and browns of the peanut field just as it was starting to bloom brought back memories of simpler times. Before this blasted war.

Thoughts of her father working the fields filled her head, his gaggle of children following in his wake, hanging on his every word as he pointed out the difference between a healthy plant and a sickly one. The togetherness of it all—that was what she missed the most.

When the kettle whistled, Rosa added the tea to let it steep. She set the kettle on a trivet in the center of the table and slid into a chair.

Olivia fell into a seat, burying her face in her hands. "I can't do this."

Rosa understood completely and would prefer to join her daughter-in-law in her tears, but she had to be strong. She had Christopher to hold her through her weeping. Olivia had no one anymore.

She gently removed Olivia's hat, putting it on the table. Stroking Olivia's hair, Rosa murmured soothing words she hoped would take away a little of the distress.

When the young lady had cried herself out, Rosa handed her a wet cloth. "Why don't you go lie down for a while? It was a long journey. Christopher and I will watch the boys."

Olivia dabbed her eyes. "You are so kind. I'm not sure what we'd do without you."

Rosa covered Olivia's hand with her own. "This is your home now too."

Chapter 32

Present day

Scott and Aury sat quietly, holding hands beside the firepit outside their house. The crackle of the fire was calming background music for the swirl of thoughts running through Aury's head.

The visitors had all been fed and were making their way back to their rooms. Most were staying at the lodge, but a few families elected to room together in one of the bunkhouses a football field away from the circle of light pooling around the center of the Eastover property.

Before she met Scott, Aury had been to Eastover multiple times with her guild for quilting retreats. After falling in love with him, it quickly became her favorite place.

Scott seemed to be far away tonight. The firelight bounced off his profile as he slid forward and poked at the wood with his free hand. The flutter of love and longing filled Aury's stomach. It was quickly followed by sharp pain of all the things they left unsaid. It had been such a peaceful evening, and she didn't want to ruin it by confronting him about all the disconnects they had had lately, but the ache of distrust threatened to snuff out the good feelings.

She was gathering her courage to speak her concerns when he stood, pulling his hand away.

"I'm going to bed. I want to get an early start tomorrow. Alan will be busy feeding all the guests, so I'm on my own."

Aury's hand felt cold already without Scott's. "I'll be here. Do you want help?"

He glanced at her then back at the fire. "Why don't you help Alan? I can finish up on my own, but then, if you're up for a walk, we can decide where we want to expand the camp and put the archery range."

Her spirits lifted slightly. Maybe she was imagining his standoffishness. "I'd like that."

"Will you take care of the fire, or do you want me to?"

"I got it. I want to sit here a little bit." She pulled a quilt over her legs to replace the heat Scott took with him when he wasn't pressed against her.

He bent down to kiss her. "I love you."

She placed her palm against his cheek. "I love you too."

The screen door closing behind him was too loud in the quiet.

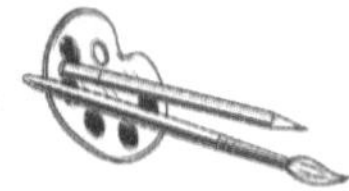

The sound of Scott's truck pulling away stirred Aury from her sleep. She glanced at the clock. Seven. Too early to be making noise on the trail when they had guests on the property.

Treasure stuck her wet nose under Aury's arm.

"Yeah, yeah. I'm getting up." She gave the dog a scratch behind her ear, then tossed off the quilt she made last year during the retreat. It had taken multiple washings after the storm, but Aury was able to save it.

She let Treasure out while she started the coffee and went through her morning routine. When it was time to head to the dining hall to help Alan with breakfast, she put Treasure inside. "Not sure why Daddy didn't take you with him, but you'll have to play inside today. Too many kids running around to distract you."

The morning went by quickly. Breakfast was efficient as always under Alan's supervision. He even made special smiling pancakes for the young at heart at the camp.

Aury peeled potatoes for lunch, then restocked the trays that would go on the salad bar. Dutifully hanging her apron back on its hook, she returned to the house to work on the books.

Treasure convinced Aury to play ball for half an hour before she secluded herself at the kitchen table to work on scheduling. After she finished the day-to-day operations, Aury treated herself by creating the online schedule for her craft classes. She still had a few holes to fill with instructors but was overall pleased with the results for the first quarter. She wanted to start slowly and add classes as the word spread, but the first priority would be for the guests who were staying on the property.

As she looked over her work, the front door opened.

"Hope you haven't had lunch yet." Scott held up a takeout bag from Aury's favorite restaurant in town.

She lifted an eyebrow. "I thought you were working on the trail?"

"Finished. I returned the stump grinder and couldn't resist a little treat. I thought we'd have a picnic."

"I could use some fresh air." Aury selected an older quilt she made expressly for picnics. Traditionally patchworked, the fabrics were worn, and each held a specific memory.

They walked hand in hand past the crafters' cottage to the area they were considering for archery. Treasure loped along beside them, occasionally darting after a squirrel before returning to their side.

Scott pointed to a heavily wooded area with thin undergrowth. "What do you think about putting the archery range there?"

"Where's the line to the camp next door?"

He indicated the approximate location of the line. "It runs parallel to this strip, so archers wouldn't be shooting into another property, but I think we should fence it off anyway."

Aury envisioned the targets downrange. "I like it. Are you going to leave the trees?"

"Most of them. I think they'll add a little more challenge to hit the target. And it shouldn't take long to cut back some of this scrub. If we hit it with a Weedwacker regularly, it should be easy to maintain."

They walked and shared more about their dreams for future upgrades to Eastover, what items needed immediate fixes, and which ones could wait.

Finally, Aury couldn't put it off any longer. "We need to talk."

"I thought we've been talking."

Aury shrugged. "Kind of. But there's also things we aren't saying."

Scott slowed to a stop. "Are you happy here?"

"What? What kind of question is that? I love this place." Aury turned to face him. "Why would you ask that?"

He shook his head. "You had a career and a life in Williamsburg until I dragged you into the middle of nowhere. You're such a social person. I'm worried you'll get bored when the work is done."

She smirked. "Will the work ever be done?"

He gave a faint smile and continued walking.

This conversation made her stomach queasy. Was he looking for an out? If she asked about his recent lies, would that be the end of them?

The morning had been going so well. The idea of mapping out plans for this camp together made her feel secure in their future. But now . . .? She was confused. Was he saying she didn't belong here?

When they reached an opening in the woods, she spread the blanket, and Scott plopped down on it. He pulled the food from the bag and handed Aury her favorite sub.

Food was a much safer topic.

After swallowing a big bite, she sighed. "I love this delivery service."

Treasure sniffed around the blanket until Scott withdrew a treat from his jacket pocket. The pup grabbed it and ran several yards away to gnaw at her prize.

Scott finished his lunch and lay back on the blanket with his eyes closed, the dappled sun kissing his eyelids.

Aury thought about when they first met: their adventure following the clues to find the treasure hidden by his ancestor. How they had gotten to know each other as they brainstormed and searched the property together. How easily she had been accepted into his family, and how much Gran loved him too.

Her heart beat rapidly, and she couldn't stop herself from leaning over to sneak in a kiss of her own.

He wrapped his arms around her, pulling her close. "We should do this every day."

"You've been extra busy lately." Aury buried her head in his chest, hoping the hurt and suspicion didn't leach into her words.

Scott sighed. "I know. I'm sorry. But we should make time. Don't we have a wedding to plan?"

She pushed herself up to a seated position.

He let her go, his words coming out in a rush. "I don't mean now. I know we have a lot going on, but we should work it into the schedule."

His crooked smile didn't put her mind at ease. *Is he trying to put off the wedding? Does this have something to do with where he's been sneaking off to?*

Scott shook her gently. "Where'd you go? Is everything all right?"

"I'm fine." Aury stood and brushed off her jeans.

Her cell phone vibrated in her back pocket. "Hey, Karmine. What's up?"

"Where are you? I have something to show you."

"Behind the crafters' cottage."

"I'm at the cottage now. Can you meet me here?"

"On our way." She disconnected and turned to Scott. "Karmine's at the cottage. She has something she wants to show us. She's pretty excited."

They packed up their picnic and walked out of the woods. Treasure raced ahead to where Karmine was waiting.

Scott put the picnic quilt on the back of a lawn chair outside the cottage. "What's this big discovery?"

Karmine held out a scrap of paper.

Aury unfolded the paper, yellowed with age. "What is it?"

Scott considered the drawing over her shoulder. "It looks like schematics."

"But for what?" Aury turned the page to examine it at different angles.

"Whatever it is, it's incomplete." Karmine pointed at the rough edge. "This was ripped, so there must be more to it."

"Where did you find it?" Scott accepted the paper Aury handed him.

A smug look took over Karmine's lovely face. "Behind the painting you left with me."

Aury's jaw dropped, and her heart quickened. "What? I didn't see anything?"

Karmine's excitement was contagious as she described her discovery. "One of the canvases was loose, so I took it out of the frame. I wanted to stretch it tighter." She paused for dramatic effect. "There were two canvases!"

Aury and Scott looked at her, confused.

"I don't get the significance," Scott admitted.

The artist exaggerated a sigh. "There's no reason to have two canvases stretched over one frame. I think this one was put together just to hide this piece of paper."

Aury took the paper back from Scott. "But what's the big deal about this? It's old, but I can't imagine it's worth anything. It's not a treasure map or anything."

Scott nudged Aury and winked. "That would be fun."

"I'm not sure what it is, but it got me thinking. The two paintings you left with me were definitely the same style, done by the same artist. I think it was even a landscape of the same location, painted from slightly different angles. So I checked the second canvas." Karmine pulled out another yellowed page.

"No way!" Aury took it gently. This paper was torn on all four sides. She spun it this way and that, but it didn't appear to fit together with the first paper.

"Yeah, I tried that too." Karmine grinned. "Do you have any more of those paintings? Seems like we're missing pieces."

"I don't think so, but we can check. Help me look." Aury rushed into the cottage. The others followed her.

Karmine searched through a stack of canvases leaning against a wall.

Scott and Aury shifted around some of the other donations to see if anything was hidden behind them.

Karmine held up a painting, scrutinized it, then put it back. She got to the last one and sighed. "No luck."

Scott shook his head.

Aury dusted her hands. "Nothing here either. Maybe Michelle has more."

"Didn't you say something went missing the other day?" Scott asked.

"That was one of mine. I was trying to imitate the style used in the paintings I left with you." She nodded at her friend. "A few more may be missing, but I couldn't swear to it. I didn't count them."

"That's strange." Karmine crossed her arms, creases forming between her brows.

Aury spread the yellowed papers out on the table. "How old do you think these are?"

Karmine rested her elbows on the surface. "I tested the paint on both the paintings. They were all natural ingredients—linseed oil with various flowers and herbs for color. I would be comfortable saying the late 1800s. In the early 1900s, paints were mass-produced, and you could get them from a Sears and Roebuck catalog."

"Do you think the papers were put in at the same time?" Aury always loved mysteries. Even if this one didn't end with a treasure, it would be fun to figure out.

"I didn't see any holes where older tacks holding the canvas to the frame would have been and then removed—on either canvas." Karmine rocked on the balls of her feet. "I think these pages must have been slid between the canvases when they were stretched. Oh, something else was strange. The paint went all the way around the frame. That's not normal. Often the sides are painted, but not the back where it attaches to the frame. There's no reason for that."

Scott leaned in to look closer. "Do you have a magnifying glass?"

Aury raised her index finger. "I believe I do."

She rummaged through a box and came up with a magnifying glass with an attached light and handed it to him. *It may be a mess in here, but it's my mess.*

He studied the documents carefully. "Definitely schematics for a machine of some kind. Hand-drawn, but no dates on these pages. Maybe if we can find the other pieces, one of them will be dated."

"Why would anyone hide something like this? Could it be worth something?" Aury thought about the money it might bring in to help Michelle maintain the Fresh Start program.

Scott shook his head. "The technology used in something this old must be far surpassed by now."

The balloon of hope that had been growing inside Aury popped. She pressed a hand to her stomach.

Karmine straightened up and looked at her watch. "I need to teach a class in Richmond shortly, but I was thinking about going by Fresh Start tomorrow to take another look at the wall murals. Do you want to meet me there? We can ask her if she has more paintings stashed somewhere."

Aury raised her eyebrows at Scott.

He chuckled. "You two do your sleuthing. I have work around here."

Aury ran quickly through her schedule for the next day. She was anxious to talk to Michelle but didn't want to leave Karmine out. It was her discovery, after all. "I'll meet you after lunch. Can I keep these papers for now?"

Karmine shrugged. "There're yours, but please let me know if you figure anything out. I'm dying to know why they were hidden."

Aury returned a wry smile. "You're not the only one."

Chapter 33

Treasure barked, jarring Aury from her dream.

The puppy ran into the bedroom, whining. She jumped on Scott's side of the bed. When he didn't respond quickly enough, she barked again.

"What is it, girl?" Scott mumbled.

"I'll let her out." Aury pushed aside the covers, shivering when the cool air touched her skin. She liked it frigid in the bedroom so she could burrow under mounds of quilts, but it was rude when she had to get up in the middle of the night. She was already looking forward to returning to her pillow.

When Aury's feet hit the floor, Treasure rushed from the room and stood at attention by the front door. As soon as the door was opened, the puppy pushed through the screen and disappeared into the night, barking as she went.

But it wasn't as dark as it should have been. The smell of woodsmoke caught Aury off guard. She glanced at the firepit, but it was cold. Treasure barked again, and Aury's eyes followed the sound.

The distant tree line that should have been shrouded in darkness danced in the flickering light from the burning building. Black clouds rose above the flames, obscuring the stars.

"Scott! Call nine-one-one!"

Aury rushed barefoot across the field toward the crafters' cottage. Yellow and orange flames licked the sky. All consideration of cold disappeared from her mind.

Scott caught up with her when she reached the blaze. He was speaking rapidly into his cellphone, trying to explain the situation while running.

Tears streamed down Aury's cheeks as her beloved cottage burned. She pulled her sleepshirt up to keep the smoke from invading her lungs. Treasure ran toward the blaze.

"Treasure! Come!" Aury's stomach clenched as she watched the black Lab rush into danger.

Treasure's silhouette stopped in front of a dark mound in the grass. She barked again, then ran halfway back to Aury before returning to the mound.

Aury squinted to make sense of what she was seeing. Nothing should be there. Only an empty field lay between the cottage and the house.

Then she was running again. "Scott! Someone's there!"

Scott continued to report into the cell, even as he moved forward with her. Aury reached Alan first. He was lying face down in a heap, hair matted to his head.

Scott thrust the cellphone into Aury's grasp and reached his hands under Alan's armpits. With a grunt, he dragged the older man away from the flames. When he was a safe distance, Scott lowered Alan to the ground and bent over him, listening for sounds of breathing.

The old man's chest rose and fell, then he was racked with coughing.

Aury took that as a good sign and ran back to the house for water. The wail of sirens followed her as she returned to the men. Scott had propped Alan up to ease the coughing.

Treasure danced around the commotion, as if anxious to make sure Alan was okay.

She tossed Scott a bottle and opened the other for Alan. Aury put the water to Alan's lips and held it until he had taken several gulps. After a few deep breaths, he was able to hold the bottle on his own.

Scott stood to meet the firetrucks. The nearest fire hydrant was near the new lodge, so the firemen began with the water their truck held while one engine ran a hose across the field. Fortunately, the cottage wasn't near any other structure on the property. There was no saving the old wood, so the firemen concentrated on containment, keeping the fire from reaching the trees.

Aury could only watch as the cottage burned.

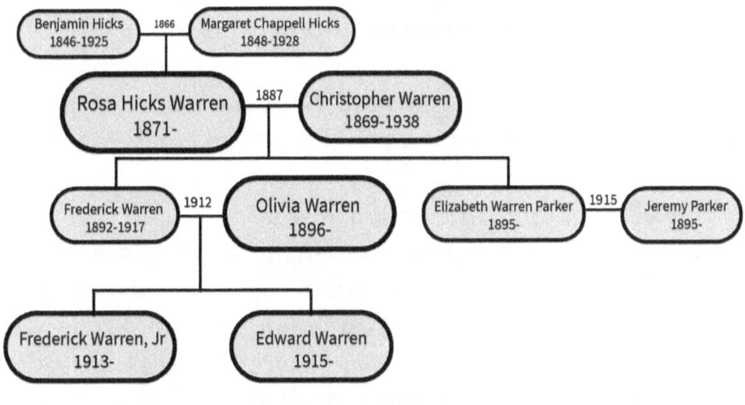

Chapter 34

Summer 1938

Rosa Warren ignored the heat baking into her black mourning dress as she stood in the circular drive in front of their Surry home. Why shouldn't her body match the sorrow in her heart? She shouldn't be here again. It was too soon.

Looking through the black netting over her face, she felt shielded from the outside world, if only temporarily. If she didn't turn around, she could imagine Christopher standing on the steps, ready to call out orders to his grandsons.

Her daughter, Elizabeth, and her husband had retired shortly after the funeral. They had traveled from Alabama by train through the night, and the events of the day had caught up with them. It was a blessing to have Elizabeth at home, even if it would only be for a short time.

Rosa's daughter-in-law stood stoically at her side, also in black. When Rosa thought about what Olivia went through, she said a prayer of thanks for the fifty-one years she had with Christopher. Oliva wasn't as fortunate. After only five years of marriage, the war had taken Olivia's husband and Rosa's son.

But at least God had granted them these beautiful boys.

Frederick's words brought Rosa out of her reverie. "Gram, I hate to leave you. Who knows what will become of this place with Edward in charge."

Edward shoved his older brother. "I've done more work on this farm than you ever have. Go back to your cushy office work."

Olivia put her arms around both her sons. "You each have a job to do, and I expect you'll do it like your grandfather taught you."

She choked up a little on her words.

Rosa placed a hand on the small of Olivia's back. She stopped herself from jerking back when she detected the sweat soaking Olivia's dress. It was nothing more than what she was experiencing in her own funeral clothes, but visions of Christopher's face, red and drenched, popped into Rosa's mind when her hand felt the dampness. His clothes had been soaked through when she finally removed them and dressed him in his best suit.

Christopher had fought until the end, not wanting to leave this life, not when there was so much work to do. Rosa held his hand as the pain racked his chest. She promised, at the very end, she would only have fond memories of him. She would forget every squabble and focus on the good life they made together.

Olivia didn't have the same opportunity to say goodbye to her father-in-law. She had been in town, arranging pickers for the following week. The doctor was leaving when Olivia breezed through the door, proud of her success and ready to share it with Christopher.

The sight of him laid out on his bed in the middle of the day had shocked her into silence. Rosa saw when the realization hit, and Olivia collapsed in on herself.

Christopher had been like a father to Olivia, and he had become the male role model the boys needed.

Edward was talking to her again. She really needed to be present for her family. "Gram, tell Frederick to get going. He's in the way of real progress."

She gazed lovingly at her elder grandson. "We'll miss your smiling face around here, Frederick."

"But not your stinky feet," Edward cut in.

Olivia sighed. "Will you ever grow up?"

"Let them be, Olivia. Enjoy them while you can." Rosa's voice was wistful.

"If you ask nicely, I'll allow you to stay in your old room when you come for a visit," Edward said to his brother.

Frederick pasted on his serious face. "Ma, I can have this runt replaced at any time. Just say the word."

Rosa took in the spectacle her grandsons were making. She suspected the show was for her benefit, to keep her from falling into despondency. It seemed to be working on Olivia as well.

The house was always livelier when Frederick visited, but it was time for him to get back to his own place in Wakefield. He had some adjustments ahead of him.

It was fitting for Frederick Junior to step into his grandfather's shoes at the peanut factory. Christopher had been grooming him for this position since Frederick was in his teens. Five years ago, Frederick had moved to Wakefield to be his grandfather's right hand. Since then, Christopher had been able to spend more time at home in Surry, and Rosa was thankful for every moment.

In 1898, the peanut crops in this part of Virginia had flourished to the point that they needed to ship their produce outside the state. Now a strapping man of twenty-five, Frederick would run the Warren Peanut Company his grandfather had built from scratch to meet that need.

Rosa ran the back of her knuckles down Frederick's cheek. "You look a lot like your great-grandfather Benjamin Hicks. He was very driven. But he also made time for his family. You remember that."

"Don't expect me to give you twelve great-grandkids." Frederick chuckled. "I don't think I could feed that many, unless they eat peanuts."

Rosa thought of the early family reunions, trying to keep all the relatives straight. It was a glorious time. Children of all ages were constantly underfoot. She was Aunty Rosa to all kids, even if they weren't actually nieces or nephews.

Now most of the family had moved away, giving up farming for other adventures—work not so tied to the unpredictable weather. She shuddered when she thought of the Great Depression. The drop in farm prices put a lot of people out of work. Many folks her age and younger were forced to move where they could find jobs other than farming. Not all of them were better off.

She and Christopher held on, not willing to give up the land her daddy had gifted them—the place where she grew up, the land and memories captured in the painting her father had gifted her. Things bounced back, even if it took a war to right the economy. And now the fields were planted, and Christopher rested beside them.

Rosa's sorrow rose to the surface again when she thought of Edward having to run the farm on his own without family nearby to help or guide him. But he was twenty-three and quite the capable young man. She and Christopher had farmed this land in their early twenties, but Edward didn't have a wife to help him yet. Although Rosa couldn't miss the looks Edward shared with that young Sophia during church services when he was supposed to be paying attention. Something was growing there.

She sighed. This range of emotions was exhausting. She turned to Edward. "You have chores to get to. Your grandfather wouldn't abide slacking, especially on his account."

Edward tipped his hat to her, then punched his brother's arm before backing toward the house.

Before Frederick could chase him down, Rosa captured him in a hug. "You take good care of yourself now, you hear? And don't wait too long to bring your gal into the family."

"I'll miss you, Gram. Whatever you need, let me know." He squeezed her tightly.

When Rosa released him, he wrapped his arms around his mother, dwarfing her in his embrace. He whispered something Rosa couldn't make out.

Tears escaped Olivia's eyes, but she gave him a wan smile. She pushed him away, and he picked up his bag. Waving over his head, he walked down the long drive to catch the bus on the main street.

Rosa put her arm around Olivia's shoulders. "Your boys are gonna do Christopher proud. And their daddy. You just wait and see."

Chapter 35

Present day

When Aury knocked on the kitchen door at Fresh Start, Michelle called for her to come in.

"Aury, you poor thing." Michelle embraced her friend. "You put so much work into the crafters' cottage."

Aury hugged her back but quickly let go before the tears started again. "It's all right. Scott says we can rebuild it. This time, we'll put in central air."

The ladies chuckled together, but Aury's heart wasn't in it. It wasn't just the loss of her dream; it was the idea that someone would come onto the property to do harm. Not to mention how easy it was for them. The fire and the attack on Alan were two more jarring events for the frightening pile. How many incidents could a small town like Surry take?

The basement door swung open. Freeman appeared, carrying an old rug, his gait a little unsteady. Aury watched him closely to determine if it was a normal response for an elderly man who just climbed steep basement stairs or if it was from alcohol. The jury was still out.

Brandon followed immediately behind the older man. His eyes scanned past Aury without acknowledgment and landed on his aunt. "There're old machine parts on the workbench in the back corner. What should we do with them?"

Michelle put her hands on her hips. "Can't imagine they're worth much, but I'll have Henry from the repair shop come by to see if he wants them."

She turned back to Aury, voice full of sympathy. "How's Alan?"

"He has a bad headache, but the doctor says he'll be fine. Someone hit him pretty hard." Aury's blood boiled at the thought.

"He's a tough old coot. Nothing will keep him down for long." Michelle patted Aury's arm. "Was everything in the cottage lost?"

The sting of tears threatened Aury again. "In the cottage, yes. Karmine still had two of the paintings you gave me. They were my favorites, so not everything was destroyed."

"That's a small blessing at least."

Aury was anxious to tell Michelle about their find but held off. "For now, we're hanging the paintings in the dining hall for everyone to enjoy."

Brandon turned to close the basement door, knocking the rug from Thomas's grasp and releasing a cloud of dust. Brandon broke into a coughing fit.

Michelle wrinkled her nose. "Drop that out back, Thomas. Then wash up. I made some cookies." She shooed him out the door. "Brandon, did you finish painting the trim upstairs?"

"Yes, ma'am."

She narrowed her gaze at him. "And cleaned out the brushes?"

Brandon hung his head. "They're soaking upstairs."

He seemed to be on his best behavior. Aury didn't detect his usual bitterness or the hostility he usually directed at her.

"Well, you go finish up. Let me visit a bit, then we can head home early."

He took the stairs two at a time.

Michelle smiled sadly. "He's trying so hard. I think this run-in with the police scared him more than he wants to admit. He's desperate to prove to me that he's changed."

"I hope you're right." Aury didn't hold out much hope about Brandon's redemption. Call her skeptical. "With any luck, this will all be over soon."

"Knock, knock." Lieutenant Elliott appeared at the open kitchen door.

Aury sighed. "Then again, maybe not."

"Come on in, Lieutenant." Michelle gestured for him to take a seat. "Would you like coffee and a fresh-baked cookie?"

"No coffee, but I would never turn down homemade cookies. Thank you." He sat at the table.

Aury joined him.

From his seat, Elliott peered deeper into the house. "I was hoping to have a chat with your nephew. Is he around?"

"He'll be down in a minute. What's this about?" Michelle placed a napkin with two cookies in front of him.

He nodded at Aury. "Just following up some leads in reference to the fire at Eastover last night."

By the time the fire trucks had finished up, the Eastover guests were on the lawn watching the spectacle. The police were questioning people when Aury went to the hospital with Alan. "What kind of leads? Did someone see something?"

"Just heard some things, is all." Elliott took a bite of the chewy chocolate cookie.

"You don't think Brandon could have been involved, do you? There's no way. He hasn't left my sight in days," Michelle insisted.

Thomas walked inside and went to the sink to wash his hands.

She glanced his way. "Well, except when he was with Thomas. And they were working in the basement."

Thomas didn't turn around but methodically dried his hands on the dish towel.

"Mr. Freeman? Do you have something you need to tell us?" Lieutenant Elliott was polite but firm.

Slowly, Freeman turned to face the table, bracing his arms behind him on the counter. "Brandon's been doing great work around here lately."

When he paused for too long, Michelle prompted him. "But?"

He sighed. "Last night he asked if he could run to the store to get snacks. He said he was feeling cooped up. I didn't see any harm in it. He'd put in a full day and evening's work."

Aury bit back the sarcastic comment she was thinking about Brandon not knowing what a full day's work looked like. She didn't think it would help the situation.

"That's okay, right?" asked Aury. "That means the store clerk can verify where he was."

Thomas cleared his throat. "He said the store was closed when he got there. He came back empty-handed."

"Thomas! How could you do this? I was counting on you." Michelle's eyes filled with tears. She turned to Aury. "He wouldn't have done this to you. He's so grateful to you for sticking up for him."

Aury wouldn't have defined it as gratitude, but she didn't think he hated her enough to burn down her cottage either. She squeezed Michelle's hand. "We'll get to the bottom of it."

Elliott lowered his voice as he told Michelle, "Someone spotted Brandon driving your van late last night. They called it into the station this morning after they heard about the fire at Eastover. Seems like the neighborhood watch is keeping an eye on him."

Brandon bounced down the steps, stopping short when he spotted Lieutenant Elliott at the table. "What's going on?"

Elliott stood. "Where did you go last night?"

Brandon looked from his aunt to Elliott and back again. Water spilled down his cheeks as he faced her. "I didn't do nothing. I swear."

"Just tell him where you were, Brandon. Please!" Michelle's lips trembled, and she choked on her words.

He swiped at his eyes. "I went to the store, like I told Mr. Freeman, but it was closed. I figured I had a little bit before he expected me back, so I stopped in to see a buddy."

"Brandon!" The cry from Michelle's mouth was torture.

"Don't say anything else." Elliott gently took his arm. "Let's go down to the station and make this official."

As they walked away, Elliott mechanically recited the Miranda Rights.

Aury put her arms around Michelle and let her cry, while Mr. Freeman had the decency to look shamefaced.

Aury wasn't sure what they should do next. Michelle didn't have the money for a lawyer. Brandon might have to roll the dice with a public defender. Did they even have one of those in Surry?

Freeman made his excuses and left the house as quickly as he could. After Michelle had dried her eyes, she and Aury sat at the table in silence, each lost in her own supposition.

Michelle's insistence that Brandon wouldn't have started the fire was based on familial ties. Aury's consideration had more to do with motive. Brandon might not like her, but she wasn't a threat to him in any way.

A knock at the kitchen door turned their focus on Karmine, and Michelle waved her in.

"Did you tell her yet?" Karmine's rushed words were directed at Aury, even before exchanging greetings.

Aury shook her head. "I was waiting for you."

"Tell me what?" Michelle looked between Karmine and Aury.

"Karmine found paper in between the canvases. A partial drawing of something. We're not sure what." Aury filled Michelle in on the little they knew or suspected. She still couldn't make the connection between the landscape and the schematic.

The artist filled in a missing piece. "I compared the paint from the mural upstairs to the paint on the canvases Aury left with me. I think they were done by the same person."

"But the style is so different." Although now that she was thinking about the rich colors, Aury could see similarities.

Karmine tilted her head and squinted at Aury through half-closed lids. "Girl, you should know people can use different techniques." She flipped back into professor mode, schooling her facial features. She held the index finger and thumb of her right hand slightly apart. "The composition of the actual paint is so close, I would put a pretty penny on the fact they were mixed by the same person. And they were homemade tints; nothing you'd pick up at the store."

There's the connection to the house, Aury thought.

"I've been playing with the colors, and I think I can recreate them close enough to touch up your mural. It won't be exact though."

"That's wonderful. At least it's a bit of good news today." Michelle's facial muscles tensed, and her lips flattened into a straight line.

Aury was worried she'd start crying again.

"Do you have any more paintings lying around? I'd like to check them." Karmine was oblivious to the troubles with Brandon and practically glowed with excitement. "We're looking for a particular style."

"You can look, but I think I got rid of all that stuff."

Aury reached out a hand to pull Michelle to her feet. Keeping her busy would give her less time to fret about her nephew. "I'd like to get in touch with Mrs. Warren. I have a feeling she's about to be a lot more interested in these old paintings now."

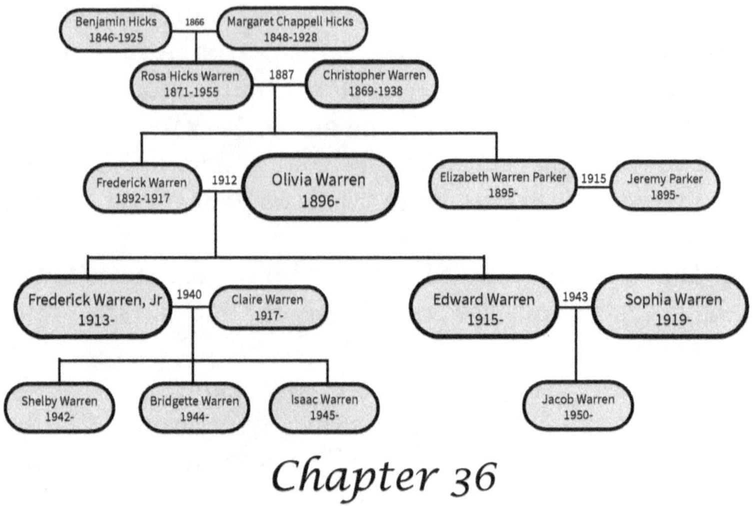

Chapter 36

Late Summer 1960

Olivia stood on the large back porch of the family home in Surry, Virginia. The sky was turning orange as the sun set over the fields. She sighed as she said a silent goodnight to her husband, as she did every night, even forty-three years after his death.

Focusing on the here and now, she rang the dinner bell.

As if by magic, the barn spewed children from its front doors. First, a tall, lanky boy of sixteen being chased by a smaller boy of ten, straw stuck in the tight curls of his jet-black hair. Two girls followed in no time.

One a young lady, Olivia reminded herself. Shelby was eighteen, after all. Her younger sister, Bridgette, was on her heels. They were carrying books, but the straw stuck to their skirts revealed they had been lounging in the hayloft.

The barn was always a favorite spot when the grandkids came to visit. From the time they were old enough to be outside alone, they were drawn to the farm equipment housed inside the earthy barn. It was in their blood.

Sophia stepped onto the porch alongside her mother-in-law and called out to the kids, "Wash up for supper. Jacob, use soap!"

The ten-year-old tagged his cousin and dashed for the house.

"You're so patient with him, Isaac. Thank you." Sophia patted the older boy's shoulder as he walked past her into the house.

"I have fun with him, Aunty Sophia. I wish I had a brother. Sisters are boring."

Olivia smiled at her granddaughters as they climbed the porch steps. "What are you reading?"

Shelby held up her copy of *A Separate Peace* by Christopher Knowles. "I got it for my birthday. Gram, it's the greatest. You have to read it!"

"She said I could read it next," Bridgette piped in.

"I'll wait in line," Olivia said.

"No books at the table," Sophia reminded them as the girls went inside. She peered into the field. "I wonder what's taking the men so long. It's getting dark."

"You know how those brothers get when they're together. Probably cooking on a new invention. It's an inherited trait from both sides of the family." Strong spice scents still threw Olivia back to her early days living in this house. Her father-in-law was constantly assessing new recipes to implement at the peanut factory. On the nights when she couldn't sleep, she would find Christopher in the kitchen, measuring and mixing freshly ground herbs. It became their bonding time together as he told her stories from her husband's childhood.

Sophia rested against the railing. "Edward's been sorting through machine parts in the barn. He thinks he found pieces to the prototype of the manure spreader Benjamin Hicks built in the early 1920s. He wants to clean it up and see if he can make it work." She gazed toward the barn. "Does Freddy miss working the fields?"

"I think he does. His wife likes living in town though." Olivia tried not to be bitter that she didn't get to see her oldest son very often.

"Is that why she's with her parents this week?"

"I suspect so." Olivia spotted two silhouettes getting larger as they approached the house. "There they are."

The men stopped by Freddy's sedan before making their way to the porch. He was carrying a large, rectangular package wrapped in brown paper.

"I hope you don't mind. Claire wanted to get rid of it, but I couldn't bring myself to just throw it away. I remember seeing paintings like this when we visited our aunts and uncles. It was like a thread that connected us all. I hate giving away part of my childhood."

"Don't worry one second about it. Your great-uncle Whitman brought one to the house before he died. Said it belonged here." Sophia addressed her husband. "Edward, will you please put it in the basement? There's room behind the canning jars."

"If you look in the attic, you'll find a few more." Olivia said. "Three of your grandma Rosa's siblings died before they had children. They each had a similar painting that ended up here."

Sophia sighed. "Somehow, it feels like fate. They were sent out with the family branches, and now they're finding their way back home."

Chapter 37

Present day

Aury received a call from Michelle early the next morning to let her know Brandon was home. She puttered around the kitchen while letting Michelle rant about her nephew.

"Lieutenant Elliott told him he needed to stay with me if he wanted to keep out of trouble. I'm so relieved. I can't imagine what was going through that boy's head." Michelle had finally run out of steam.

"You're doing everything possible for him. Lieutenant Elliott will sort it all out." Aury murmured further words of encouragement, then hung up.

"Was that Michelle?" Scott put down the papers he was working on.

She nodded. "She's really worried about Brandon, and I can't blame her."

"After everything you've told me about him, I wonder why she keeps him around. The sensible thing would be to ship him back to his mother. Michelle has enough going on."

Aury poured herself a cup of coffee and topped off Scott's cup. "We should see if Alan's feeling up to going over our project list. I need to get the budget done for next year."

"The insurance adjuster is coming by this morning to talk to us about the cottage. After we get the check, you can start designing the layout for the new cottage."

She bit the inside of her cheek. "Maybe we should put that money toward higher priorities. We already wasted enough of your resources trying to fix it up the first time around."

Scott bent his head, not meeting her eyes. "If you think that's best."

A pain began building in the back of Aury's throat. She was hoping for more assurance from Scott that their relationship was not as shaky as it felt to her right now. He didn't even correct her use of "*your* resources."

A knock startled her. She opened the door to find Gran dressed in a long, flowing dress and a hat with a band of the same material. Her hug was exactly what Aury needed at that moment.

Scott stood and kissed Liza's cheek. "What brings you out so early?"

Gran waved a fistful of sticky notes in the air. "I did some more digging."

Aury got Gran a cup of coffee while the elderly woman settled at the table.

Gran sorted through her notes, sticking them on the table in an order that made sense only to her. "I got to thinking about the drawing you found in between the canvases. Then I remembered the odd machine we saw in the microfiche. The first time, we were only looking for pictures of the house. This time, I printed the one with the men standing in front of that strange contraption."

Gran held out a copy of an old, creased, black-and-white photo. "Could your drawings be of this? The date Karmine gave you for the paint and the date of this picture are about the same time."

Aury studied it closely. She handed it to Scott and went to get the pieces of paper Karmine gave her.

Scott hummed. "The curves look right."

Gran got up to scrounge for cookies in the cabinets. "That all looks like scribbling to me. Let me know if you figure it out."

After handing Scott the slips of paper, Aury opened her laptop and typed in "copy of patent by Benjamin Hicks of peanut picker 1900." A few clicks later and the original patent complete with a diagram popped up. Aury enlarged it on the screen.

Scott held the two pieces of paper up to the monitor. "They aren't exact, but I think you might be onto something, Liza."

Gran returned to her seat, placing a plate of cookies in the center of the table. "But if it's a drawing of the peanut picker, why cut it into pieces and hide it in a painting?"

Aury agreed. "The schematic was filed with the patent office. It's not a great secret, even back then."

"Ah, another mystery." Scott grabbed a cookie.

"Want to see what else I found?" Gran pointed to her scrawled notes on a sticky. "The caption said the writing on the back of the original picture had been smeared, so not all the people were identified. One was definitely Benjamin Hicks. Researchers were able to cross reference his photo with others taken about the same time. His eldest two sons were named as well as his son-in-law, Christopher Warren. Another man leaned against the side. His name wasn't listed, just initials: TF."

Something stirred in Aury's memory. She inspected the photo closely. Had she seen this somewhere else, or was she just remembering the first time they searched the microfiche?

Aury snapped her fingers. "I saw a photo like this at Mr. Freeman's house. He told me his family had owned his house for years. It would make sense that Benjamin Hicks and a Freeman ancestor would know each other if they were neighbors."

"I think you might be right. There was an eight-year gap between when Benjamin Hicks moved to Vicksville and when Christopher Warren took possession of the house. It took quite a bit of digging, but I found a lease to Talmadge Freeman for the house and farmland during that time. Payment records show Freeman was in debt to Hicks when Warren took over the house."

Gran relocated one of the sticky notes. "On a hunch, I researched the ownership for the house Thomas Freeman lives in now. Hicks owned that too, but Talmadge Freeman moved in there when he left the bigger house. Freeman eventually paid off his debt, and Hicks sold him the smaller house."

Aury crossed her legs and sat back. "I wonder if it's Talmadge in that picture. It would make sense."

"So they were neighbors. What's the big deal?" Scott asked. "He could have been one of the sharecroppers who helped with the harvest using the peanut picker."

"I guess." Aury's right foot flexed and unflexed as she put her mind to work on the connections. She wasn't in a great position to ask Mr. Freeman.

Gran reached over to rub Aury's arm. "I know you've been busy with the fire, but have you put any more thought into Izzie's death? Do the police think there could be a connection?"

"Lieutenant Elliott hasn't come right out and said so, but it's an odd coincidence. He called in an arson investigator from Williamsburg. I'm waiting to hear more."

"But he did pull Brandon in for questioning." Scott got up to rinse out his mug and place it in the dishwasher.

Aury bit her lip. "For Michelle's sake, I hope they aren't connected."

Scott ran a hand down his face. "Did you ever clear Michelle? I mean, you know nothing about her before she came to Surry."

"That woman might be running from something she doesn't want coming out, but I'll bet my quilt stash that it's not anything *she* did." Gran's words brooked no argument.

"Well, in that case, you might have to brace yourself. If it was Brandon, he's got a lot of strikes against him. They won't go easy on him because you're friends with his aunt."

What Scott said made sense. Brandon was in the house immediately following Izzie's death, his fingerprints were on the murder weapon for Willard's murder, and he had no alibi for the fire. "Brandon doesn't seem to like me much, despite what Michelle says about him being grateful."

Gran waved her hand dismissively. "Child, that boy is a money grubber. He thinks Michelle has it, and you're a threat to him getting his hands on it."

Aury shook her head. "Michelle said her will leaves everything to the Fresh Start organization, so it will outlive her."

"Wonder if her nephew knows that." Gran took another cookie.

"Even if he didn't, burning down the cottage doesn't get him any closer to Michelle's money."

"Maybe Michelle gave you something from the house that Brandon wanted," Scott suggested. "He was selling off items. He could have taken it back and set the fire to cover up what was missing."

Aury's thoughts immediately flew to her missing painting. Brandon might not have realized it was Aury's work, especially if he didn't know much about art or he was in a hurry.

Gran stabbed at the table with her index finger. "It distracts you from your course. You set out to catch the killer. I think you need to wrap this up."

"I gathered a bit of information too." Scott shifted in his seat. "Hamilton Moore *did* try to buy the Warren and Freeman houses. It's zoned for residential and commercial, I think because it used to be a farm. Maybe they had a shop or something at one time."

"Ah, I knew that snake had to be involved somehow." Gran slapped the table.

"He's really not that bad," Scott said.

Aury looked at him out of the corner of her eye. She didn't realize they knew each other. *I wonder why he's never mentioned it.*

Just one more thing to add to the ever-growing list.

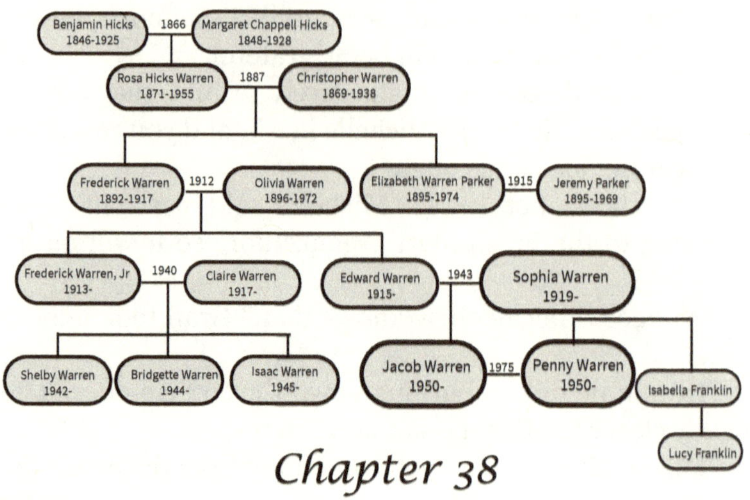

Chapter 38

Spring 1975

The church bells rang as the young couple floated down the outside steps. Birdseed rained down on them from the many well-wishers, catching in Penny's bonnet and veil. But she didn't care. This was the happiest day of her life.

Her face glowed as Jacob took her in his arms beside the car and kissed her passionately for all the world to see. His voice was husky when he said, "Mrs. Warren."

"Mr. Warren." She kissed him again. When they finally separated, she said, "Let's go home."

He held the door open for her, and she slid into the front seat. The crowd cheered when Jacob honked the horn as they drove away.

It was only a ten-minute drive to Goodson Path and their home, which had been in the family for a hundred years. Over time, most of the surrounding land had been sold off to farmers still willing to work the soil, although the Warrens only kept a few acres for a personal garden.

When they reached the front door, Jacob gathered Penny into his arms. "I'll love you forever."

She nestled against his neck. They exchanged kisses. Breathlessly, she pulled away. "We have to be ready to receive guests in thirty minutes."

Jacob stole another kiss and grumbled, "Who planned this party anyway?"

She gave him a playful shove. "We did. Let's get changed before the family arrives."

A quick wardrobe switch later, Penny was drawn to the dining room by the wonderful aroma. Seeing her mother-in-law, she felt twice blessed. Jacob's family had immediately accepted Penny as their own, and she became the daughter they never had. "I can't believe all this food! It looks wonderful."

"We all pitched in. That's what family does," Sophia reassured her. She straightened the napkins and centered the flowers on the table.

Penny took Sophia's hands. "You really don't have to leave tonight. This is your house too."

"You deserve a week without your in-laws around. We'll have plenty of time together. Besides, it'll be good to visit Freddy's family. Seems we only see them at weddings these days." Sophia squeezed her hands before letting go. "Your mama will be here soon. Let's get the peanut soup from the kitchen."

After a whirlwind of visitors came and went, the newlyweds stood between the dining room table with remnants of food and a sideboard piled with gifts. Penny tried to absorb it all, but her energy was starting to lag. "Folks were mighty generous."

"And awfully hungry. I was hoping to feed on those leftovers all week." Jacob picked up a sliver of ham and popped it in his mouth.

His mother swatted his arm. "We left you plenty in the icebox."

Penny's mom made a shooing motion. "You two go put up your feet. Let us clean this up, then we'll get out of your hair."

Jacob took Penny's hand and led her into the living room. He plopped onto the couch and pulled her into his lap.

A woman burst into the room. "Have you seen Lucy? I can't keep up with her."

Penny sighed. She could count on her sister to intrude on their moment. "I think she's in the barn with the other kids. That's their usual hangout."

"The barn? In her best dress?" She rushed out of the room.

Penny shook her head. "We'll need to have Lucy over more often, just to give her some semblance of a childhood. My sister is on the uptight side."

She rested her head on his shoulder, breathing in the spice and nutty smell from the peanut factory. He had shaved that morning, but dark stubble was already making his cheeks prickly. She rubbed her palm down his face absently as she stared at the opposite wall.

The greens and browns inside a frame caught her eye. "What's that painting from?"

Jacob shrugged. "I'm not sure. It's been there as long as I can remember. There's a few more like it in the attic. Isaac and I found them once when we were playing hide and seek."

She got up to take a closer look. "Did someone in your family paint them?"

"Not sure. I don't think so."

Penny searched the corners of the canvas, looking for a signature. Very faint, on the lower right side, she found the scrawl of initials. "Is there anyone in your family with the initials LF?"

"You'd have to ask Ma. If you don't like it, we can put it in the attic with the others or get rid of it all together." He joined her next to the painting.

"No, it's nice."

Jacob squinted at the greenery in the woman's hands. "I think that might be a peanut plant. Maybe that's why we still have it. Reminding us of our roots, as it were."

Chapter 39

Present Day

Aury sat impatiently in the dark. Her mind swirled, bouncing from one idea to the other. *Too much coffee. I should have known better.*

The new moon made the night inky-black, and the starlight didn't provide much illumination through the windows. She could barely see her hands in her lap.

She focused on her breathing to slow her racing heart. Faint music drifted from the lodge, but there were no other human sounds. The crickets and frogs sang their own songs. The greasy odor of fried fish from dinner still permeated the air.

Click.

Was that her imagination? Her body tensed, and she strained to hear anything out of the ordinary. The blower from the heater kicked on, and Aury jumped. Laughing at herself for being so edgy, she went back to counting her breaths. Her mind strayed again, wondering where Scott's head was. She had to confront him about all the lies. She couldn't live like this . . . again.

A dim red glow sprang into life in the other room.

Aury's attention jerked back into place. She watched as the light came closer and closer to the doorway. She held perfectly still; only her eyes followed the beam's progress across the floor.

Although they were now inside the room with her, Aury still wasn't able to make out the figure holding the flashlight. She instinctively reached for Treasure, but the pup wasn't with her tonight.

A circle of red light arched across the wall opposite from where she sat. It hesitated for a moment on the needlepoint work from Proverbs 15:7 reminding everyone that "He who is greedy for gain troubles his own house."

It darted away, quickly panning the wall to the corner and back. This time, the glow found one of the paintings Aury had hung for safekeeping. The figure moved until they were directly in front of it.

Aury held her breath.

The flashlight was placed on the ground facing the wall, and the figure stretched to take the painting off the nail where it was suspended. It caught momentarily, and the figure whispered a curse. After some jostling, the painting came down and was placed beside the light.

The *snap* of metal clicking into place was audible just as the blower from the heater shut off. A flash of silver was illuminated before the figure bent over the canvas, their back still to Aury. Moments later, a pocketknife was tossed aside as the figure maneuvered their arm, reaching for something.

In the red spotlight, a piece of paper appeared between two pinched fingers.

Aury flipped on the light switch.

The sudden, glaring light blinded the figure, and he froze.

When Thomas Freeman opened his eyes, Lieutenant Elliott, Aury, and Scott sat at a table in a far corner of the room.

Chapter 40

Michelle was dumbfounded. "But how did you know Thomas would take the bait?"

She, Scott, and Aury sat at the diner, apple pie with cinnamon ice cream sitting untouched in front of them.

Aury blushed. "Mostly a feeling. The Warren house had to be at the center of it all. Starting with Izzie being in the wrong place at the wrong time."

When Michelle cringed, Aury rushed on. "At first, I wasn't sure if the target was Izzie, you, or the house. No one benefitted from Izzie's death, not even her ex."

"But me? Why would anyone go after me?"

"I looked at the Fresh Start angle, but that didn't seem likely. It's a great organization but without a lot of capital." Aury's face heated up as she admitted, "I also considered your finances."

Michelle snorted a laugh. "You quickly saw that was a dead end."

Aury smiled an acknowledgment. "Then Willard was killed. He was only in town because of the house, so I narrowed the motives to the house or something inside it."

"Hamilton Moore was also interested in the house. He tried to buy it from Mrs. Warren," Michelle said.

Aury tore bits off her paper napkin as she spoke. Something still bugged her about Moore, but it didn't fit into this mystery. "Moore isn't a great human being, but he's a businessman. I did some digging after Willard was killed to be sure. Moore had alibis for both murders, although I didn't put it past him to hire out the dirty work."

"And that's where you thought Brandon came in." Michelle focused on eating her dessert with unusual intensity, refusing to meet Aury's eyes.

Not sure what to say, Aury quickly ran through her options. Brandon *was* a frontrunner suspect for quite a while.

Michelle looked up. "Oh, don't try to snow me. He had to be on your suspect list. I admit he was on mine for a little while there."

"Well, he had to be considered." Aury sipped her water. "But when my car was broken into, it shifted my attention. It happened when I was supposedly transporting paintings from the Warren house. Only you, Brandon, and Mr. Freeman knew I had them. If Brandon wanted them, he could have taken them at any time. He . . . acquired other things."

"It's okay. You can say stole." Michelle shook her head. "He took things without my permission or knowledge and sold them. He didn't want me to find out how much money he owed to the wrong people. We're dealing with that."

Aury kept her thoughts to herself on that topic. "When paintings were stolen from my cottage, I was sure that had to be the connection to the Warren house. The similarities in my painting—while not at all the quality of the originals—were enough to tempt Mr. Freeman into taking it. He replaced it with another landscape, hoping I wouldn't notice. To him, the artwork wasn't the point, so he assumed no one would think anything about it."

The idea that anyone would mistake her novice work for a finished piece baffled her, but Aury chalked it up to the thief being in a hurry. "When I took Mr. Freeman that pumpkin bread, I saw a painting similar to the others you gave me. At first I thought you might have given it to him."

Michelle shook her head. "I didn't give him anything."

"I went on that assumption because the frames were different. Then I couldn't get it out of my head how improbable it was that he would own a painting by the same artist."

Aury pushed her plate aside. She was too wound up to eat. "Freeman also had a framed, black-and-white photograph in his sitting room, like the one Gran and I saw in the archives at the historical society."

"The one next to the peanut picker?" Michelle asked.

"Yep. When I tried to get a closer look, he ushered me out of the house in a hurry. If it's out in the open, it isn't a secret, so it must have been something he didn't want me in particular to notice."

Scott pointed to her pie. "Are you going to eat that?"

Aury rolled her eyes affectionately and slid the plate in front of him.

"Gran went back to Richmond to get more details about the pictures." Aury filled Michelle in on everything Gran had shared.

Michelle held her fingers to her temples. "So why would Thomas care if you knew his ancestor was in a picture with Hicks?"

Aury rested her chin in the palm of her hand. "The only thing I can come up with is that he didn't want me to tie the peanut picker to his family until he got all the paintings."

Michelle flopped back in her seat. "Why in heaven's name would he want the paintings?"

Scott gave a Cheshire grin. "Because of what was *behind* them."

"Those old pieces of paper you told me about?" Michelle asked. "How did he even know about them?"

Aury chuckled at Michelle's reaction as she continued. "That stumped me at first too. Mr. Freeman thought enough of his painting to have it reframed recently, whereas Mrs. Warren donated hers alongside the house. When I called to ask her about them, she said they had been in the house for years. She vaguely remembered the family lore about an ancestor on her husband's side who had them commissioned for his children so they could take a piece of home with them. Since she didn't have any children, she didn't have any sentimental attachment to them. She also confirmed she hadn't given one to Mr. Freeman."

"If she didn't care about them, Thomas could have just asked her for the paintings," Michelle said.

"He might not have even realized there were more paintings until he helped you load the canvases into the van to bring to me. I doubt he even thought much about *his* painting until he had it reframed and discovered the hidden paper."

Scott scooped a dab of ice cream and chunk of pie onto his spoon. "He had to know the paper he found was only a part of a bigger piece, just like Karmine did. He probably saw the initials of the artist on your paintings and realized they were done by the same person—one of his ancestors. He had to get his hands on the other paintings to see if there were other fragments behind those canvases."

"But they weren't anything worth killing for." Michelle looked close to tears again.

Aury stared out the window as she tried to follow all the different scenarios they had come up with. "I don't think he planned to kill Izzie or you. I suspect he went looking for you, but he had had a few too many—I smelled whiskey on him when he was talking to the lieutenant—and confused Izzie for you. She had earbuds in and probably didn't even hear him come in the room."

Tears escaped, running down Michelle's cheeks. "So Izzie's death *is* my fault!"

Aury covered her hand. "It's no one's fault but Freeman's. He was drunk and might have already been on edge when he saw Izzie. Maybe being ignored set him off, and he blew up. It was more likely rage than premeditated."

Michelle dabbed at her eyes. "But why burn down the cottage? How did that help him?"

"My guess is to cover up the theft of more items." Scott pointed his spoon at Aury. "Aury had recently returned from visiting with Karmine. Maybe Freeman figured she had picked up the paintings."

Aury nodded. "After Mr. Freeman's arrest, the police searched his home. They found my painting where I was trying to recreate the technique. It had been stripped from the frame, but then discarded when he didn't find what he was looking for."

Michelle's eyes ping-ponged back and forth between the couple as they took turns explaining.

"Besides the painting hanging on his wall, there were also four more hidden in his basement," Scott said. "My guess is he found them when he was helping clean out your house and snuck them away when you weren't looking."

"The canvases had been removed from their frames, and the pieces of the document were found tucked inside an old journal," Aury said.

"The police let Karmine check the other canvases. That's when she spotted a distinct pattern between the paintings." Scott spoke with his mouth full. "The colors were the same, especially around the edges. We lined them up, matching the colors like a jigsaw puzzle."

"Then I finally understood why the perspective was so interesting. Each painting was only part of a whole. Like a quilt." Aury sat back and folded her hands in her lap. "Granted, we still don't have all the pieces, but maybe Mrs. Warren will help us track them down."

Michelle's lips dropped into a frown. "The shame is, I would have given him the paintings. I had no use for them."

Aury agreed. "Same here. If he said they meant something to him, I would have been happy to hand them over."

Scott wiped his mouth and tossed the napkin on the table. "After he killed Izzie, Freeman couldn't very well show too much interest in anything of potential value in the house. It might show he had motive for the murder, however far-reaching."

"Did you save any pie for me?" Lieutenant Elliot smiled down at them.

Michelle scooted over in the seat to make room for him.

The waitress came by, and Elliott ordered pie and coffee. "Did I miss anything good?" he asked.

Michelle inclined her head toward Aury and Scott. "They were trying to help me understand why Thomas would resort to murder."

Elliott shook his head. "He didn't set out to kill anybody."

"That's what they said. Izzie was an accident, but then he didn't stop. What makes someone do such horrible things?"

Aury continued, "Apparently there's some resentment between the Freeman family and the Warrens going back generations. Gran researched the Freeman family line. Talmadge Freeman leased the Warren house for a short time. Then Christopher Warren and his bride, Rosa Hicks, moved in. Talmadge moved into the smaller house next door."

"So you think the Freemans got booted to make way for Warren?" Elliott asked.

"Looks like it." Aury sipped at her now tepid coffee and made a face.

Scott pursed his lips. "That could certainly stir up bad blood. But to last this long?"

The waitress returned with Lieutenant Elliott's pie and refilled the coffee cups around the table.

Michelle was more animated now, as the pieces were falling in place. "Thomas has had some bad breaks. The nuclear plant let him go with very little to live on. When Penny Warren donated the house, it must have sparked his ire to think she had enough money that she didn't need to even sell the house. Especially when Moore would only buy Thomas's house if he could get the Warren house too."

"But enough to resort to murder? That's extreme." Scott didn't sound quite convinced.

Elliott swallowed a bite of pie before adding to the conversation. "When we interviewed Freeman, he fessed up to killing Izzie." The lieutenant nodded at Michelle. "He wanted to persuade you to give him the paintings, because he was convinced there was evidence in them that he needed to make a claim on the Warren fortune. He didn't want to come right out and ask you. Freeman thought if you knew about their possible worth, you'd turn them over to Mrs. Warren."

"The alcohol didn't help his reasoning, I'm sure." Aury sniffed in disgust.

"When you," Elliott used his fingers to make air quotes around the word you, "ignored him, things got out of hand. His temper took over, and he lashed out."

Scott picked up and then put down his mug without drinking. "What about David Willard? That couldn't have been an accident. He was killed in his hotel room."

Elliott raised an eyebrow at Aury, giving her a chance to answer. When she held up her hands in surrender, he explained, "Willard knew Freeman was looking for something in the house but didn't know what. Willard was trying to blackmail him with the threat to spill the beans to Michelle."

"So it was his greed that got him killed," Scott said.

"Then why did you accuse Brandon of killing Willard?" Michelle's voice rose an octave.

"Brandon was working on Willard's behalf to get you to give up the house so Willard could sell it to Hamilton Moore." The lieutenant looked at Aury. "You were right. Moore is looking to build in Surry."

Michelle clenched her jaw, and her nostrils flared. "Another discussion to have with my nephew."

Elliott stirred sugar into his coffee. "Brandon's and Willard's were the only fingerprints on the statue. The DA's charging Freeman with premediated murder because he must have worn gloves, intending to do harm. Freeman admitted he recognized the statue from the house and figured Brandon must have given it to Willard. That gave him the idea to frame Brandon. He thought you would give up the house for sure after that."

Scott stared at the coffee mug as he spun it around and around between his hands. "Why was he still after the house?"

"He had no way of knowing how many paintings there were or if more proof existed inside the house. Besides, if he could buy it up cheap and sell it to Moore with a markup, he'd be set for the rest of his life." Elliott tucked his napkin under his plate.

"Proof about what?" Michelle sounded exasperated.

Aury understood that feeling. "The pieces of paper were each part of a puzzle too. We didn't find all the pieces, but when we put together the ones we had, they formed an early sketch of the schematics for the peanut picker. It wasn't the final that was submitted to the patent office, but it was close."

Picking up the thread, Elliott went on, "Freeman found the paper from his painting last year when he had it reframed. He recognized it as part of a schematic. His grandfather had told him stories about how Benjamin Hicks, a distant relative of the Warrens, had stolen the idea of the peanut picker from their family and patented it, making their fortune. Freeman thought the proof that his family owned the idea was hidden behind those paintings, and he could somehow make money from it."

Aury couldn't imagine how that would be possible after so much time. Surely there was a statute of limitations on something like that.

Elliott was still speaking. "When he saw the paintings Michelle gave to Aury, he picked up on the similarities and wanted to get his hands on them to see if they held more clues. So when he overheard Aury say she was taking the paintings to a friend in Williamsburg, he broke into her car looking for them, but Aury had already dropped the paintings off.

"He didn't have any luck there, but then he ran across a few more in the basement of Fresh Start. When he checked those, he found more pieces of the diagram for the peanut picker. He was convinced that's why his family handed down the painting from generation to generation. Apparently it's been written in his ancestors' wills that the painting has to stay in the house. No one ever knew why."

"If his ancestors owned even a portion of that patent, it would have made them very wealthy, considering how well the Warrens have done over the years," Scott said.

Aury frowned. "The Warren money came from the peanut factory though. Probably only a small portion came from Hicks's inheritance. He had eleven kids, for goodness sakes."

"Did the Freemans have anything to do with the peanut picker?" Michelle asked.

"There's no proof of it. I pulled the patent when I was creating the brochure for the history of the Warren house. No other name was mentioned except Benjamin Hicks." Using her finger, Aury made swirls in the condensation left on the table by her water glass.

"And it's far too late now. If the Freemans thought they had a claim and didn't take legal action within years of the patent being filed, there was no hope Thomas Freeman would get anything. He didn't think this through or do his research." Elliott finished his coffee.

Scott shrugged. "Maybe he was hoping to guilt Mrs. Warren into recompensation."

Michelle rested her head against the back of the booth and closed her eyes. "Who did the paintings and why?"

"Freeman told us about a diary he found in his attic." Elliott crossed his ankles, stretching his long legs into the aisle. "It appears to have been written by an ancestor named Letitia Freeman. Benjamin Hicks commissioned her to paint twelve paintings—one for each of his children and one for her to keep."

"The pieces all together make a beautiful landscape." Aury pulled out her phone and passed it to Michelle. "Of course, some squares are missing, but you can imagine the full picture."

Michelle used her fingers to enlarge the photo and move it around on the screen.

"It's amazing. Who would have thought?" She passed the phone back to Aury.

"But why the schematics?" Scott asked.

Elliott shrugged. "The only thing I can think is sentimentality. The drawing isn't worth anything, even if they had all the pieces."

After Aury's parents died, Gran gave Aury a patchwork quilt that had belonged to Gran's mother. It was only valuable to the people who would appreciate it. "Maybe it was just another thing for Hicks to share with his family. The peanut picker is what he's most known for, after all."

She wondered if Mrs. Warren would be more interested in the paintings after she learned more about their history. "Why would Letitia have one if the Freemans didn't have anything to do with the patent?"

"Letitia covers that in her diary. She was good friends with Benjamin Hicks's daughter Rosa Warren. They were neighbors. That's how Hicks learned she could paint. Apparently she did something in one of the rooms."

"Oh!" Michelle cried out excitedly. "My office! She's the one who painted the jungle scene."

Aury smiled brightly. "I think you're right."

"Hicks only had eleven surviving children. He thought the painter should get to keep the extra piece." Elliott sighed. "I'm sure he never imagined it would turn into such a deadly decision."

"Who would?" Aury shook her head. "Such a loving sentiment turned into something so ugly."

She thought about the first time she saw the painting of the small plant cupped in a woman's hands. The brushstrokes were casual but captivating, an amateur painting with love. It had called to her. This terrible business with Freeman didn't deserve to be the Hicks legacy or the painter's. "Michelle, I think we should add to the mural in your office. Let's extend it so the vines wind down the hall."

Michelle clapped her hands, and her eyes brightened. "Oh, I love that idea! You can paint birds, lizards, and even monkeys. The children will love it."

Aury pictured how the large leaves and thick green stalks would drape over the doorways. Maybe she would even add some peanut plants along the baseboards.

"The vine can symbolize the shelter and protection you're giving these women as they get on their feet, just like Benjamin

Hicks gave his children a little piece of himself when they went off into the world. Something that kept them tethered to this house as long as they needed it."

Michelle sat back in her seat. It had been a while since Aury had seen her so relaxed and happy.

"The women will be planting the seeds of their new life at Fresh Start, so they can go off into the world stronger. I like the sound of that," Michelle said.

Elliott raised his coffee cup. "To a fresh start."

Scott winked at Aury as he clinked his mug to Elliott's. "To Fresh Start."

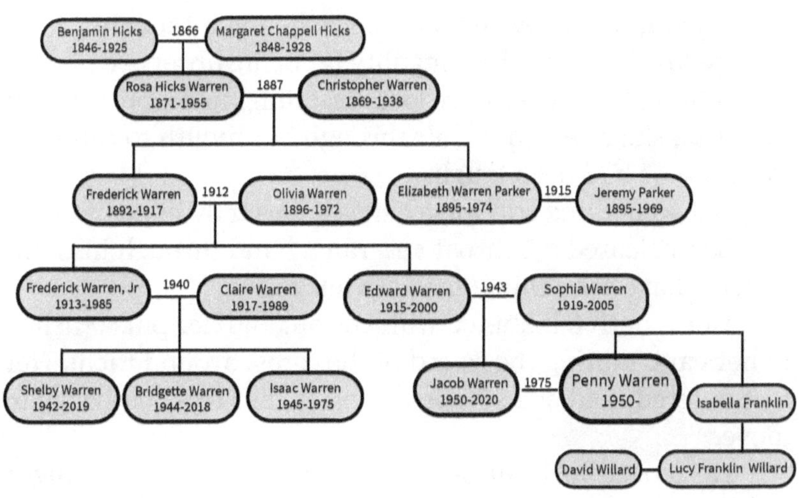

Epilogue

Aury and Scott walked the path to the beach in silence, each lost in their thoughts.

She had to admit a sense of satisfaction at helping to solve Izzie and Willard's murders, even while the senselessness of it all appalled her.

A pang of sorrow stabbed her when she thought of the cottage fire, but then she felt guilty for being upset over such a trivial thing when lives were lost. Breathing in deeply through her nose, she released the air through her mouth to calm her mind as she had been taught.

But something still wasn't sitting correctly in her core.

Scott cleared his throat and ran a hand through his hair. "Aury, I have something I need to tell you."

Her mouth felt stuffed with cotton, and her pulse rushed in her ears, muting the sound of the forest around them. Her feet faltered, and she stopped in place, her legs too heavy to move.

He moved in front of her and took her hand, kissing it before opening her palm to trace the lines with his finger. He didn't meet her eyes. "I know you didn't go to college to keep books for a retreat center that's barely keeping its lights on. It's not fair to you."

This is it. He was breaking off their engagement.

"I've tried to find extra work around here." He lowered her hand, looking everywhere but at her face. "I reached out

212

to the firm I worked for in DC. There's an opening at the same pay level I left."

Aury couldn't breathe. He was leaving her to go back to DC.

"I know Gran is here, but it's not that far. Or maybe she'd be willing to move to DC with us."

Air escaped Aury's lungs in a whoosh. He wanted her to move to DC? She shook her head to clear the cobwebs.

Scott was still speaking. "But I understand if that's not the lifestyle you were counting on."

Aury stared at him so intently that he must have felt her pull and met her gaze. "What are you really saying, Scott? You want to give all this up and move to DC? You love it here."

"But I love you more. If you don't think we're making enough money—"

"When did I ever say anything about money?"

It was Scott's turn to look confused. "Well, you're spending every spare second trying to get the craft cottage up and running so you can give classes. You don't seem to want to even talk about the wedding."

She put a finger to his lips to stop him. "I want to teach classes because I *like* to teach classes. To be able to craft for a living is my dream job. This is much better than the accounting I learned in college."

She placed her hand over his heart. "I'd marry you if we were broke. Money isn't a factor at all."

"Then why have you been putting off the wedding?"

She dropped her gaze. "I'm scared. I've been through this before, and I'm afraid once we get married, you'll lose interest and go looking for someone else." She choked back a sob. "You've been very cagey lately. I know you haven't been working on the trail as often as you say."

He took her chin in his hand and peered into her eyes. "I am not Todd. I love you and want to spend the rest of my life with you."

Her eyes sparked. "Then what are you hiding from me?"

He sighed and dropped his hand. "You aren't going to like it."

"I don't like the secrets."

After taking a deep breath, he let it out in a rush. "I've been working on the side for Hamilton Moore."

This was not at all what she was expecting.

"I know you don't like him, and honestly, he's not my favorite guy either, but he pays well."

"What are you doing for him?"

"Inspecting some buildings he's thinking about buying, mostly. After hearing you and Gran dragging him through the mud, I didn't want you to think of me like that."

"Scott, I would never." She pushed her fingers into her temples to ward off the headache she knew was coming. "Moore's known for building extravagant structures that no one needs or can afford."

"He knows he has that reputation, and he's trying to fix it. I'm helping him make better choices and build things that current residents can afford. We're even looking at putting a new daycare center in an empty storefront downtown. The bones are solid; it just needs a facelift."

"But why did you start working for him to begin with? You're always saying you don't have enough time to do everything you want to do around here."

He hung his head. "I thought maybe you were putting off the wedding because you didn't think we had enough money."

She smiled lovingly. "Do I come across as some kind of princess to you? I don't want or need anything elaborate. I think a big tent in the middle of the field would be a dream wedding."

"So you don't want to move to DC?"

She kissed him lightly. "Not in a million years."

His eyes blazed, and he pulled her in close for a deeper kiss.

When they came up for air, Aury asked, "What do you think about a spring wedding?"

######

Author's note

The rabbit holes are the best part of writing the Eastover Treasure Mystery Series.

As I'm writing the first draft, my characters ask questions, many of which I don't know the answers to, so I have to research. The internet is a wealth of information, but libraries are a place to escape. If you haven't visited your local library lately, I highly recommend the road trip. It's amazing what many of them have grown into.

Now, about the historical part of the story. The area from Surry to Suffolk, Virginia, is well known for growing peanuts. Suffolk has hosted a Peanut Festival since 1941, honoring the city's agriculture heritage and devotion to peanuts. If you're in the area in October, I suggest checking it out. https://www.suffolkpeanutfest.com/

Peanuts aren't native to North America but are believed to have gotten their roots in Virginia in the early 1700s when Africans forced into slavery brought them to North America.

At first, peanuts were only used for animal feed, but during the Civil War, Union soldiers picked them up in the south and took them north. In the late 1800s, P.T. Barnum's circus traveled across the country selling hot roasted peanuts as a novelty.

Benjamin Hicks (1846-1925) is a real character, although I took some liberties to flesh out his story. Not a lot is known about him. He was born in Courtland, Virginia, in May 1846 to an enslaved woman, Lottie Ricks, and an unidentified man.

In 1849, Virginia passed the emancipation law, which allowed owners to free their enslaved people through two methods: by a last will and testament or by a deed recorded in the court of their county or corporation. The three-year-old Benjamin Hicks was freed.

Hicks married Margaret Chappell in 1869, and they had eleven children. They lived in the Vicksville area, which is in Southampton. He was well respected in the community and earned his living as a farmer and blacksmith. As in my story, Benjamin was creative. He was skilled with the anvil, forge, and woodworking tools and constantly tinkered to improve farming techniques.

He contributed to the development of the peanut harvester, which combines removing the peanut plant, separating earthly elements, handling seedlings, and picking the product. But he's most well-known for his 1902 patent of the gas-powered machine for stemming and cleaning peanuts or peas.

Peanut Picker
Photo used by permission © Dennis Mook

Benjamin Hicks also patented a manure spreader, important to farmers of the time. Through these inventions and his farming techniques, Hicks helped revolutionize peanut farming in the Southampton area.

Interest in peanuts was further advanced when George Washington Carver introduced over 300 food, commercial, and industrial uses for peanuts. If you've ever been to a ballpark, you've probably tried Virginia peanuts, the largest and most flavorful.

Through the use of an ancestry site, I found the real names for some of Benjamin and Margaret Hicks's children. I changed their birth order to fit my storyline. I followed the family tree where I could; in that line, there were many more girls than boys to carry on the Hicks name.

The Warren house in Surry is totally fictitious, although the history of Blacks becoming sharecroppers is true. In some cases, they didn't have any other choice, not being allowed to own property of their own. It was another form of slavery.

As I progress with the Eastover Treasure mysteries, I find it's difficult to come up with different hiding places for treasure that haven't already been written about. There's a delicate balance between too obvious and too farfetched. I welcome new suggestions.

If you have enjoyed *A Killer Donation,* we would love a review on whatever platform you are most comfortable with.

https://books2read.com/AKillerDonation

If you want to learn how Aury and Scott met, checkout *Eastover Treasures.*

Chapter 1

September 10, 1861

Mary's long skirts swished as she hurried into the dining area. *Where do I even begin?* she thought.

James had already transported some belongings, but he left her to sort out household items. How could she decide what was worth saving and what wasn't?

If she cleared too many objects, they would suspect items were hidden and go searching. She must be selective. Opening the drawer of the buffet, she withdrew a handful of items, then opened the next drawer, slamming them shut as she moved on. She repeated this process until she had a small pile.

Brushing the loose hair off her forehead, she turned to the next room. *I don't know why he has to leave now. We are supposed to be plowing a new garden.*

Outside the window, the reins clinked as James hitched the horse to the wagon. Swiftly, she shifted her attention to the parlor and took the painting from over the mantle. A lighter rectangle was left on the wallpaper where it had been. Muttering words her mother wouldn't approve of, Mary replaced the painting. She spun to take in the rest of the space.

Everything is a treasure to me! How can James not understand that?

Mary's frustration was clouding her concentration. She needed to take a minute. She stopped in the library, admiring their collection of books. Her father was a generous man and often sent treasures he found on his trips to Philadelphia.

With the fighting between the north and south, no packages had come recently. She picked up the leather-bound volume he had given her when she and James moved to Virginia.

I need to get back to my writing. Father will expect to hear all the details about country life when we travel north next.

But when will that be?

Looking around, she took a mental inventory. A drop of sweat threatened her eyes, but she wiped it away with the back of her hand. Then she heard the thunder of the boys' feet across the wood floor. They skittered into the room.

"Momma, can Frederick and I go to the river to catch frogs?" nine-year-old Thomas asked.

She put on a brave face. "What are you going to do with them once you catch them?"

"We can eat them," Frederick offered.

Thomas punched his arm. "That's foul."

"No, it's not. It's living off the land. You eat what you can catch. Isn't that right, Ma?" Frederick was only ten, but already starting to talk like his father.

She smiled at the towheaded boys. "Let's save the eating until it's necessary."

"But if those secesh take our house, we may have to live in the woods. Pa said so," Thomas insisted.

"Where did you learn that kind of language, young man?"

"Noah," both boys said together.

Mary rolled her eyes. "I'll have a talk with your brother. You may go down to the river but take a basket and bring some berries with you when you come back."

The boys were out the door before she had a chance to say anything else.

"Sarah?" Mary called.

The fourteen-year-old entered the library, carrying her latest sampler. "Yes, Ma."

"Will you get some of the quilts from the upstairs closet and bring them down?"

"Yes, ma'am."

Mary replaced the book on the shelf and plucked out another one, placing it on the side table. Then another.

"Momma?" Sarah's voice cut through Mary's wild purge. "We aren't moving all those books, are we?"

"And why not? Books have value." Mary turned away from the shelf and took in the overflowing stacks she had subconsciously built.

Sighing, she began replacing some volumes. "Why don't you help me pick the best ten to save?"

Chapter 2

Present Day

The breeze picked up as Aury St. Clair sat on the back deck of the rustic motel checking the latest weather forecast on her phone. The hurricane had shifted again, this time moving up the east coast of Florida. There was a fifty-fifty chance the weather that accompanied a storm of that size would miss their slice of Virginia all together.

Aury held the cell phone loosely in her lap and prepared to say goodbye to the solitude she had with nature. The breeze rustled the bushes surrounding the pond, sending a ripple across the water. The frogs were especially loud. Maybe they sensed the impending storm.

The phone's buzz joined Mother Nature's song, and Aury picked it up again. The cell reception was so bad this far into the woods that she was usually bombarded with text messages that had been waiting to find her phone as soon as it could get a signal. From the porch, she at least had a bar or two.

She glanced through them, answering a few from the accounting firm she worked for. They seemed to disregard the fact that she was on vacation. She tucked it away again, rising from the picnic bench.

As Aury opened the door, she was immediately flooded with the cacophony of sounds emanating from the women jammed into the open floor plan of the activities room. The concrete walls did little to absorb the sound, bouncing it around the hall until only emphasized syllables and harsh laughter could be discerned.

Aury slid into place behind her sewing machine, which rested on a table butted against three others. The ladies continued their banter.

"Finished with your phone sex?" Debbie asked.

"I was. Don't know about him," Aury answered, just as straight-faced.

Debbie cackled. "Guys have a harder time faking it," she said, reloading her bobbin and snapping the door closed on the casing. Her soft, gray curls framed a round face that was always quick with a smile, but it was her brightly colored sweatshirts that Aury appreciated. They usually had a quick-witted line printed on them in bold colors. Today was no different: "I'm glad no one can hear what I'm thinking" was printed in neon pink.

Pat gave Aury a speculative look. "What's the weather?"

"The hurricane is scheduled to hit the east side of Florida. They still don't know if it will turn, but it's moving fast."

Debbie shook her head. "I could be a weatherman and do a better job than those bozos."

Pat ignored her. "Do we need to consider packing up sooner than planned?" A tall woman with a dry sense of humor, Pat's imposing nature hid her inner spunk. It had taken a while for Aury to figure her out. Thankfully, Pat saved her sharpest retorts for Debbie.

"No way," Linda said from the next table. "I paid for six days, and I'm going to use all six." The hum of her machine charged over the fabric in a practiced clip. "My husband would never let me get this much done at home. I'm taking advantage of the getaway."

Aury turned her gaze to the sunlight streaming through the windows. "Looks like another beautiful day."

"You just never know with these storm patterns," Suzanne commented from across the table. "Hurricanes are fickle." She stood from her machine and limped toward the ironing board.

Aury tried to focus on one of the many projects she brought with her for this quilting retreat. She had been looking forward to it for so long, but now the projects were overwhelming, and she had trouble concentrating.

"Sam said he thinks we should head back early in case they shut the ferry down," Carla added. "Taking the twenty-minute ferry will be a lot better than the extra hour it would take if we had to go up toward Richmond and back down the peninsula."

She didn't sound worried, though. At least twenty years older than Aury and six inches shorter, Carla was a sweet soul with a positive attitude. She'd find the bright spot in the toughest situation.

"If it comes down to it, we'll close up shop. Anyone can leave whenever they want if they're nervous." Aury had spent months planning this retreat. She would hate for the weather to mess it up.

She looked around the room at the fifteen heads bent over their sewing machines and projects in various stages. Aury knew she needed to get some work done. When she got home, there would be many other projects that drew her attention away from her quilting. She wanted to get her entry for the Mid-Atlantic Quilt Festival completed before the week-long retreat ended.

At thirty-eight years old, Aury was one of the youngest in the room. Reconnecting with her grandmother through her quilting had proven a useful hobby to distract her from the what-might-have-beens that kept her awake at night. After her parents had died in a car crash four years ago, she had been wracked with guilt. They had been on their way to visit her because she was upset after yet-another argument with her husband. They drove through the night instead of waiting until the next day. A drunk driver crossed the centerline and ended their lives upon impact.

Even with her grandmother's constant assurances that it wasn't her fault, Aury still felt responsible. And her husband gave her no emotional support. She had followed him to

Williamsburg when he was offered a job, more to be near her grandmother but also as a last chance to make their marriage work. It ended less than a year later.

Now her grandmother was her best friend, and she loved spending time with her. Liza St. Clair had taught her to sew when Aury was only eight years old. They had made clothes and quilts for dolls when Aury visited on vacations. It wasn't until visiting a quilt show that Aury began to value quilting as an art, not as a necessity.

Aury leaned down to search through her fabric bag as a pretense to hide her welled-up eyes from the ladies at her table. Thinking of her grandmother stuck in the rehab hospital broke her heart. Liza was spry for eighty-one and would take on most challenges. It would be unfair to be taken out by the flu. Aury had tried to find someone else to take over the retreat so she could stay and care for her, but the old lady insisted she go. She said Aury would do more good there than at her bedside.

. . . to be continued.

PB&J Quilt Pattern

You know I love scrappy. This rail fence pattern can be made in so many ways. To make the Peanut Butter & Jelly pattern, I just made the two outside blocks the same color for the "bread."

1. You can keep within the same color pallet or mix it up. Use the same "bread" on your sandwich, but mix up the sandwiches within your larger block 8.5" block, or you may end up with a swastika symbol.

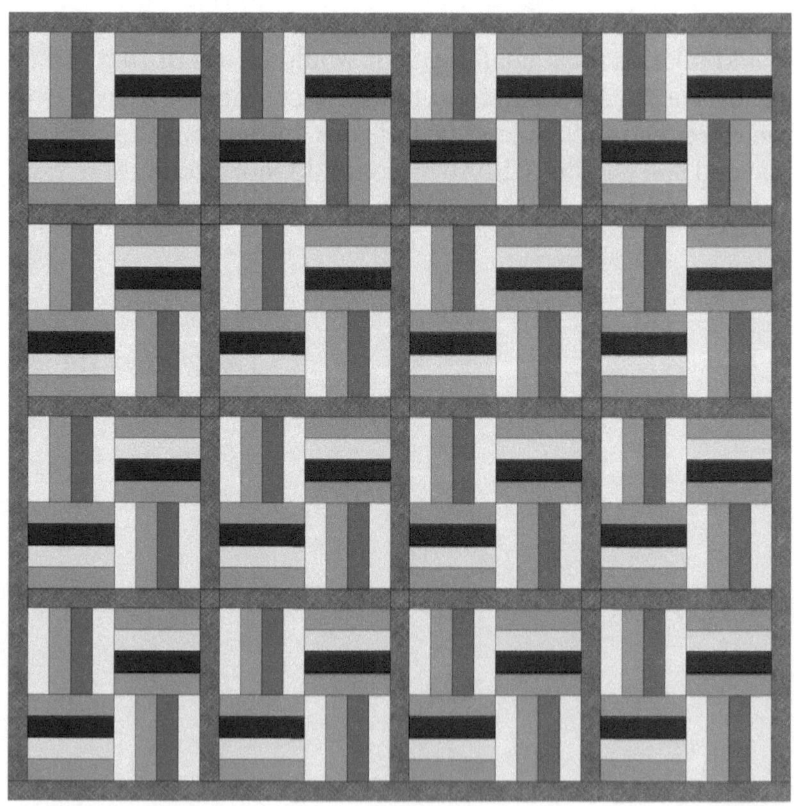

2. Check out my website for color variations and a printable coloring sheet so you can come up with your own pattern:

https://DawnBrothertonAuthor.com/PBJ.

Bread (B): light
Peanut Butter (PB): medium
Jelly (J): dark

This quilt can be made any size. I've listed some sample sizes for fabric requirements.

The yardage assumes 42" WOF.

Seams are 1/4".

You can piece strips together.

Material Requirements

	Throw: (5x7 blocks) 46x64" w/ sashing 42x58" w/o sashing	Twin: (7x9 blocks) 64x 82" w/ sashing 58x74" w/o sashing	Queen: (8x10 blocks) 73x91" w/ sashing 66x82" w/o sashing
Bread 1-color scheme: 3-color scheme: Scrappy:	1+3/8 yards 1/2 yard each 280 pieces	2 + 3/8 yards 1 yard each 504 pieces	3 yards 1 yard each 640 pieces
Peanut butter 1-color scheme: 3-color scheme: Scrappy:	3/4 yards 1/4 yard each 140 pieces	1+1/4 yards 1/2 yard each 252 pieces	1+1/2 yards 1/2 yard each 320 pieces
Jelly 1-color scheme: 3-color scheme: Scrappy:	3/4 yards 1/4 yard each 140 pieces	1+1/4 yards 1/2 yard each 252 pieces	1+1/2 yards 1/2 yard each 320 pieces
Sashing (optional)	1 yard or 86 pieces	1 + 5/8 yards or 162 pieces	2 yards or 209 pieces

Making the blocks

1. Cut 1.5" strips of each color, WOF

2. Sew 1.5" strips together on the long end in order: B, PB, J, B

3. Press seams the same direction

4. Cut across all four strips to make 4 1/2" block

5. Layout the block. Create variations with the colors.

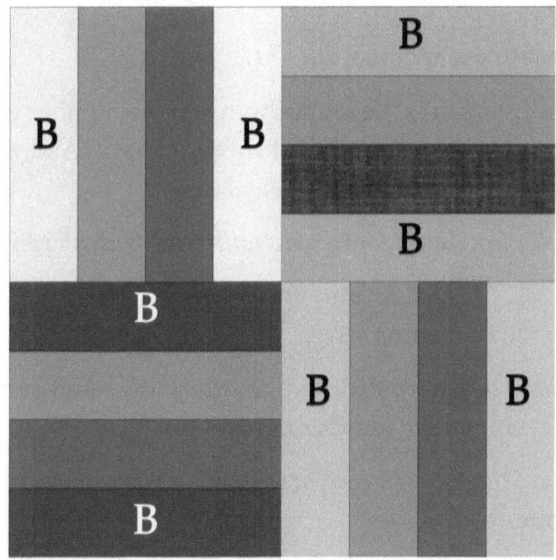

6. Sew together

7. Repeat until you have the appropriate number of blocks

8. Trim blocks to 8.5x8.5"

9. Layout on a quilt wall or something similar so you can rearrange in the pattern that looks best to you

See my website for various layout examples.

https://DawnBrothertonAuthor.com/PBJ.

WITHOUT SASHING

1. Sew blocks, RST, for the number of blocks to make one row.

2. Repeat 1 until you have all the rows complete.

3. Press seams for even-numbered rows one direction and odd-numbered rows the opposite.

4. Sew rows, RST, nesting the seams.

5. Press.

6. Jump to borders.

SASHING

1. If you elect to use sashing, cut 1+1/2" strips WOF.

2. Cut strips into 8+1/2" segments to reach the number of blocks you have minus the number of rows you have (And you thought you would never use algebra!)

   Example: for 8x10 blocks, you will need 70 sash segments (80 blocks-10 rows)

3. Set aside the remaining strips.

4. Sew sashing segment, RST, to one side of the number of blocks you have minus the number of rows you have

   Example: for 8x10 blocks, sew sash segment onto 70 blocks (80 blocks-10 rows)

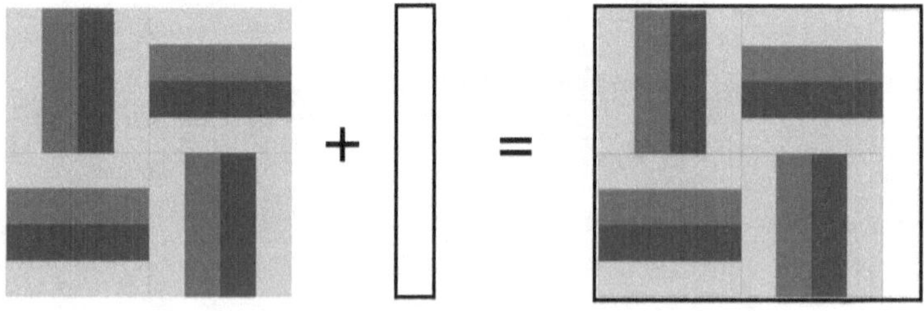

5. Sew blocks with sashing together, RST, with sashing in between until you have the proper number of blocks per row minus 1 block.

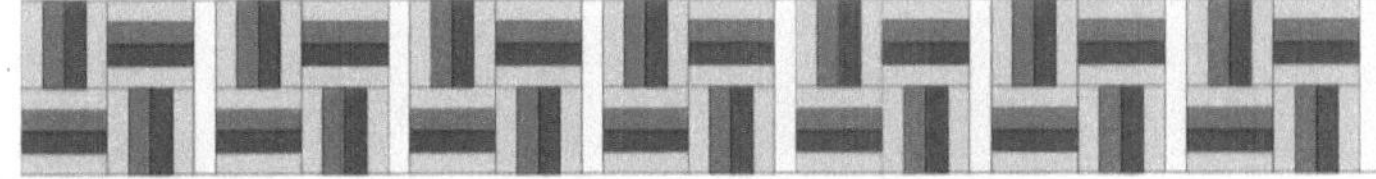

6. Sew a block WITHOUT SASHING to the end of the row to complete the proper number of blocks.

7. Press seams all one direction.

8. Repeat for remaining rows.

9. Press seams. With sashing, nesting isn't an issue. Alternate seam pressing per row to keep the bulk from forming a line, or you can press sashing out toward blocks.

10. With the sashing strips you set aside, cut the number of rows minus 1, the width of one row.

    Example: for 8x10 blocks, 9 strips 71" long (each block w/ sashing is 9". 9x8=72-1 inch for the last block which doesn't have sashing)

TIP: I recommend cutting all the strips the same length before sewing them to the row to help block your quilt. You can piece your strips together as needed.

11. Sew sashing strip to the bottom of each row, RST. You will have one extra row.

12. RST, sew rows together with sashing in between.

TIP: To line up the sashing, using a ruler, line up with the edge of the block and draw a small line within the seam allowance on the sashing. Match those lines to the stitch lines on the other row.

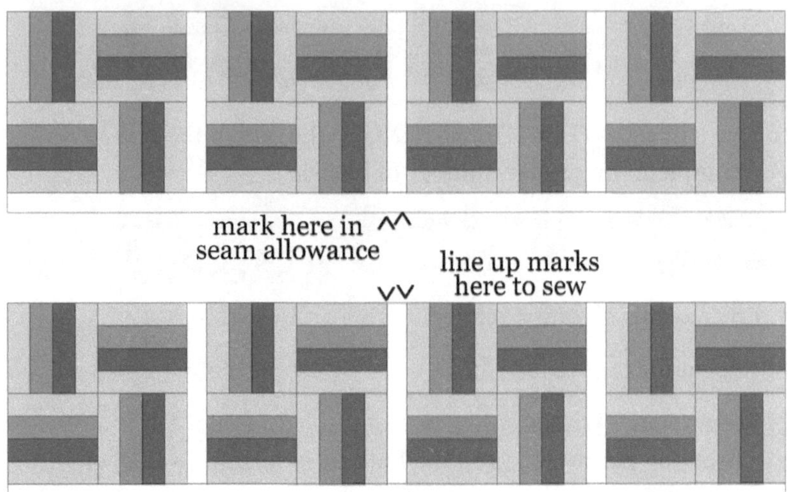

13. Sew your last row without sashing to the bottom of the quilt.

14. Press toward sashing.

BORDER

1. You can add as many borders as you would like at any width. That's the glory of making your own project. Using the same material as you did with the sashing will be a different look than using a complementary color.

2. Measure the length of your quilt at each side and down the middle (You would think it should be exactly the same, but you never know with so many seams).

3. Take the average and cut two strips that length.

4. Sew, RST, to either side of your quilt.

5. Press toward border.

6. Repeat steps 1-2 with the top and bottom of your quilt.

7. Press toward border.

About the Author

Dawn Brotherton is an award-winning author, Air Force veteran, and avid crafter. When she isn't writing, she can be found in her sewing room, designing new creations with either fabric or paint.

When it comes to exceptional writing, she draws on her experience as a colonel retired from the US Air Force as well as a softball coach and Girl Scout leader. Her variety of interests has led to a variety of genres including mystery, romance, young adult fantasy, middle grade sports, picture books, and nonfiction.

Keep in touch with Dawn

Website:

https://www.dawnbrothertonauthor.com/

Facebook:

https://www.facebook.com/DawnBrothertonAuthor

Instagram:

https://www.instagram.com/dawnbrothertonauthor/

Bookbub:

https://www.bookbub.com/authors/dawn-brotherton

Other Books by Dawn Brotherton

Eastover Treasure Cozy Mysteries
Eastover Treasures
Oaky With a Hint of Murder

Jackie Austin Mysteries
The Obsession (also available on audio)
Wind the Clock
Truth Has No Agenda

Romance
Untimely Love

Children's Books
If I Look Like You
Scout Goes to School
Scout's Feast with Friends
Scout and Her Friends Activity Book

Lady Tigers Series
Trish's Team (book 1)
Margie Makes a Difference (book 2)
Nicole's New Friend (book 3)
Avery Appreciates True Friendship (book 4, written by
Paige Ashley Brotherton)
Tammy Tries Baseball (book 5)

Nonfiction
Baseball/Softball Scorebook
The Road to Publishing

Contributing Author to Anthologies
A-10s Over Kosovo
Sisters in Arms
Water from Wellspring
Coastal Crimes 2: Death Takes a Vacation